WIDE ORANGE BEAMS
SHOT OUT FROM THE NOSES
OF TWO THIN SHIPS . . .

. . . cutting a swath of intense red flame through the crops. Instinctively Kerdoch, the Klingon farmer, flung himself to the side of the path and rolled down into the shallow ditch on the right. Behind him, from the direction of the colony center, came loud explosions. Kerdoch stood up and spun around. His family, his wife, his home were near the center. Instantly he was climbing out of the ditch, running toward his farm, intent on saving his family.

And paying back in death whoever was doing this. . . .

STAR TREK®

TREATY'S LAW

DAY OF HONOR

BOOK FOUR OF FOUR

DEAN WESLEY SMITH
AND
KRISTINE KATHRYN RUSCH

POCKET BOOKS

New York   London   Toronto   Sydney   Tokyo   Singapore

An *Original* Publication of POCKET BOOKS

POCKET BOOKS, a division of Simon & Schuster Inc.
1230 Avenue of the Americas, New York, NY 10020

ISBN: 0-671-00424-7

First Pocket Books printing October 1997

10 9 8 7 6 5 4 3 2 1

POCKET and colophon are registered trademarks of
Simon & Schuster Inc.

Printed in the U.S.A.

This one is for Jeff, Kelly, and Rich.
Thanks for all the great times.

TREATY'S LAW

Prologue

KERDOCH MOVED with a steady, solid pace across the large family room to his chair. He wore the same clothes he had worn on this day twenty cycles earlier. Frayed work clothes that still fit, even though his body had thickened with age. They were the clothes of a proud Klingon farmer, but on that special day twenty cycles ago, they had also been the uniform of a warrior.

The air was warm and still full of the smells of the huge meal prepared and eaten earlier. The tension of anticipation of a wonderful story about to be told blanketed the room, coloring everyone's sight with a special glow, as if Kahless himself were about to visit them. Kerdoch felt it. He let the sensation fill him with strength, reinforcing his tired old bones, bones worn by a lifetime of working the fields to feed the

1

warriors of the Empire. His job was a proud one. He and his family were respected in the region.

The seventeen Klingon adults and the thirty-one Klingon children who filled the room were silent, almost not breathing. Waiting.

Kerdoch settled himself in his big chair, then looked over the group. They were his family. His *entire* family. Around his feet, his youngest grandchildren sat cross-legged, staring up at their grandfather. They too anticipated his story, and he knew it.

They all knew the story by heart. Kerdoch had repeated the story every year on the same day, and he had never tired of it. His children and grandchildren were not tired of it, either; that much was clear. A good sign for the future, in his opinion. His story was important, about a day and a fight of honor that should be remembered by all Klingons.

Kerdoch's black eyes never missed a detail, not in the fields, and not in this large room on this special day. His gaze bored through his grandchildren and his older children until it came to rest on his wife, standing near the back. He smiled, and she returned his smile. She also remembered this day twenty years earlier. It was a day on which she feared she had lost her husband, her children, and her own life. She too knew the importance of his story.

The tension in the room seemed to grow as everyone knew the story of the great fight was about to begin. The excitement of hearing it again was almost too much for the younger children to bear. Many of them squirmed and shifted their position. Kerdoch forced himself not to smile at them.

He took a deep breath, then started, letting his deep

voice fill the room as he took himself and his gathered family back to that time of battle twenty cycles earlier.

To a time when he, Kerdoch, had been a warrior. And when the Klingon Empire had learned about the honor of its enemies.

Chapter One

KERDOCH GRUNTED SOFTLY as he stood upright, stretching the soreness out of the tight muscles in his back. He had been a farmer for almost thirty years, and each passing year wore on his body a little more. But it was a price he was more than willing to pay.

He studied his work. The field of tIqKa SuD spread out before him like a calm ocean, blue-green stems drifting back and forth like gentle waves at the touch of an unseen wind. The health of his crops radiated from every stem.

On the horizon K'Tuj, the larger of the two yellow suns had dipped below the horizon, leaving only K'mach's faint yellow light to illuminate his work. Already the chill was returning to the air, pushing out the intense heat of the day. Kerdoch knew that within the hour the cold would settle in for the short night.

Back in the farming colony the lights of the streets and in the domes would be on, the fires lit.

He and the rest of the colonists had been on this planet now for five years. They had named the planet Qul' Tu. Paradise. He loved many things about this new home, but he loved most of all the nights around the fire, letting the ale and the flame hold back the cold and soothe his tired muscles.

He turned slowly, surveying his field and his work. Not a black stalk of Qut weed could be seen above the blue-green stocks of his crop. He had again won the day's battle. The pride of a fight well fought filled him for a moment. And he let it.

Then, as the second sun touched the horizon, he focused on the tasks of tomorrow, the struggle for the approaching harvest. Feeding the Empire was a never-ending battle that must be fought every day, or the war would be lost. Kerdoch was proud of his place in the Empire. Throughout the sector he was well respected for his work and his land's output. He enjoyed that respect and had every intention of gaining more.

Moving through the plants without breaking even one stem, Kerdoch made his way to the open area between fields, then turned and headed for home down a dirt path between two shallow ditches. His family would be waiting. Dinner would be ready, the fire popping and crackling like a celebration. A celebration of a day's battle won.

Suddenly his thoughts of family and the next day's tasks were broken by the searing sound of two aircraft flashing overhead. They were low, not more than ten of his height in the air. He couldn't tell what type of craft they were. They did not look like any of the colony ships. These were flat and diamond-shaped, nothing like any Klingon ship he'd ever heard about.

The intense wind in their wake rocked him, staggering him until he caught his balance. Around him his plants whipped back and forth as if being brushed by a large unseen hand.

In his five years on this land, on this planet, he'd never seen a craft fly over his fields, even at a great height, let alone low and fast. Without doubt there would be crop damage from this foolish act. He would make sure the persons responsible would pay.

He glanced around in the dimming light to see if he could locate any damage. But it was too dark. And the night chill was settling in. His assessment would have to wait for morning.

In the faint light Kerdoch caught sight of the two craft making a high, very tight turn above the glowing orange of the sunset. They finished their turn and headed back toward him, coming in low again and very fast, two thin silver slashes in the sky.

He stopped, too startled to move.

His mind fought to make sense of what he was seeing.

The ships appeared to be making an attack run.

In his youth on the planet T'Klar he had seen such action from aircraft in the great battle of T'Klar. His mother had been killed in just such an attack led by a cowardly pilot not willing to look his prey in the eyes. Kerdoch had managed to survive and see his mother's murderer killed two years later. Revenge had tasted good that day.

Wide orange beams shot out from the noses of the two thin ships, cutting a swath of intense red and blue flame through the crops.

It *was* an attack mission!

They were heading right at him.

Instinctively Kerdoch flung himself to the right side of the path and rolled down into a shallow ditch. He trusted his heavy work shirt to protect his body. He used his arms to cover his head.

Almost instantly the two aircraft were over him and then gone past.

The concussion from their passing pressed Kerdoch into the ditch, pushing his face into the mud as an added insult. The pilots of these ships would pay for this action.

Before he could move to push himself up he felt an intense burning on his shoulder and back. He was on fire from their flame weapons.

He rolled over, rocking back and forth on his back as hard and as quickly as he could in the dirt and mud of the ditch, letting the coolness of the ground smother the flames of his clothing. Many mornings he had cursed the cold ground as his aching joints worked it. Now he thanked it.

When he was sure the flames on his back were out, he stood, ignoring his pain.

For fifty paces on either side of him, his crops were nothing more than smoking ashes illuminated by small flickering fires along the edges of the destruction. In the distance through the smoke Kerdoch could see the two aircraft as they continued their burning run through his neighbors' crops.

Who were they?

Why burn his crops? The Empire's food?

There was no sense to this action.

Behind him, from the direction of his home and the main colony center came loud explosions.

He spun around. Flames shot into the air as more strange aircraft attacked the colony.

His family, his wife, and his home were near the center of the colony. Instantly he was running, intent on saving his family.

And paying back in death whoever was doing this.

Captain James T. Kirk crossed his arms and leaned against the wall in the tiny office. The office belonged to Commander Bracker, who ran Starbase 11, one of the smallest starbases Kirk had ever been on. Small and uncomfortable. This office barely accommodated Kirk and Bracker, let alone the four other people in the room. The size of the office didn't help Kirk's mood.

He glared across the desk at the smiling face of his friend Captain Kelly Bogle of the *U.S.S. Farragut*. Bogle was standing behind Bracker, somehow making himself the center of attention in the small space. He had arrived before Kirk and taken the place Kirk would have had. The place Kirk had had when both captains arrived on the starbase.

Bogle's position was symbolic of his recent victory over Kirk. Kirk adjusted his arms, but he couldn't relieve the tension in his shoulders. He had lost. And he hated to lose, even in a friendly game of catch-the-thief. But worse, he hated to lose to Kelly Bogle, his friend and former shipmate on the *Farragut*. That galled Kirk even more.

Captain Bogle stood only three inches taller than Kirk, but to Kirk the difference had always seemed much greater. Bogle somehow carried himself with a straight-backed posture that always made him seem like the tallest man in the room, even when he wasn't.

His light brown hair was never out of place. Kirk also knew that straight-backed posture and perfect hair were consistent with the way Bogle captained his ship. He did everything by the book. But in a fight, Kirk couldn't honestly think of a better ship, crew, and captain to have at his side.

He liked Kelly Bogle, partly because Bogle was one of the few people who could get the better of Kirk. Rarely, to be sure. But Bogle could do it, and he could do it by the book.

Near the door, two red-shirted *Farragut* crew members held a tiny, childlike, and extremely thin humanoid between them. The prisoner wore regulation starbase children's clothing—probably stolen—and a small duck-billed cap. He was the first member of the Liv Kirk had ever seen, but he'd heard a great deal about them over the past few years. They were reported to be a race of thieves, although Spock claimed that for an entire race to turn to theft was not logical. Logical or not, the Liv stole on every planet, every starbase, every ship they appeared on.

They were fair creatures who appeared, at first glance, to be human children. They had porcelain skin, bright blue eyes, and no body hair. The tallest member of the race most likely wouldn't have reached Kirk's chin, and this one was far from the tallest: he came up to Kirk's waist.

They were known as the "child-race," "the kids from Liv," "troublemakers," as well as by a dozen other names. They traveled in small ships of their own or stowed away on other ships. They had an uncanny ability to hide in places where hiding didn't seem possible. And they looked so sweet and childlike that unsuspecting adults of all species usually took them in, soon to be robbed blind.

"It seems," Commander Bracker said nervously, "that our situation is now resolved."

Kirk glared at Bracker, a stocky red-haired man who was clearly nervous as he sat between the two starship captains. It was obviously the last place Bracker wanted to be. But he had caused his own discomfort. He had sent a message to the *Enterprise,* which was close by at the time, asking for some quick help with robberies at the station. Kirk had felt it would be a good excuse to give his crew a few days' shore leave and had agreed to help. But just minutes before the *Enterprise* reached the starbase, the *Farragut* had arrived unexpectedly for repairs.

The contest to catch a thief had started the first night in a bar, with a friendly wager between members of the two crews. Actually, some of the *Farragut* crew had said that the *Enterprise* couldn't catch anything if they tried and a few of Kirk's crew had objected. Loudly, from what Kirk had come to understand.

The argument had grown even louder between Kirk and Bogle in the officers' mess. Then the two captains had laughed, made a friendly wager, and bought each other a drink.

When the drinks were over, both men had hurried back to their crews. Shore leave was called off until the cause of the disappearances was found.

It had taken both crews a full day of searching the small station to find the Liv, hiding in a locker in a main hallway. His loot had been stashed in a dozen places around the station.

Captain Bogle smiled at his security detail. "Escort our prisoner to the station brig."

Then Bogle turned to Kirk. "Well, Captain, I'll collect that drink in the bar anytime you are ready." Bogle did not quite manage to keep the smirk off his face, even though he was trying.

Sort of.

Kirk shook his head. The game had been all in fun, yet some pride and ship's honor had been involved. It irked him that his crew had lost.

He still wasn't sure why they had lost. He knew Bogle too well to suspect an underhanded move, but he still felt uncomfortable—and a bit responsible. He had intended to check the lockers himself, but he had been detained, talking to a yeoman in the bar.

She was worth being detained for.

She was not worth losing a bet over.

It galled him to lose, but he had no one to blame but himself. Even so, the bet had been a nice diversion from the last month, which had been filled with routine. The sector of space they were in had provided nothing new, not even an interesting debris field or an unusual moon.

He smiled at Bogle, but his smile had an edge. Bogle had won this bet, but he wouldn't win the next.

"I could use a drink right now," Kirk said. "Care to join me?" With a wide sweeping gesture he indicated the door.

Bogle laughed. "I'd be glad to."

Both nodded to the relieved-looking station commander, then turned and headed for the door side by side.

Kirk liked Bogle, and even with the ribbing for not catching the thief first, drinking with his friend would be enjoyable. Just what Dr. McCoy had ordered for him and the rest of the crew.

But before the captains had taken two steps, their communicators went off simultaneously.

Kirk had his up and open first, instantly wondering what emergency would cause both starships to call their captains at the same time. "Kirk here," he said.

Beside him Bogle turned his back on Kirk and said, "Bogle," in such a stern tone that Kirk glanced over at him.

"Captain," Spock's voice came loud and clear over the communicator. "We are receiving a distress call from the agricultural planet Signi Beta. They are under attack and asking for assistance from anyone nearby."

Signi Beta was the Federation name for the Klingon farming planet QI' tu'. Just the name Signi Beta annoyed Kirk. The Federation farmers had lost the planet to the Klingons in a fair and honest contest.

But losing to the Klingons galled Kirk more than losing to Bogle did.

The planet was not in dispute, though. Why would anyone attack it?

Behind him, he heard Bogle get the same news.

"Mr. Spock," Kirk said, "notify the crew that shore leave has been canceled. Order them back to the ship immediately. Then set a course for Signi Beta. On my mark, beam me aboard."

"Aye, Captain," Spock said.

Kirk snapped his communicator closed at almost the same moment Bogle did. The two captains turned and faced each other, all thought of the rivalry and the drinks gone. Now they were both efficient working Starfleet captains with the same problem.

"How long until you can get under way?" Kirk asked. He knew that the *Farragut* had taken a beating during a run-in with a subspace anomaly. They had to repair their warp drives as well as bring weapons and shield systems back online.

"The starbase crew told us we had to dock here for at least twenty hours," Bogle said. "But knowing my engineer, Projeff, we can get out of here in fifteen."

Kirk grinned. Projeff was one of the few engineers who could give Scotty a run for his money. "I'll keep you informed as to what we find."

"Good luck," Bogle said, his eyes intent on Kirk.

"Thanks," Kirk said, knowing that Bogle was saying much more. They ran their ships in very different manners, but the respect between the two captains was there. Kirk extended his hand, and Bogle shook it. "That drink will have to wait."

Bogle smiled. "I don't mind you owing it to me. Just make sure you stay alive to pay it off."

"Oh, I'll pay you back," Kirk said, laughing. "And then some." He flipped open his communicator. *"Enterprise.* One to beam up."

Sixty seconds later the *Enterprise* was headed at warp five for Signi Beta on the edge of the Klingon Empire.

"Dinna give me any trouble, Doctor," Chief Engineer Montgomery Scott said, clutching his right arm as he sat on the edge of the medical cot. Dr. McCoy was standing beside him, holding a tricorder and frowning. "I woulda been here sooner, but I had a project to finish."

"Do you realize how filthy this wound is, Scotty?" McCoy snapped. "If you'd waited much longer, it would have become infected. I could have treated it, but it would have taken a lot longer."

"Ah, time. That's the ticket, isn't it, Doctor?" Scotty said. "We're headin' into Klingon space and I've got parts and pieces all over her innards. I gotta get back to Engineering and put things to right before we reach that planet."

"You'll let me finish," McCoy said. "And you'll tell me how you got this mess while on shore leave at a starbase."

"Well, now, I didn't exactly get the cut on the Starbase."

"Wound," McCoy said. "This is too big to be called a cut."

Scotty shrugged but didn't look at his arm. The sleeve of his uniform was torn, and beneath it the skin had been flayed to the bone.

"So you're telling me it happened right here?" McCoy asked.

"No, not really," Scotty said.

"You aren't telling me anything. Are you afraid I'd go to the captain?"

"We weren't doin' anything wrong," Scotty said with all the dignity he could muster.

"'We?'" McCoy asked.

"Aye, Doc," Scotty said. "Projeff 'n' I."

"Projeff?" McCoy asked. "The engineer from the *Farragut?*"

"The same," Scotty said. "We had a wee wager."

"A wager," McCoy said. "I suppose it had nothing to do with the thefts."

"Naw. That's Security's business. And the captain's." Scotty smiled his wide, impish smile, the one that had gotten them into trouble on more than one shore leave. "This was over the lassies."

"The ships? What about them?" McCoy finished cleaning and sterilizing the wound.

"Projeff claims that he found a way to use the power from hydroponics to enrich the oxygen content of the environmental controls."

"We don't need more oxygen."

"I didn't say we did. But supposin' she got herself in a fix, and we were havin' trouble with the environmental controls. We could use . . ."

Scotty launched into an explanation so technical that McCoy, who prided himself on understanding most things scientific—especially when they touched on fundamentals, like oxygen—couldn't follow a word.

"So you were testing it?"

"Lord, no," Scotty said. "We were building models. The *Farragut*'s environmental system is one of the worst I've ever seen. A pile of junk-heap parts that needs to be replaced, if you ask me. 'Twouldna be fair to Projeff to attempt a modification on that scrap heap."

"So you were building computer models."

"Actually, we were using some of the base's supplies as parts for small scale models. I made some modifications to Projeff's proposal and we wanted to see who could get his model running quicker."

"I don't see why you had to take the *Enterprise* apart to do that."

"I dinna, Doctor," Scotty said. "I was merely showing Projeff some of the finer points of our environmental system so that he could improve the *Farragut*'s."

"I see," McCoy said, even though he didn't. "I still

don't understand how you wounded yourself building models."

"I slid me arm up a miniature jeffries tube," Scotty said. He flushed. "To adjust the cabling. It got stuck."

"Why didn't you get help, man?"

"What, and let Projeff see me dilemma? No, sir! Montgomery Scott solves his own engineering problems, he does."

McCoy shook his head. "Next time, get one of the medical staff to help you out," he said.

"There won't be a next time," Scotty said. He glanced at his arm. There was no sign of the cut. McCoy's healing powers had worked again. "We're heading to the outskirts of Klingon space. There won't be time for models and such."

"But that won't stop you from working on them, will it, Mr. Scott?"

Scotty grinned. "If I have time ta build models," he said, "then all will be right with the world." He slid off the table and headed for Engineering before McCoy could caution him to keep the arm stable for the next few hours.

McCoy sighed and went to his desk. He doubted all would be right with the world. The captain had asked McCoy to inventory the medical supplies and order up more from storage if need be.

And Jim only did that when he was expecting trouble.

Chapter Two

THE ATTACKING SHIPS had moved on by the time Kerdoch made it into the center of the colony. Most of the dome buildings were damaged. Flames and smoke filled the air. The only newly constructed wood building in the colony, the meeting hall and tavern, had been completely destroyed. Kerdoch could see a number of bodies in the smoking piles of timbers and furniture, all of them far beyond his help.

He took a deep breath of the smoke-filled air, calming himself, as his father had taught him to do. Then he forced himself to really look at the details of what was happening around him. A battle was won in the small details, his father had said. Kerdoch had always remembered those words, both in the battle to grow crops and now.

Smoke billowed out of the house of his friend, Kehma, but Kerdoch could tell the home was in no

18

danger of burning down. Flames also flickered on or near almost every other dome building in the colony. Yet none of the main panels of which the domes were constructed had caught fire. He knew they were designed to withstand almost anything. He was very glad now that they did just that.

Through the smoke Kerdoch could see his neighbors and friends fighting the fires or helping the wounded. He could do nothing to help any of them at the moment.

The colony was withstanding the attack fairly well so far. The domes had not been designed with combat in mind, but they had been built to hold against harsh weather and high winds on dozens of planets. There would be dead, but not too many, because of the standard colony construction he had sworn he hated so often in the past. He would never curse it again after today.

He turned and at a full run headed for his own home. It too was one of the standard-issue Klingon domes that the colonists had been using during the five-year test period. Now that the planet's future was ensured, he had been preparing to build his family a real home, outside of town on his own land. Now he would also keep the dome, if they lived through this cowardly attack.

His home showed damage from a direct hit, but it was still standing. There was no sign of his wife and five children. That fact relieved him. If they were still alive they would be inside, door blocked, ready to defend their home as best they could. He would have to be careful going in or they'd fire on him.

He tried the front door and found it securely

locked. That meant someone was alive in there. The door didn't lock from the outside.

He moved around to the side, tossing burning roofing away from the walls of his home as he went. The colony living quarters had only one main door, but they were also equipped with a hidden emergency entry that could be opened from the outside.

He yanked open the small hatch and, without putting himself in front of it, shouted, "It is I, Kerdoch!"

Inside he heard sudden movement; then his wife said, "Kerdoch? Son of whom?" Her voice was full of courage, testing to make sure that no one but her husband would enter her home. She was a solid, stout woman, and Kerdoch could imagine her standing inside, weapon aimed at the emergency door.

Kerdoch smiled. "Kerdoch, son of KaDach, beloved one."

"Enter, my husband," she said.

Inside, in the dark, he hugged his wife and five children as the ground shook.

The enemy ships had returned on another attack run.

Dr. Vivian Rathbone watched as the turbolift doors slid open with a hiss. She slowly stepped through and onto the *Enterprise* bridge.

She was amazed at how nervous she felt as she smoothed her commander's uniform. This was her first time on any starship bridge, and in the six months she'd been posted to the *Enterprise,* it had never occurred to her that she would be ordered to any of the officers' areas, let alone the bridge.

She had hoped to see the bridge someday, while in

space dock, perhaps, or on a tour. To suddenly be called there during an emergency was not at all what a colonial agronomist would expect. Her job was to study any planets the ship discovered for possible future colonization and food-production ability. During red alerts her most important duty was to report to her lab and stay out of the way of crew members who had important things to do.

Behind her the door hissed closed, and she stopped. Captain Kirk sat in his command chair facing the main screen, seemingly deep in thought. She had seen him from a distance when she was first assigned to the ship. Then he had seemed like any other Starfleet officer, hurrying about his business. Now, though, he seemed larger than before. A man in his element. A man who accepted his power as he accepted the design of the bridge.

A man no one should trifle with.

The stars of warp space flashed past on the screen, but nothing else was visible. The slight beeping and clicking sounds of a working bridge were the only sounds around her, but they seemed extra loud to her in her heightened nervousness.

Spock had his head pressed against a scope at his science station. She'd passed the Vulcan science officer a few times in the halls, and every time was impressed by his stern demeanor. This time was no exception.

Lieutenant Sulu and Ensign Chekov were at their stations. She had spoken to both of them before. They had seemed nice enough, but concerned with the business of the day. She'd had a sense she failed to make an impact on any of them, although she was honored just to share the same starship with them.

Lieutenant Uhura swiveled in her chair, put a hand to the device in her ear, and smiled at Vivian, who smiled back. She and the lieutenant had become occasional three-dimensional chess partners. They played when they were both off duty, which rarely happened at the same time. But they did enjoy the games they were able to play. They were evenly matched, and Uhura was cunning. Vivian appreciated cunning; it added surprise to the game.

Uhura's smile helped. At least Vivian didn't feel entirely alone on the bridge. But she did feel vulnerable.

In all of Vivian's forty-two years she couldn't remember a moment this tense. Even finishing her doctoral thesis hadn't been this draining. She smoothed her uniform again and then patted her brown hair to make sure it was in place.

Calm.

Calm. She repeated the word over and over silently. Just stay calm, damm it.

"Captain Kirk," Uhura said, nodding toward Vivian. Uhura obviously understood how nervous Vivian was. "Dr. Rathbone is here."

Sulu, Chekov, and Captain Kirk all turned to look at Vivian at the same moment. Spock kept his face to his science scope.

Vivian felt as if a dozen spotlights had been turned on her and she was under close inspection. After a short moment Captain Kirk sprang from his chair and moved toward her, smiling. The man's movements were all fluidity and grace.

And energy.

His presence was overwhelming.

"It's good to meet you, Doctor," he said.

She managed to acknowledge his greeting with a nod of her head. Somehow his smile melted her tension, and she managed to smile back. She'd been in the presence of many powerful and famous people over the years, but never one with such charm. Now she understood why there were so many stories about this young captain. Judging from this brief meeting, the stories most likely were true.

Before she could respond, Kirk motioned for her to step down beside his captain's chair.

"Spock," the captain said. "Put our destination on the main screen for Commander Rathbone."

"Aye, Captain," Spock said.

The captain sat in the command chair and indicated that Vivian remain beside him.

After a moment the picture of a green and blue and orange planet flashed on the screen. Vivian stared. The planet was very familiar.

"Signi Beta," she said, shocked. She'd spent over four years of her life on Signi Beta, in the Federation farming community on the southern continent. But that community had been disbanded six months before, and she had been posted to the *Enterprise*. She had never expected to see Signi Beta again. Or really ever wanted to.

"Correct," Spock said. "Signi Beta, now the Klingon farming planet QI'tu'. Translated, the name means 'Paradise.'"

"I prefer not to remember," Vivian said, obviously not shielding the bitterness from her voice. "But that planet is far from a paradise by any definition."

Both Kirk and Spock stared at her. Spock's right eyebrow went up, giving his stoic face a questioning look.

"Your personnel file shows that you were a member of the Federation agricultural team stationed on Signi Beta," Kirk said.

Vivian took a deep breath and forced herself to look away from the damned planet framed on the main viewscreen. "I was, Captain," she said, looking into his powerful gaze. "For the first two years I was the colony's assistant chief agronomist, and for the last two years I was the chief."

"So," Captain Kirk said, his intense gaze very serious. "What happened?"

"The Klingons beat us," Vivian said. "That simple."

She could tell that Kirk didn't much like her statement or the short, curt way she said it.

"There is nothing simple about Klingons, Commander," Kirk said.

She opened her mouth, but before she could speak, Spock looked up from his scope.

"Doctor," he said, "it would aid our understanding of the situation if you supply details about the planet."

Vivian nodded and took a deep breath, forcing her feelings of anger toward what had happened on Signi Beta aside. "I'm sorry Sir," she said. "My time there . . . it's a touchy subject for me."

"So I understand," Spock said, without sounding understanding at all. "But so far you have told us little more than what our computer records."

"We were hoping," Kirk said, his voice suddenly gentle, "that you could provide us with some insight."

"Insight?" she said.

24

"Into Signi Beta."

Insight. How could she give them insight into years of work followed by intense frustration? How could she let them know that she—that the entire Federation colony—had underestimated the Klingons?

She took a deep breath and decided to start from some sort of beginning. "For a number of years, Signi Beta was a disputed planet between the Federation and the Klingons. Then, five years ago, a test was set up. Two colonies—one Klingon, one Federation—would work the planet to see who could manage it in the best fashion."

"Manage?" Spock said.

She nodded. "Manage. Raise crops and plan the future use of the planet's resources."

"And the Klingons von?" Chekov asked. He had spun in his chair, his eyebrows raised.

"Ensign," Kirk warned.

Vivian nodded. "They won under the terms of the Organian Treaty. Fair and square, according to the judge."

"And who judged this contest?" Kirk asked. "Certainly not the Organians."

Vivian shook her head. "Ambassador Ninties, a Sandpinian, was picked as the final judge by both sides and approved by the Organians."

"A Sandpinian?" Kirk asked, glancing at Spock.

Spock nodded. "The Sandpinians are relatively new members of the Federation. Sandpinia is covered with sand dunes, swamps, and oceans. The Sandpinians' immense agricultural talent helped the race survive there. It is my understanding that their entire culture developed around those dunes. Their transportation system, for example, is made up of small cartlike vehicles that travel on narrow paths at very slow speeds. They have developed a new branch of agriculture called—"

"All right. That's enough, Mr. Spock," Kirk said, holding up his hand to stop the information flow. He seemed to smile slightly as he did so.

"There is one other important fact, Captain," Spock said.

"Yes, Spock?"

"I believe the Sandpinians were chosen as much for their mental development as for their agricultural talents."

"Mental development, Mr. Spock?" Kirk sounded confused, which echoed the way Vivian felt.

"Humans and Klingons cause Organians mental distress."

"Ah, yes," Kirk said. "I remember that."

"Sandpinians do not."

Kirk frowned at his first officer and turned back to Vivian. "Commander, I take it Ambassador Ninties ruled in favor of the Klingon colony?"

"Yes, sir," she said. "Unfortunately. The Federation Colonization Authority underestimated the Klingons' botanical expertise. They beat us soundly."

"I do not believe Klingons could grow a turnip, let alone farm a colony," Chekov said.

"Even Klingons have to eat, Mr. Chekov," Kirk said.

"Yes, but have you seen their menus? Live worms. Blood pies. This is not the food of a ciwilized people."

"It may not be," Vivian said, "but they can make barren land fertile in a shorter time than we can. They sustain higher yields, and they lose less to insects and weather-related causes. They succeeded partly because Klingon agriculture is better suited to Signi Beta's environment and partly because they approach agriculture as they do war—succeed or die; there is no room for failure."

"Amazing," Kirk said. "I've learned never to underestimate a Klingon, but it never crossed my mind that a warrior race could be so good at farming."

"To be honest, Captain," Vivian said, "we all felt the same way, right up until the moment Ambassador Ninties presented the plans, findings, and proof from both sides, then ruled in favor of the Klingons. In his place, I would have ruled the same way, I'm afraid."

"I can see why this is a touchy subject for you," Captain Kirk said, frowning.

"Captain," Sulu said. "We are ten minutes away from the planet."

Kirk seemed to snap to attention. "Shields up. Yellow alert," he ordered.

Vivian started to turn to go to her lab when Captain Kirk said, "Commander?"

She stopped and turned.

"Stay here on the bridge," the captain said, indicating a position beside his chair. "We might need you."

"Sir?" Vivian said, her stomach twisting even tighter than it had when she first walked onto the bridge. Why in the world would Captain Kirk need her on the bridge of the *Enterprise?* And during a yellow alert?

Captain Kirk nodded, seeming to understand her

confusion. He turned back to the main viewscreen. Then he said, "The Klingon colony on Signi Beta is under attack and we're responding."

Under attack? By whom? All Commander Vivian Rathbone could do was stand near the rail, her mouth open, staring at the viewscreen as the *Enterprise* dropped out of warp near Signi Beta.

Chapter Three

KERDOCH LISTENED for a moment. The silence was broken by the crackle of fire, a few distant cries, and nothing else. The attack had ceased, at least for the time being.

He stepped out from behind the makeshift shield of furniture he had built to protect his family from the possibility of the dome collapsing. The dome had taken at least one direct hit but had remained standing. They were lucky, nothing more. They had survived through the night and into the morning. He imagined that was more than many of his neighbors and friends had done this night.

His wife brushed the dust from her vest as she stood and faced her husband. "Who are they?"

"Cowards" was all Kerdoch said. The anger in his voice was harsh.

He glanced around at his home. The roof still held,

but everything inside was in ruins. Smoke poured from cracks in the side of the domed plating, filling the area with a thick cloud.

He turned to his wife who was helping the younger children. "Put out what fire you can. Then prepare for another attack. Use more furniture to build extra shielding."

"Understood," she said, then nodded to him. "I will see you after the fight."

She knew him all too well. They were a good team. She would defend their home. He would defend their home as well, but he would be defending their home, the planet.

It would not be easy.

The colony had four disrupter cannons in position around the perimeter, but during the fight he had heard none of them being fired. Perhaps they had been destroyed or no one had made it to them in time. It had been at least six months since the cannons had even been tested, so it would take time to get them operating. A stupid thing to have done. The colonists should have been prepared. If they survived this, they would not be caught unprepared for battle again. He would make sure of that.

He nodded to his wife, then turned and ducked out the emergency exit of the dome. Behind him his wife and two oldest children emerged and began putting out the fires on and around the structure.

The sunlight on the colony was clouded and dimmed by the smoke of a hundred fires. Women, children, and some men were emerging from the domes to fight the fires or help the wounded. Ahead Kerdoch saw two other farmers, KaHanb and Kolit, heading in the same direction he was—toward the disrupter cannons on the south side of the colony. The cowards who attacked from the sky might have gotten away with two attacks, but they would not launch a third.

He could feel his blood coursing through his veins; his heart was light, his breath steady. He felt ready, his anger turned with focus to the task at hand.

On the bridge of the *U.S.S. Farragut*, in stationary orbit above Starbase 11, Captain Bogle took three long-legged strides in one direction in front of his captain's chair.

Turn.

Three back. He knew it drove his crew crazy when he paced, but at that moment he didn't much care. The *Enterprise* had left fourteen hours before, and since then every available person had been assigned to repairs on the *Farragut*. Bogle's little voice told him Kirk was heading into a mess. Granted, James T. Kirk was one of the best captains in the Federation, especially in unusual and messy situations. But even the best needed some help at times. And being stuck at starbase wasn't the sort of help Kelly Bogle wanted to give his friend Kirk.

Richard Lee, the *Farragut*'s science officer, looked up from his scope, frowning—an unusual look on his normally smiling face. "The *Enterprise* should be arriving at Signi Beta any moment."

Bogle stopped pacing and punched the comm link on his chair. "Engineering!"

"We're ready," Chief Engineer Projeff replied, as if the announcement were just another report.

Bogle smiled. This time Projeff had beaten his own best repair-time estimate by two hours. The man was a wizard.

"Status?" Bogle asked.

"Full warp drive coming online now," Projeff said. "Two hours and we'll have weapons back up. Ten hours and I could make her dance around a flagpole."

Captain Bogle dropped down into his seat, half laughing to himself. "Nice work, Projeff. Stand by for full warp speed."

"Yes, Captain," Projeff said. "Standing by."

Bogle punched off the comm link to Engineering. "Is the course for Signi Beta plotted and laid in?" he asked his navigator. He knew it was, since he'd asked the same question five hours earlier.

"Yes, Captain," Lieutenant Michael Book said, his bald head not turning away from his board.

"Warp five," Bogle said. "Now."

The *Farragut* turned away from Space Station 11 and jumped to warp in an easy, smooth movement.

"Comm," Captain Bogle said to Lieutenant Sandy at Communications, "Inform the *Enterprise* that we're under way."

"Yes, sir," the lieutenant said. "With pleasure."

Bogle sat back in his chair and took a long, deep breath for what seemed like the first time in fourteen hours.

Kirk faced the main screen as the *Enterprise* sat some distance away from the planet. Kirk had factored in the distress call, making certain the *Enterprise* had maneuvering room should she encounter a fleet of Klingon battle cruisers.

But none showed on the screen. The planet itself looked exactly like the file images: a calm-looking, blue-green Class M, vaguely Earthlike, deceptively pastoral. There were no visible signs of problems.

He clenched a fist. He didn't like the feeling he was getting.

"Are we alone up here?" he asked.

"According to our instruments, we are," Spock said. He sounded vaguely perplexed. "However, the Klingon colony shows signs of heavy damage."

"From what?" Kirk demanded.

"Unknown," Spock said. "Fields have been burned; wells and farming equipment have been destroyed. The colony itself has sustained heavy damage and casualties. It appears from the damage patterns that the colony was attacked from the air by a fairly large force."

"And that force is now gone," Kirk said.

"If the attack came from space," Spock said, "then the attacking force has left. If the attack came from the ground, I cannot say with accuracy whether or not the colony's adversaries have left."

"Spock," Kirk said, "surely you can tell me if the damage came from a starship or not."

"Not without further study," Spock said. "I can tell you that the attack was sudden. The Klingons did not even have time to mount a defense. I have never seen such damage to a Klingon colony."

"They're farmers," Rathbone said. Her voice was shaking. "They might have been Klingons, but they were farmers first. And Signi Beta was protected by a treaty. They wouldn't have expected an attack."

Kirk swiveled in his chair. Rathbone was an attractive woman who had clearly suffered a great loss when she left Signi Beta. She also seemed quite nervous to be on the bridge. But she looked straight at him when she spoke, and despite her nervousness and her visible distress at the condition of the colony, she spoke with authority.

"Why would anyone attack a farming community?" Kirk asked, thinking out loud.

Rathbone turned her attention to the screen. She shook her head. "I don't know," she said. "I honestly don't. All of us in the Federation colony were upset, angry, and bitter over the Sandpinian judgment, but not enough to do something like this. There's simply no—"

"Captain!" Chekov said. "Klingon battle cruiser!"

Suddenly the entire ship rocked as it took a first hit against the shields. Kirk nearly lost his balance. "Spock! I thought you said there was no one else up here!"

"They did not register on my equipment, Captain." Spock sounded all too calm for a man who was gripping his scope as tightly as he was.

Kirk settled in his chair as the viewscreen showed a Klingon battle cruiser opening up on the *Enterprise.* "Evasive maneuvers, Mr. Sulu."

Three more hits rocked the bridge, the sound roaring like a huge wave about to engulf them.

"Aye, sir," Sulu shouted, his fingers dancing over his board like a concert pianist's.

"It was a trap," Chekov muttered as another hit rocked the ship. "This distress call, it was a trap."

Kirk didn't think so. Such a trap, using a distress call, wasn't the Klingon way. They tended to fight in a straightforward manner, at least in his experience.

And besides, it was clear that the Klingon colony had been attacked. Unless this was a rogue Klingon ship, which was always possible.

"Spock," Kirk said, "did that battle cruiser attack the colony?"

Spock glanced at the captain, then seemed to understand what Kirk was thinking. He quickly checked his scope as two more hits rocked the *Enterprise*.

"Shields at sixty percent," Sulu said.

"No, Captain," Spock said. "That ship did not attack the colony. The weapon patterns are all wrong."

"Lieutenant Uhura," Kirk said. "Hail the battle cruiser."

She pressed one long fingernail against the board, then looked at him. "There is no response, sir."

"Mr. Sulu, arm the photon torpedoes," Kirk said as the Klingon battle cruiser turned to make another run. "Full pattern."

"They're armed, sir," Sulu said.

"Fire!" Kirk shouted as the battle cruiser moved past and above the *Enterprise*.

The quick successive thumps of the torpedoes firing felt faint but reassuring to Kirk.

The *Enterprise* rocked hard and violently with the impact of two more Klingon disrupter blasts. Kirk managed to hang on and stay in his seat, but Rathbone lost her grip and was tossed against the rail. Her head smacked against the floor, and she seemed to be out cold.

Kirk couldn't spare anyone to check her. The battle cruiser was getting ready for another attack. He punched the comm button. "Dr. McCoy to the bridge. We have an emergency."

"Captain, the shields are at fifty percent," Sulu said.

Then Chekov, who had been monitoring the fighting, raised a fist. "We hit them! They are hurt!"

But the Klingon battle cruiser didn't look badly damaged to Kirk as it swung around and held position facing the *Enterprise*.

"Open a channel to that Klingon ship," Kirk said tightly. "If this was intentional, this will be the last time the Federation answers a Klingon distress signal."

"The channel is open, Captain," Uhura said.

Kirk stood and took a deep breath. "Captain of the Klingon ship, this is Captain James T. Kirk of the Federation starship *Enterprise*. Are you too much of a coward to face your enemy?"

He smiled to himself. If that didn't work, he didn't know his Klingons.

"Sir," Uhura said, "we have an incoming message."

"Put it on-screen," Kirk said, cutting off his smile.

Quickly the image of the battle cruiser was replaced by the sneering face of a very familiar Klingon. Kirk would have recognized that roundish face and those dark eyes anywhere. It was Kirk's old foe, Commander Kor.

"So, Kirk," Kor said, doing nothing to cover his sneering tone. "You attack what you cannot earn fairly."

Kirk snorted in surprise. So the Klingons were going to blame the attack on the Federation. If he hadn't trusted Spock's analysis of the damage, he would have sworn that the Klingons had set up this entire affair.

"We're not responsible for the attacks on your colony," Kirk said. "We answered a distress call."

"Lies," Kor said. "We Klingons repay the loss of a life with a life. You will pay for what you have done to our colony."

"Look, Kor," Kirk said, stepping toward the screen. "Arguing won't get us anywhere. It—"

"I do not want to hear more of your lies, Kirk."

"Then look at the proof," Kirk snapped. "Analyze the attack patterns and weapons residue on the colony. Take a look at the damage. It will become clear that we couldn't have done this."

He was gambling. Spock hadn't been that specific about the damage to the planet. And Kirk had no real way of checking before he made the claim. But he had bluffed before with Klingons, and he had won.

Kor sneered, but he made a motion with his hand that was barely visible at the bottom of the screen. So he was having an officer do the test. While he waited, he said, "You could have disguised your weapons. The Federation is known for such trickery."

"Look at the proof, Kor," Kirk said.

Someone spoke to Kor off-screen. He turned away slightly, then turned back, his small eyes narrow. "Perhaps you have a weapon we do not know about."

Stubborn pigheaded people. Kor had the evidence, but he refused to believe it. How could a man talk to people like that? Forcefully. With a firmness they cannot dispute.

"Kor," Kirk said, "if you damage my ship, I'll damage yours, and we'll keep fighting until only one of us remains. But that won't help your colony. If we're fighting each other, we won't be able to defend this planet from the real attacker, who's sitting out there laughing at us."

"We do not need the Federation's help in battle," Kor said, but he didn't sound as convinced as before. It was clear that Kirk's words were making their point to the Klingon commander.

"That may be so," Kirk said, trying not to let his frustration show. "But if we talk to the survivors we might find out who the real enemy is."

Kor nodded. "I will beam one of the colonists up to my ship. You are welcome to join in the questions, but the invitation is for you, Kirk. Alone."

Kirk glanced over his shoulder at Spock, who was staring at him. Kirk's heart was beating hard. This was the sort of challenge he loved, but he could tell that Spock didn't like the idea at all.

"We could withdraw from the area and leave you to your own devices," Kirk said, "but I am as curious as you are. I will come alone. Stand ready."

Kor nodded.

The screen went blank, then returned to the image of the Klingon battle cruiser hanging in space facing the *Enterprise*. Behind the Klingon ship the blue-green planet looked calm and peaceful, but Kirk knew better. That calm planet could prove to be the end of the Organian Peace Treaty if he didn't work this right.

Kirk took a deep breath and then turned to Spock. "I think that went well, don't you?"

Spock only raised an eyebrow.

"Forgive me, Captain, but I do not think this is wise," Chekov said. "Klingons are well known for their deception. They could—"

"They could what, Mr. Chekov? You think they

staged this whole thing so that they could lure me to that battle cruiser and kill me?"

"No, sir. But—"

"You think they plan to pick off starship captains one by one and simply started with me?"

"No, sir. But—"

"But what, Mr. Chekov?"

"But I do not like this. I think it would be wise to send someone with you."

It probably would be wise. But Kirk was unwilling to do that. "I said I would go alone and I will," he said. "If something happens to me, Mr. Spock can handle the *Enterprise*. Starfleet Command will have to get involved. Any more 'advice'?"

"None," Spock said. "However, as this is a Klingon planet, and Commander Kor's vessel is here, it would be logical to allow them to handle the distress call alone, as you yourself suggested."

"It might be logical, Mr. Spock," Kirk said. "But they already suspect the attack was initiated by Starfleet. Leaving now might seem to prove their suspicions. We have a treaty to protect whether or not we like its terms."

He turned to see McCoy kneeling next to Rathbone. She was still unconscious.

"McCoy activated a scanner. "What happened to her?"

"She hit her head," responded Kirk.

Dr. McCoy studied his instrument briefly, then looked up at Kirk. "I'll say she hit her head. That's quite a bump. But she'll be fine."

"Good," Kirk said, returning to his chair.

Spock approached Kirk. "Captain," Spock said

softly, "as your first officer, I must inform you that beaming alone onto a Klingon ship might not be a prudent course of action."

Kirk held up his hand for Spock to stop before he read him regulations regarding the imprudence. Beaming over to Kor's ship seemed to be the only choice they had at the moment. The *Enterprise* hadn't attacked that colony. And Kirk would have wagered anything that Kor hadn't either.

That meant another force had. And that force might return at any moment.

Chapter Four

KERDOCH STOOD ON the edge of the disrupter-cannon platform taking a break while two of his neighbors continued to work behind him. The smell of smoke was thick in his nostrils. The colony would stink of it for days. He thought of it as an incentive to work harder and faster.

He and two others had gotten one disrupter cannon on the outskirts of the colony almost ready. Another group worked on a second cannon on the west side of the colony. The other two cannons had been destroyed in the night attacks. If the cowards returned for another run in their thin ships, they would have a fight on their hands.

Kerdoch took a deep, long drink of water from a jug. The day had turned hot under the two suns, and Kerdoch felt the sweat caked to his back and arms. In midmorning his oldest boy had brought water and food for him and his neighbors.

His son had reported that the fires were out and that his mother had completed building a shelter inside their dome. He then asked if he could stay and fight with his father on the cannon. Kerdoch ordered him to return to his mother's side, where he was needed to defend her and their home. After the boy left, Kerdoch felt proud. He had taught his children well. He hoped they all lived long enough to pass on the lesson.

He took another drink from the jug and was about to return to work when he felt the odd sensation of a transporter beam. It had been years since he felt one, but the feeling was not easily forgotten.

"Kerdoch!" his neighbor shouted, jumping toward Kerdoch as if he might hold him and pull him from the beam. A fruitless but generous gesture.

"Be prepared," he managed to say to his friends before he was gone.

Kerdoch's only thought as the transporter took him was that he wished he had a weapon in his hand. At least that way he could have died fighting.

But when the transporter released him, he found himself on a Klingon battle cruiser. He'd been on two before and instantly recognized it. But how? And why? He fought to remain calm and prepare himself for what would come.

He stepped slowly down from the pad to be greeted by a nod from the Klingon warrior running the transporter. Then through a door strode another warrior, clearly the commander of this battle cruiser. "I am Kor," the warrior said.

"Kerdoch." He hoped his shock didn't show. Kor

was a famous commander, known for his fighting skills.

"Good," Kor said, nodding his respect to the farmer. "In a moment we will talk."

"I understand, Commander," Kerdoch said.

Behind Kerdoch the sound of the transporter filled the room. He turned as a human form reassembled itself on the transporter pad. Could the humans be behind this cowardly attack? That was a possibility Kerdoch had not considered. The humans in the Federation colony had been more than friendly during the years they shared QI'tu' with the Klingons.

What was a human doing on a Klingon battle cruiser?

This was very confusing. Kerdoch shook his head. After this day and last night, nothing would seem impossible ever again.

This human was puny, but then, all humans seemed puny to Kerdoch. This human also had strength; that was evident in the way he moved, the confidence with which he carried himself. He was a warrior, just as the Klingons were.

The human stepped down from the transporter pad and nodded to Kor. "Commander."

Kor nodded back. "Captain."

A Federation captain! With Kor. It was obvious to Kerdoch that these two knew each other—and didn't like each other. That he might have expected, but what was the human captain doing here? And why had they picked him, Kerdoch, off the surface? Questions. Too many questions.

"This way," Kor snapped, turning and moving out of the room without waiting for a response.

The human captain stepped in behind Kor, and

Kerdoch followed the human. Fourteen hours before, he had been walking the dirt path in his field when the attack began. Now he walked the corridors of a Klingon battle cruiser with a Federation captain and one of the Empire's most famous warriors.

Someone was stabbing her in the side of the head. She was sure of it. Waves of pain kept bouncing around inside her skull, and she'd have given anything to have them stop.

"The pain'll ease in a moment, Doctor," a solid, almost harsh male voice said above her, as if reading her mind. "Just lie still."

The voice was right. The pain was slowly diminishing from stabbing to pounding.

She forced herself to try to remember what had happened. The floor under her back was hard and a little cold. She could feel the hum of something working through her shoulder blades. Around her she could hear voices, but she couldn't make out the words. Where was . . . ?

Then she remembered. She was on the bridge.

She had passed out on the bridge of the *Enterprise*. The thought was like an electric shock through her system.

Her eyes snapped open, and she tried to sit up.

"Wait a minute," the voice said. "No dancing until I say so."

No dancing? It took her a second to realize that was a joke. And as she did, she felt a hand push her back until she lay flat.

She agreed with the disembodied voice. Her vision was a blur of spinning colors. She closed her eyes, and the spinning quickly stopped. Her head was clearing, and her memory was coming back.

The *Enterprise* had been under attack by a Klingon ship above Signi Beta. They had been hit, and she'd lost her grip on the railing and hit her head on the floor. That was all she could remember.

That and the pain. She forced herself to take a deep breath, which helped wash the pain back yet another notch. This time she slowly opened her eyes without moving. After a moment the face of Dr. McCoy came into focus above her.

"You're all right," he said, his hand firm on her shoulder. "You had a nasty fall, but you'll be fine."

She'd worked with the gruff McCoy a few times on data she'd gathered from planets. He was an amazingly smart man who liked to call himself just an old country doctor. He was far from that. In her opinion, he had one of the most skilled medical minds in the Federation. Besides that, she liked him, gruffness and all. And he had seemed to like her, too.

"Thank you, Doctor," she said after a long few seconds. Her voice sounded odd to her ears, but speaking didn't cause any increase in pain.

The Doctor half snorted and gently held her arm to help her to her feet. "Go slow, now," he said. "The swelling has receded and the pain should go along with it. You tell me if it doesn't."

"Okay," she said, being very careful she didn't nod in the process. She managed to stand and hold onto the rail. The same rail she'd lost her grip on in the first place.

After a moment of making sure she wasn't going down again McCoy let go of her arm and turned to face the main screen.

Around her the bridge was functioning normally, none of the crew paying her the slightest attention. Science Officer Spock stood at his panel, face buried in his scope. Chekov and Sulu both attended their controls. Lieutenant Uhura sat facing the communication panel, intently listening to something on her earpiece. Only Captain Kirk was missing.

And on the main screen was the Klingon battle cruiser.

"What's going on?" she half whispered to McCoy.

"The captain's on that damned Klingon ship." He sounded annoyed. And slightly worried. "We're to wait here until he returns."

Slowly, keeping her head as still as possible, she turned to completely face the front screen. The Captain on a Klingon ship? What was going on?

She leaned back against the railing and forced herself to take a deep breath. The pain in her head lessened even more, but the questions remained.

Captain Kirk could not identify the type of room he found himself seated in. Federation starships had exact configurations. Captains' quarters had a different look from ensigns'. Each room was designed for a specific purpose.

This room could have been the officers' mess or an emptied crewman's quarters. It certainly didn't seem like a meeting room. The lights were dim, as they were all over the ship. Klingons seemed to prefer dark colors as well, giving the whole place the feeling of something underground, something slightly unsavory.

Something dangerous.

The small room was also hot and stuffy. Kor had placed a pitcher of fluid in the center of the table, but no cups. No one had asked for any either, and Kirk wasn't about to be the first. He wasn't even certain he should taste anything on this ship, no matter how hot and thirsty he got.

The chair, however, was surprisingly comfortable. It had arms that encircled him, and the cushion, while not soft, wasn't hard, either. It was, however, a bit larger than he was used to—and he had always thought his command chair was large.

He sat in that chair for some time, while Kerdoch told his story. It sounded like the Klingon farmer and the other colonists had had a very long night. They were more than lucky to be alive.

The farmer spoke in precise detail. His memory was astounding, his ability to recall the trivial, trying. But like a good soldier, he assumed all details might be important.

Finally, the farmer finished telling his story of the night of flames, as he called it.

"Thank you, Kerdoch," Kor said, nodding in respect as the farmer stopped talking.

The farmer nodded back and wiped the sweat from his face with his sleeve.

Kirk had been surprised during the last ten minutes at the respect Kor showed the colonist. It seemed that even in a warrior race like the Klingons, those who supplied the food and built the ships and weapons were highly regarded and respected. It was an eye-opening detail of the Klingon culture that a Federation officer would normally never get a chance to see.

Kirk had seen many other things since he'd been on the ship, things he doubted any other Federation officer had seen. Kor had tried to keep him away from the main areas of the battle cruiser, but Kirk had sneaked a look into various sections, making a mental note of their layout and size.

Kor turned to Kirk, showing no respect at all now for a Federation captain.

"Well, Kirk," he said, his voice low and mean, "was this attack from one of the Federation's mongrel races? Do you deny it?"

"Of course I deny it," Kirk said, forcing himself to keep his voice level and not play Kor's game. "If we wanted to destroy the colony, we wouldn't have used small ships to do it. And if the attackers were rogue members of the Federation, we would have had warning. I would also have recognized the type of craft used. I don't. When I return to the *Enterprise,* I'll search our database for crafts like that. But I can tell you now, I've never seen or heard of diamond shaped ships of that size and configuration."

"You would lie to protect your own," Kor said.

"No, I wouldn't," Kirk said. "If members of the Federation made this sort of cowardly attack, I'd want to catch them and punish them as much as you." Kirk kept his gaze focused on Kor's eyes.

The silence stretched until finally Kor laughed. "So you would defend a Klingon planet to keep Federation races under control?"

Kirk held his temper. "Of course not, Commander," he said, keeping his voice level and cold and staring at Kor as hard as he could. "I would defend this planet because it sent out a distress call. Commander, the Organian Treaty would mean nothing if I refused to enforce it."

"You are a strange human," Kor said, shaking his head in disgust. "I will accept your word for the moment. But do not cross me, Captain."

Both men stared at each other until finally Kerdoch said, "Commander, I would like to return to defend my family in case of another attack."

Kor slammed his fist on the table and stood. "Of course, Kerdoch. I will send men with you to help."

"So will I," Kirk said. He flipped open his communicator before Kor could say a word. *"Enterprise,* have Dr. McCoy, Dr. Rathbone, Lieutenant Sulu, and a security detail meet me in the transporter room. Stand by to beam me aboard."

"Aye, Captain." Spock's voice came back clear enough for all in the small room to hear.

Kirk turned to the farmer. "Kerdoch, if the cowards who did this return, I will be at your side to defend you and your family."

"As will I," Kor said.

Kerdoch looked first at Kirk, then at Kor. There was a puzzled, intent look in his eyes. But after a moment he nodded his agreement.

"Good," Kor said, slapping the farmer on the back.

Kirk flipped open his communicator. *"Enterprise,* one to beam aboard."

Then he turned to Kor and Kerdoch. "I will meet you at the colony."

Kor laughed, again shaking his head in mock amazement as Kirk beamed out.

But for Kirk, there was nothing to laugh about—at least not until they discovered who attacked this colony.

Chapter Five

FOR THE SECOND TIME in under two hours Kerdoch felt the effects of a transporter. Only this time he knew exactly where he was being beamed to: the center of the colony.

Back to his home.

Beside him stood Commander Kor and four warriors. Kerdoch had never felt so powerful before. Pride filled his heart and made his blood surge through his veins. He had been given many honors over his years as a colonist, but never one that pleased him as this did.

As the transporter released them in the open center courtyard of the colony, a shout went up from those nearby.

"Kerdoch has returned," one yelled.

"With help!" a woman's voice added.

Kerdoch stood proudly beside Kor as his neighbors

and friends rushed toward them. The colony had suffered even more damage than Kerdoch had remembered. Beside him Kerdoch noticed that Kor frowned as he surveyed the remains of a once proud Klingon farming community. He must have been shocked at the destruction.

Kerdoch waited for a moment until his wife reached his side, and he hugged her. Then he held up his hands and waited for the crowd to calm.

"This is Kor," he said, "commander of the mighty battle cruiser *Klothos* of the Imperial Fleet."

At his mention of Kor's name there were several swift intakes of breath and one gasp. Suddenly everyone was again talking as the relief of having warriors and a battle cruiser here to help defend the colony grew thick in the air, and warriors led by a respected and much honored commander such as Kor.

Kerdoch's wife squeezed him, as if he were the hero responsible for bringing Kor.

Kerdoch, however, felt a distinct unease, as if the winds had shifted and things were not as right as the others might think. He looked over the smiling faces of his neighbors, but saw nothing. So he turned to Kor.

"Sir," Kerdoch said, "we must prepare."

Kor slapped Kerdoch on the back. "You are right, my friend. We must."

In front of them the air shimmered. Weapons came up and were trained on the spot as the Federation captain and several other humans appeared.

Around him Kerdoch could sense the tension returning like a thick fur blanket tossed over the crowd. Only Kor's men lowered their weapons. The colonists did not.

There were five humans with the Federation captain. One was a woman.

The human captain strode up to Kerdoch and Kor. "Do you have wounded?"

Kerdoch nodded. "Many."

"Can someone lead the doctor to them?" The human captain indicated a thin man with a bag over his shoulder who stood off to his left.

Kerdoch turned to his wife and indicated that she should help the doctor.

"This way," she said, with only a questioning glance at her husband.

The human captain turned to his people. "Commander Rathbone, you and Lieutenant Sulu scout the surrounding fields, see if you can discover what was done to the crops, with what kind of weapon, and why. Ensign Chop, Ensign Adaro, you two stay with me."

The human captain then turned to Kor. "We are here to help defend your colony. What needs to be done to get ready for another attack?"

Kor laughed at the Federation captain. "Kirk, you are still the fool. But for the moment we will gladly take advantage of your foolishness."

Kor turned to Kerdoch, who stood straight under the commander's gaze. "Do you have disrupter cannons?"

"Two are working," Kerdoch said "They are on the southwest and northeast perimeters."

"Good," Kor said. "Two are better than none. Kirk have one of your men join one of mine and one colonist at each gun."

One of the colonists put a hand on Kor's arm. "Do you think the humans can be trusted?"

Kor looked down at the offending hand. The colonist removed it quickly. "Are you questioning my judgment?"

"No, Commander," the colonist said. "It is just that when we had humans on this planet, we were instructed to keep them away from our weapons and our technology."

"That is normally a good rule," Kor said, "but I think I can handle Kirk."

The human captain rolled his eyes, but said nothing. He turned to the two humans in red shirts. "Ensign Chop, you take the southwest cannon. Ensign Adaro, take the other."

Kor turned again and faced Kerdoch. "From which direction did the ships make their attack runs?"

Kerdoch glanced around at his neighbors, who were watching.

"Most came directly from the west," Katacq said, and others around him nodded.

"Then we will set up a defensive position on the western edge of the colony," Kor said.

The human captain nodded his agreement, and without hesitation the two captains turned and moved toward the west, matching each other stride for stride.

After a moment Kerdoch realized that he and the other colonists should follow.

Dr. Vivian Rathbone forced herself to take a deep breath as she followed Lieutenant Sulu around a few of the damaged colony domes and out into the burnt fields.

Above them both suns kept the air thick and extremely hot, almost choking with the drifting smoke and black ash. The sky was the same pale blue and pink she remembered, but until now she'd forgotten how really hot it could get on Signi Beta. And how miserable. A person forgot such matters when five years of work got tossed away.

They moved a few hundred steps into the closest field and then stopped. She was having a very hard time believing she was in a landing party with Captain Kirk. And even a harder time making sense of the fact she was back on Signi Beta.

It didn't smell like Signi Beta.

The smoke filled her eyes with tears. Such destruction. And of crops. She had read about such things when she was studying history; she knew that sometimes war parties attacked supplies. But she had never seen it.

It looked as if a fire had made a selective rampage through the crops. The destruction looked all the more terrible since she knew it was deliberate.

Sulu crouched and used his scanner on the remains of the crops while she stood staring across the distant smoking fields, trying to take in what she was seeing.

She'd visited the Klingon colony twice during her years on this planet. Both times she had been struck by the beauty of the waves of blue-green crops, lush and supple even at the hottest time of day. Now those crops had been reduced to black ash. A crime.

"This is strange," Sulu said, shaking his head.

"What is?" Vivian asked, kneeling beside him. She knew why the captain had sent her and Sulu to investigate the destruction of the crops: she had lived and worked here, and Sulu was widely known for his botanical hobbies. In fact, she had hoped to someday talk to him about it. Once this mission was over, maybe she'd get the chance.

"I'm getting some strange readings here, Commander." He held up his tricorder for her to look at.

She glanced at the numbers and then smiled, impressed. "Good work, Lieutenant," she said. "It took our scientists almost two months to identify that same problem."

"You mean this is planetwide?" Sulu asked, turning to face her.

She nodded and stood slowly so as not to start her head spinning. "This planet, in its distant past, had a very different form of plant life, obviously native to these heat and soil conditions. Then something happened here about eight or nine hundred years ago that altered the planet's climate, and a second, biologically different form of plant life appeared, which slowly melded with and then overran the first."

Sulu stared at his readings, shaking his head. "Amazing."

"It is that," she said. "Now the Klingons have imported a third form of plant life that is blending with the first two. We did the same thing in our experiments on the southern continent. The Klingons were more successful than we were. That's one of the many reasons they won this planet."

Sulu stood, still studying his tricorder. "Any indication of what caused the first plant shift?"

Vivian shook her head. "Most likely it was a natural event such as a meteor strike, though some scientists think the plants were artificially introduced by a lost culture. Knowing the true story might have helped us win this planet."

Sulu nodded. "As Mr. Spock would say: Fascinating."

Vivian laughed. "That it was. And still is, I imagine, to the Klingons." Even she could hear the bitterness in her voice.

Sulu ignored her comment and moved his tricorder in a wide circle.

She watched for a moment, then bent down and used her own tricorder to study the remains of some of the plants. They had been almost flash-burned with a high-intensity heat source of some type. She picked off a stem and smelled it. "Plasma," she said.

"Exactly, Commander," Sulu said. "My guess is that this was done with a wide-focus plasma beam."

"Do you know of any ships that use wide-focus plasma beams?" she asked.

"Not a one," Sulu said. "And I can't imagine why any ship would use them unless it wanted to do this kind of damage."

Vivian looked out over the field for patterns, just as she had done when a fungus outbreak threatened the Federation crops. What she saw now was a systematic pattern of destruction that targeted only the Klingon crops.

"Look," she said to Sulu, pointing out a few distant areas. "No natural vegetation has been touched, only the Klingon fields."

Sulu frowned, focusing his tricorder on where she had pointed.

"You're right. This *is* strange." Sulu snapped his tricorder shut and turned to face her. "Let's report back to the captain. He is going to want to know this."

She nodded. "Maybe Captain Kirk can figure out what's going on here. I sure can't."

Sulu laughed. "Nothing about this seems to make sense, does it?"

"Nothing," she said. "That much I'll agree with. And I mean that in more ways than one."

Kirk turned from his work digging a bunker near the western edge of the colony to see Dr. Rathbone and Sulu approaching from the fields and Dr. McCoy coming from the center of the colony.

Kirk stopped and wiped the sweat from his forehead with the back of his arm. He'd have to make sure all of his people got enough water in this heat. Otherwise they might not survive until the next attack.

Kor and two of the colonists, including Kerdoch, were about twenty paces away, digging another bunker. They'd left him on his own and every so often laughed at him from a distance. But alone Kirk had managed to dig a fairly decent bunker that would provide some protection.

"Jim," McCoy said before he even reached Kirk, "the Klingon doctor has everyone all fixed up."

Kirk could tell that his friend was annoyed. "So that's good, isn't it?"

"Yeah, fine," McCoy said. "But the damn superior Klingon attitude is going to make me mad someday."

"Insulted your ability, did he?" Kirk asked. He managed to hide his grin from McCoy.

McCoy snorted, then said, "He can't insult my ability. He's working with patients who have constitutions like tree trunks. It would take a meteor strike to seriously damage these people."

Kirk cocked his head. "Are you saying no one was badly injured?"

"Of course not," McCoy said. "There were several serious injuries. But, dammit, Jim, the Klingon physique is built to withstand damage. I've never seen anything like it. When one part breaks down, another kicks in. Klingon doctors lack the finesse of human ones."

"Apparently they don't need finesse," Kirk said. "We are fragile creatures."

"You're telling me. This heat is reminding me with each breath."

"I thought you grew up in the heat, Doctor."

"And I live in a controlled environment for that reason, Captain," McCoy snapped. "No intelligent creature would subject himself to temperatures like this on a daily basis. And he certainly wouldn't dig ditches in this climate."

"Bunkers," Kirk said. "I'm digging a bunker."

"Well, make sure you drink enough water. The last thing I need is a captain with heat stroke."

"Yes, sir," Kirk said, smiling. "If you're worried, you can stay here and help me dig."

"Didn't I just say I didn't want to be out in the heat?"

"I don't think you have much choice, Bones." As Kirk finished the sentence, Sulu and Rathbone reached him. "I take it you two have something to report."

"The destruction," Sulu said, "was caused by a wide-focus plasma beam and focused only on the Klingon crops, leaving the natural brush and plants surrounding the Klingon fields standing."

"Wide focus?" Kirk asked.

Sulu nodded.

Kirk glanced around at the colony's domed buildings. No wonder most of them were still standing. Wide-focus plasma beams had very high heat but very little destructive power. A hand phaser could do more damage than the weapon Sulu was describing.

"It makes no sense, does it, Captain?" Sulu said.

"Not if you're trying to destroy a colony," Kirk said. "But if you just want to burn everything down without doing serious damage to the ground, it would be a good method. Right?"

"That's right," Rathbone said. "Like burning grass off a field. It clears the unwanted stubble, kills the pests, and returns most of the nutrients to the soil."

"I wouldn't let the Klingons hear you call them pests," McCoy said.

Sulu laughed, but Kirk managed to keep focused on what they were talking about. "We need some more answers." He climbed out of the bunker and strode toward Kor and Kerdoch.

"Captain," Kor said, "you seem to be lagging behind in your building. Too much work for you?"

Kirk noticed that Kerdoch didn't laugh with Kor and the other colonists.

Kirk smiled at Kor. "You might want to put a roof over your bunker," Kirk said. "Might save you a few burns in the coming attack. The weapons used the first two times were wide-focus plasma beams."

"What?" Kor said, jumping up from the bunker and facing the humans. "What fools would attack a colony with such a weapon?"

"The fools who attacked your colony," McCoy said.

"And they only targeted your crops," Kirk said. "The natural plants and brush near your fields were not harmed."

Kor shook his head, obviously puzzled. "This makes no sense."

Suddenly Kirk's communicator demanded attention. A fraction of a second later so did Kor's. Kirk wanted to laugh, but he was worried about the incoming message. Twice in twenty-four hours he and another ship's commander had been called at the same moment while away from their ships.

He flipped open his communicator. "Kirk here."

Behind him Kor said something in Klingon.

"Captain," Spock's voice came through clear and as calm as always. "Six alien ships are approaching the system at high speed. I do not recognize their type and class."

"Go to red alert," Kirk said. "We'll batten down the hatches here."

"Yes, sir," Spock said.

"And Spock," Kirk said. "Keep her in one piece."

"She would not function efficiently any other way, sir," Spock said.

"Good. Kirk out."

Chapter Six

KELLY BOGLE sat in his captain's chair staring at the stars flashing past in warp. He'd spent the last six hours sleeping, then had a quick breakfast, and was now back on the bridge. Waiting.

He hated these times of waiting. They were the worst part of being a starship captain as far as he was concerned. Especially the times when a starship was covering an incredibly vast expanse of space to reach an emergency. Those times seemed to stretch so that every minute was an hour and every hour a day. He would never get used to it, no matter how long he sat in this chair.

Now they were rushing to be at the side of the *Enterprise.* Kirk had already had a skirmish with the Klingons, but had managed, in pure James Kirk fashion to get them to work with him. How long that would last Bogle didn't even want to venture to guess.

But what worried Bogle even more was the fact that they still didn't know who had attacked the colony.

Behind him his communication officer, Lieutenant Sandy, twisted around in his chair. "Sir, a message from the *Enterprise*. They, along with the Klingon battle cruiser and the Klingon colony, are under attack by a large unknown force."

"How long until we reach scene?"

Science Officer Richard Lee said, "Six hours, ten minutes, sir."

Bogle stabbed his finger on his communication button. "Engineering? Projeff, can you get me any more speed?"

The reply came back quick and short: "Not if you want to get there safely."

"Understood," Bogle said, and clicked off the communication button. That was the third time he'd asked Projeff for higher warp. The first two times Projeff had managed to nudge their speed upward. But clearly not this time. The third time *wasn't* the charm.

Bogle turned to Sandy. "Inform the *Enterprise* of our location and time of arrival."

"Yes, sir," Sandy said.

"And, Lieutenant," Bogle said, leaning back in his chair and staring at the stars flashing past.

"Yes, sir?" Sandy said.

"Wish them luck."

Spock stood beside the captain's chair, his attention completely focused on the screen and the image of the incoming ships. All six of the approaching ships were twice the size of the *Enterprise*. They seemed to be designed in a wedge, almost winglike, thin and pointed in the front, expanding into two thick structures in the rear. A very efficient and logical design.

The Klingon battle cruiser *Klothos,* under the command of Subcommander Korath, had turned to face the incoming fleet beside the *Enterprise.* Both ships had gone to battle-ready status.

"Sir, we have had no response to our hails," Lieutenant Uhura said.

"Keep hailing them on all channels and frequencies, Lieutenant," Spock said.

"Aye, sir."

Spock moved up to his science scope and ran a quick computer check of the approaching ships. Again the computer told him what he already knew: these ships were unknown to the Federation, and—if Korath could be believed—to the Klingon Empire as well.

He stepped back down beside the captain's chair, but did not sit down. As he watched the screen, the six ships broke smoothly into three units of two. One unit turned and moved toward a high orbit over the planet while the other two units headed directly for the *Enterprise* and the Klingon battle cruiser. It would be a logical move if the two ships in high orbit intended to attack the colony on the planet again.

"Lieutenant, have we had any response to our hails?" Spock asked again.

"No, sir," Uhura said.

"Arm photon torpedoes," Spock said. "Mr. Chekov, prepare for evasive maneuver Beta Six."

"Torpedoes armed," Chekov said. "Standing by."

Spock said nothing, just stared intently at the screen. The four ships seemed to be making a standard attack formation, working to pinch the two defenders between them. Now it would be only moments before their intentions became clear.

At the moment Spock had expected, phaser beams shot out of the four approaching ships. The *Enterprise* rocked from the impact, but Spock managed to hang on to the captain's chair and keep his feet. There was now clearly no doubt of the ships' hostile intentions.

"Return fire, Mr. Chekov," Spock said. "Then break off and follow the two ships heading for planetary orbit."

Spock didn't say it, but he was concerned for the captain and the landing party. If Spock's calculations were correct, those two ships carried atmosphere-capable craft, ready for another attack on the colony on the surface.

Four photon torpedoes hit the two attacking ships as they passed by, exploding against their screens. The screens flared bright blue but withstood the force. Spock noted that the new ships were not only efficiently designed but were well armed and protected as well.

The *Enterprise* turned and moved up and to the left, working to be in a position near the two orbiting ships. The move caught the two attacking ships by surprise as they banked to turn in the wrong direction.

"Screens at eighty-five percent," Chekov said. "We hit them twice, but they sustained no damage."

Spock had already gathered as much.

The Klingon battle cruiser was taking a different approach. Korath seemed to care nothing of his Commander on the planet. He was dogfighting with the two ships that had attacked him, taking more punishment than he was handing out.

On the main screen the two orbiting ships seemed

to split in half along the thick back edge as huge doors opened.

"Docking bay doors, sir, they are opening," Chekov said.

Spock had already identified the doors as part of a docking bay. He didn't need Chekov's help on that. But he did need Chekov's help conserving firepower. He was glad the ensign was a good shot.

Dozens of smaller craft emerged from each alien ship and turned toward the planet's surface.

"Fire on the smaller craft, Mr. Chekov," Spock ordered. "Ignore the larger ones."

"Aye, sir," Chekov said.

The phaser shots streaked across the blackness of space. Four shots fired in rapid succession. Apparently the mother ships had not expected the attack. The smaller ships weren't shielded.

Four of them exploded as the phaser shots found their targets.

"We got them!" Chekov cried.

"Mr. Chekov," Spock said, wishing the ensign's emotions were as well controlled as his aim. "We 'got' nothing. Continue firing."

"Mr. Spock," Chekov said. "I think we have trouble."

Spock looked at the screen as the two mother ships turned to face the *Enterprise*.

"I think we have had trouble since we arrived in this sector, Ensign," Spock said.

Two more shots destroyed two more smaller craft. But Spock noted there were still over twenty headed for the colony.

"Sir," Mr. Chekov said, "the other two ships are coming in behind us."

Mr. Spock nodded. There would be no logic in destroying the *Enterprise* in a fight of four against one. That would not save the captain or the colony below.

"Take us back toward the Klingon ship," Spock ordered as the ship rocked with direct hits from the two mother ships. "Heading 238.72. Half impulse."

"Screens at sixty percent," Chekov said as the starship turned and sped toward the battle between the Klingon battle cruiser and the two strange craft.

Again the move caught the ships pursuing the *Enterprise* by surprise. The two orbiting ships stayed in position.

One of the alien craft fighting the Klingon battle cruiser seemed to be damaged, but it was clear that at the moment the *Klothos* was taking a beating. It was also clear that Subcommander Korath would not retreat. The Klingons needed help.

"Lieutenant," Spock said, "hail Korath."

Uhura pressed a few buttons on her station, then turned to him. "On-screen, sir."

When Korath's face appeared on the screen Spock gave him no chance to speak. "On my mark focus all your firepower on the ship closest to our position."

Korath glared at Spock for a moment, then nodded. "Understood."

"Ensign Chekov," Spock said, "focus our full phaser array on that ship. Fire on my mark."

"Aye, sir," Chekov said, his fingers dancing on the board.

"Now," Spock said, both to Chekov and Korath.

The full force of weapons fire from the Klingon battle cruiser and the *Enterprise* knocked the alien ship's screens down almost instantly. In a moment the huge ship exploded in a bright flash of orange and red.

"Got him!" Chekov shouted.

Spock did not admonish him this time. There was no containing the ensign's enthusiasm.

"Take us to a position beside the battle cruiser," Spock said.

"Yes, sir."

As the *Enterprise* dropped into position, the three attacking alien ships turned away, moving back between the *Enterprise* and the planet. They took up positions near the other two, forming an effective blockade of the colony on the surface below.

"They're breaking off the attack," Chekov said, his voice excited.

Spock nodded. It was logical. They had lost a ship. They would guard their ground forces while they took time to assess the battle that had just occurred. He would have done the same thing given the chance.

0 Spock punched the comm button on the captain's chair. "Mr. Scott, are we within transporter range of the landing party?"

"No, Mr. Spock," Mr. Scott said.

Spock cut the connection.

"Lieutenant," Spock said. "Hail the captain."

"Aye, sir," Uhura said.

Within a moment the familiar "Kirk here" rang out on the bridge.

"Captain," Spock said, "twenty small enemy ships are entering the planet's atmosphere. We have destroyed one of their transports, but we are being held outside transporter range by five others."

"Five?" Kirk said.

"Yes, sir," Spock said.

"Is there damage to the *Enterprise,* Mr. Spock?"

"No, sir. Our shields have lost some power, but I expect to regain it shortly," Spock said. "The Klingon battle cruiser will need some repairs, but it is still functioning. The *Farragut* will arrive in six hours and two minutes."

"Understood," Kirk said. "Do not put the *Enterprise* in any undue danger, Mr. Spock. That is an order. We will hold out here until the *Farragut* arrives. Keep me informed. Kirk out."

Mr. Spock stood beside the command chair, staring at the five ships on the screen and the blue-green planet beyond. The captain's orders were logical, but as the captain had said a number of times, that did not mean there might not be a better, even more logical way. It was just up to Spock to find it.

He tapped the communications button on the arm of the captain's chair. "Mr. Scott, would you report to the bridge."

"Aye, sir," Scott's voice came back strong.

"Lieutenant," Spock said, turning to Uhura, "inform the *Farragut* of our situation. Scramble the message. Include in that message full sensor scans on the invading ships. Then tell them speed is of the essence."

"Aye, sir," Uhura said.

Spock turned back to face the five ships and the planet beyond. There should be a way to get the captain off that planet.

Or at least help him.

Kirk flipped his communicator closed. Beside him stood McCoy, Sulu, and Dr. Rathbone. All watched him with wide eyes and sweaty faces. Kor and Kerdoch had stepped a few feet away, and Kor still talked to his ship.

"Well, they're on their way," Kirk said, trying to put some hope in his voice, even though he didn't feel any. "Spock says there are twenty ships."

"How long?" Dr. Rathbone asked.

Kirk shook his head, then rubbed sweat from his eyes. "They should come through the atmosphere in about five minutes. Maybe less."

Kor snapped his communicator back onto his belt. "The attack comes," he said to Kirk.

Kirk nodded. "We need to warn the colonists to take cover."

"I will do it," Kerdoch said. He turned and, with the other colonist who had been helping him dig, headed at a full run toward the domed structures of the colony.

"I will go to the western disrupter cannon," Kor said. Without another word he also turned and moved off, striding as if it were just another normal day instead of the day he would most likely die.

Kirk glanced around at the two bunkers they had built. Shallow holes in hard dirt. Nothing more. Against plasma-beam weapons, the bunkers would be useless. They at least needed covers.

Scanning the area quickly, Kirk saw what might work. The colony domes had been constructed of prefabricated panels about four feet wide by eight feet long. If they were light enough to be carried, they might do the trick.

"Quickly," he said, gesturing for his away team to follow him.

At a run he made his way to the edge of the colony and to a mostly destroyed housing dome. The body of a Klingon man, clearly dead, was pinned inside. Kirk hoped that the man wouldn't mind them using his home to survive.

With a quick yank he pulled one prefabricated panel free and studied it. About the size of a normal door and four inches thick, it weighed no more than twenty pounds. The panels were much lighter than they looked—a nice piece of Klingon design. They would never withstand a direct hit from any major weapon, but they would serve just fine as heat shields.

He turned and handed the sheet to Rathbone. "Use this as a cover for the bunker—the one the Klingons dug."

She struggled with it for a moment, also clearly surprised at the panel's light weight. Then she picked it up, lifted it over her head, and moved off.

"Didn't know she was that strong," McCoy said, watching her go.

Kirk turned and, with Sulu's help, yanked another panel free and tossed it to the Doctor.

McCoy grabbed at it. "That explains it," he said as he easily picked it up and followed Rathbone.

Within another few seconds Kirk and Sulu had freed two more and were headed back to the bunker.

Rathbone had managed to get her panel across the top of the waist-high trench and was frantically pushing dirt over it to camouflage it.

McCoy was fitting his beside the first. Within another thirty frantic seconds they had the four panels covering the open bunker and enough dirt on top of them to make them look almost natural. The bunker was open on either end, but there wasn't enough time to do anything about that now.

Kirk took a deep breath of hot air and scanned the

bright horizon. Through the heat waves, in the distance, low and just above the small foothills, he saw several bright cuts in the sky, as if someone had painted silver lines on the horizon.

Alien attack ships. They were just as Kordach had described.

"Take cover!" Kirk shouted.

With Dr. Rathbone and McCoy in the center and Sulu near the other open end, Kirk took his place, phaser in hand. He doubted there was much he could do with a phaser, but at the moment it felt good just holding it.

Chapter Seven

KERDOCH HEADED INTO the center of the colony at a full run, his hard steps kicking up the dust between the domed colony homes. "Take cover," he shouted every few steps. "The enemy returns."

His voice carried far ahead of his running pace and as each neighbor in turn heard his warning, they paused, then went into quick action.

Women and children scrambled for the cover of their prefabricated homes.

Husbands took up weapons and ran for the perimeter of the colony, ready to fight with anything they could find.

Kerdoch continued his mission, running and shouting his warning through the center of the colony until he reached his own home. His wife stood outside, obviously having heard his call. She now waited for him. His children were already inside, out of sight. He knew, however, that his oldest son stood guard just inside the door and would hear him.

He stopped in front of his wife and took her shoulders, looking deep into her eyes. Her muscles were firm under his grasp and for an instant he never wanted to let her go. Then he took a deep, hot breath and said, "Get yourself and the children as far under cover inside as you can. There are many ships coming."

"You go to the guns?" she asked.

"I will fight," he said. "In any fashion I can."

She nodded. "I will guard the children and our home. Fight well, my husband."

"We shall not let these cowards take our land," Kerdoch said. And inside he felt it. Deeper than he'd ever felt anything before. And with more anger and force than he had ever felt.

He still worried about his wife and his children, but he did not fear for his own life. If he died fighting on this hot afternoon, he would have died well.

He squeezed his wife's shoulders with both hands one more time, then turned and at a full run headed for the fight.

But he was too late.

The first wave of ships flashed over the colony before he'd run another hundred steps, their flat hulls gleaming like mirrors in the light of the two suns.

They were firing as they went, the same wide beams as before.

Kerdoch instinctively ducked and covered his head with his arm, but this time he didn't make it to the ground. The explosions and concussion wave from their high speed knocked him backward, picking him up and tossing him into the air like a leaf in a very hot, very strong wind.

The last thing he remembered as he was thrown into the remains of a dome was being angry that he had not reached his place on the big gun.

Very angry.

Then his head hit something hard as he crashed through the dome, and the blackness took him.

Kor could see the gleaming cuts in the sky headed his way—at least ten small ships flying in a tight wedge. Good. A tight formation was the flight of idiots. It would increase the chances of a hit from the big gun.

He stood behind a chest-high earthen wall that had been quickly erected to help protect one of the colony's large disrupter cannons. Beside him were six colonists, hand weapons aimed at the coming ships as if they might bring down a ship with one. Kor acknowledged their courage. They were true Klingons. The Federation man also stood in the bunker beside him, phaser in hand. He too had courage.

Behind Kor the cannon stood no more than a man high on a thick concrete platform. One of his men and one colonist grasped the gun. It would take both of them to track and fire at the small fast-moving ships. The disrupter cannon had been designed to defend against attacks from the air. It was not extremely accurate, but the force was powerful enough to knock almost any craft from the sky.

"At my command," Kor said to those on the gun base, as across the hot surface of the planet the ships became more distinct. Then, quicker than Kor had time to react, the ships were on and over them, a fast wave of shining metal firing wide-focus plasma beams. He had been caught by surprise before, but never like that. The ships' speed was at least ten times what he had been expecting.

The impact of the plasma beams and the shock waves of the passing ships caught Kor as he instinctively turned away, smashing him down into the dirt at the base of the big gun. In all his years he had never felt such a force, like a giant's fist pounding him square in the back.

But soon the giant stopped pounding.

Kor fought his way back to his feet. An extra sensation of heat covered his right arm and shoulder, and it took him a moment to realize his uniform jacket was on fire.

In one quick motion he stripped off the jacket and tossed it aside in disgust, leaving only his shirt on.

Beside him the colonists behind the earthen burn were shedding their shirts and jackets or rolling on the ground to smother the flames. The federation crewman lay in the bottom of the bunker, a nasty gash across his forehead.

Kor glanced around. The first wave of attack craft already beyond the colony and out of range of the big gun. He cussed at them. If they returned, he would be ready.

His officer and the colonist who had manned the gun were lying together in a burning heap about twenty feet from the gun. They had been standing in the open, and the full force of the plasma beam had caught them. Kor knew he had been lucky to be behind the earthen burn. The barrier had most likely saved his life and that of the other colonists.

He glanced quickly around. In the distance a second wave of craft dropped down out of the sky and became shimmery slits in the sky headed for the colony.

He started to stand his ground, then thought better of it. There was a time to face an enemy and a time to duck an enemy's blows. This was a time to duck, so that he could throw a blow of his own later.

"Get down!" he shouted to the colonists. "Now!"

He barely had time to drop to his stomach and cover his head as the second attack wave struck.

This time the heat and the force of the ships' passing smashed him flat into the dry ground, knocking the wind from him. But that blow just served to make him angrier.

The moment the force let up, Kor jumped back to his feet. No other wave of ships seemed to be forming, so he turned to follow the last wave as they burned more crops and then climbed into the sky, disappearing into the distance.

Slowly the intense rumble of their passing faded, leaving only the crackling of fires and the cries for help from the wounded. Behind him the colonists staggered to their feet, patting out random flames on each other's clothes.

Kor stared at the destruction throughout the colony. Everything seemed to be burning. He stepped up on the platform base to see if the big gun still functioned. A quick check showed that it was operable. But before the next attack they would need to protect it better.

Suddenly a faint rumbling sound spun him around.

Gleaming slits in the low sky filled the horizon.

"Kor!" one of the colonists shouted. "Get down!"

He dove for the protection of the bunker, but for the second time that day Kor was caught by surprise.

The impact twisted him through the air. He landed hard and rolled, pushed along by the force of impact wave from the ships.

Part of his warrior brain said that rolling was the right thing to do. Rolling would put out the flames on his clothes. The other part of his mind said he should stand and fight.

The instant the shock wave let go of him he rolled up and onto his feet, balanced to fight.

Everything around him spun, and a sharp, biting pain cut through his chest.

"You will pay," he said to the swirling images of the departing ships.

Then the blackness swirled in from all sides, and there was nothing he could do to stop it.

Or his fall toward the ground.

Nothing.

Kirk had thought the day hot before. Now it had suddenly turned into a roaring inferno as the alien craft sped by over the covered bunker. He'd seen them as small cuts against the sky forming a wedge low on the horizon. He'd counted ten of them. If Spock's count was correct, and it usually was, that left at least ten more to form a second attack force. He wondered where they were and exactly what they were attacking.

Almost before he could get his head back under the cover the ships were over and past.

The ground shook like an earthquake, and heat washed through the open-ended bunker like a blast of fire.

McCoy shouted over the rumbling, "Cover your eyes!"

But Kirk already had his arm over his face, protecting himself. He hoped Rathbone beside him had done the same thing, because he could feel the burning against his forehead and scalp. If they survived this, they would have very strange-looking sunburns.

Then as suddenly as the intense heat and loud rumbling had hit them, it was gone, leaving somewhat cooler air swirling into their small shelter.

And quiet. Ear-ringing quiet.

Sulu and Rathbone instantly began coughing, but both indicated to McCoy that they were all right. They'd just swallowed some of the hot air, and their lungs were reacting.

"Stay under cover," Kirk said, then stuck his head out and did a quick scan of the surrounding area. The alien force was obviously using the wide-focus plasma weapons again, since just about every building was left standing, but everything that could burn was afire.

Luckily the Klingons had made the prefabricated sheets for their domes fireproof. Otherwise there would have been nothing left standing and no one left alive, including them. "If I live through this, I'll write a note of thanks to the Klingon who invented these panels," he said to himself.

He eased himself out of the bunker to check the direction the ships had gone. They were already out of sight. Kirk scanned the horizon, looking for them.

Nothing but burning buildings and fields almost as far as the eye could see. It wasn't until he'd turned back in the direction from which the first wave of ships had come that he saw the second wave dropping down toward the horizon to make a run at the colony.

"That explains where the other half of the ships went," he said to himself. "Right here.

"Cover yourself!" he shouted to the others as he dived back under the prefabricated panels that served as a cover for their bunker.

He hit the dirt, face down beside Rathbone, as the ground shook and the second blast of heat smashed into them. Kirk was amazed his clothing didn't just burst into flames. He'd felt that level of heat before, but only when opening an oven to remove a freshly roasted real turkey. And that had been years ago, back when he still had time to cook, and a kitchen to cook in.

Then, again as quickly as they had come, the ships and the intense blast of heat were past, leaving swirling dust and smoke in their wake.

Kirk sat up, his face instantly dripping wet, his clothes sticking to every inch of his skin. Beside him Rathbone also sat up and leaned back against the dirt wall. Her face was streaked black with grime and sweat, and her brown hair was plastered to her head.

"Not my kind of sauna," McCoy said, trying to pull his shirt away from his skin.

"You mean you get this hot on purpose?" Sulu said.

McCoy only snorted.

"We're going to need water, Bones," Kirk said. "How much do we have?"

"Not enough for this kind of heat," McCoy said. "But whatever you have, everyone, drink it now. Doctor's orders."

Kirk and Bones didn't have canteens, but both Sulu and Rathbone each had carried one. The four of them split the contents of the two canteens, while staying under the cover of the bunker.

As they were finishing Rathbone said, "Do you think the attack is over?"

Kirk had been wondering the same thing. It didn't make sense to end the attack with just two runs at the colony. Unless that was all the firepower the small ships could carry. But plasma weapons didn't take up that much room, so Kirk doubted that was the case. If Spock were here, he'd tell them exactly what the odds were for another attack.

Suddenly the ground around them shook, and they barely had time to cover their faces before the intense heat hit them again, this time smashing them into one another, since they weren't braced. Kirk found himself being pushed over Rathbone, his head ending up on McCoy's back.

After the attack eased, Kirk pushed himself up and away from Rathbone. "I think that was your answer. Everyone all right?"

"I was hoping for a different one," she said. She pushed some wet hair out of her face. "I'm fine, I think."

"What kind of ships were those?" McCoy asked.

"I have no idea," Sulu said. He pulled out his tricorder and assessed the area around them. "Those aren't standard plasma weapons, either. They've been modified somehow."

Kirk gazed at his crew. He was proud of them. They instantly returned to business. Rathbone looked shaken, but she was fine as well.

They had never faced anything quite like this before. No wonder the Klingons had been upset. No wonder they had tried to figure out what was happening, and no wonder they had blamed the Federation at first. These attacks were deliberately aimed at the colony, as if someone did not want the colony on the planet.

"Dr. Rathbone," Kirk said. "Signi Beta was uninhabited when the Federation planned the settlement, am I right?"

"Of course," she gasped, as if her lungs still hadn't recovered from the searing heat. "We'd never colonize a settled planet."

"I doubt the Klingons would either, Jim," McCoy said. "They might have conquered it, but they wouldn't have colonized it."

Kirk gazed up at the now empty sky. "Those attacks were meant for the colony. Who would attack farmers? And why?"

"Who knows?" McCoy said. He was checking the people around him, making certain they weren't seriously injured. "Maybe we should find out who the Klingons have angered lately and who would like to attack them," McCoy said.

"Destroying a food supply is the best way to get to the heart of a culture," Rathbone said.

Kirk looked at her. She was right. He had no data points besides this one. For all he knew, Klingon farming communities all over the sector could be under attack. He shivered despite the heat.

"Well," he said, "they gave us a small reprieve. Let's see what we can do with it."

He knew the ships would be back. They seemed to use a concentrated attack formation, and they had a scorched-earth policy—something he'd studied at the Academy, something Earth hadn't seen since the twentieth century.

Barbaric.

And dangerous.

And effective.

It destroyed the defenders' ability to mount an attack, and destroyed morale by injuring home, hearth, and kin.

Kirk wiped his hand over his brow. He was sweating profusely. He wasn't used to the heat, and neither were his companions. Their water was gone.

And the attacks weren't over.

This was going to be a very long and very hot afternoon, and if they didn't get water soon, it would be their last.

Chapter Eight

THE ATTACK on the colony lasted just under two hours. Twenty-four passes of the attack fleet, never varying their direction or the intensity of their fire.

Kirk had never seen anything like it. It was as if the colony was nothing more than a spot they wanted removed from the surface of the planet, and they were going to keep wiping and wiping at it until it was gone.

After the tenth attack, Kirk had contacted Spock and asked him if he could get sensor readings on the five main ships to let him know when the smaller ships returned. Spock said he could.

Fourteen intense heat waves later, Spock informed him that the smaller craft had returned to the mother ships.

Kirk managed to drag himself out of the bunker and stand up. He was light-headed and enormously thirsty. The skin on his arms felt like leather and was very sensitive to his touch.

Dr. McCoy climbed out the other side and stood beside Sulu. "Jim," he said, his voice almost a whisper, "we need water. Quickly."

Kirk nodded, too tired and dry to talk. He helped Rathbone to stand. Then the four of them staggered toward what was left of the colony.

Kirk could barely force his legs to move one in front of the other, and from the way the others beside him were staggering, he knew he wasn't the only one having problems. If that attack had lasted much longer, they might never have climbed out of that bunker.

He had never felt so useless. The plans they had made before the attack hadn't worked. Neither he nor Kor had expected such a sustained assault. Nor had he expected to have the *Enterprise* rendered useless overhead.

The enemy they were facing was greater than he expected.

Over a third of the colony buildings were in piles of burning rubble. Not once during the attack had Kirk heard any fire from the disrupter cannons, so there was no telling what had happened to Kor and his men and to Ensigns Chop and Adaro. The chances were good that they were all dead.

They passed the bodies of two Klingons, one a woman, one a young boy, as they moved around a pile of rubble. Both bodies were burned beyond recognition. The woman's clothes and most of her flesh were gone, leaving only blackened bones and a charred black pile of what had been her interior organs. All her blood and other fluids had boiled away hours before.

"We were lucky," Sulu said.

"Very," Bones said, taking Rathbone by the arm and pulling her forward away from the bodies.

"This way," Kirk said, indicating that they should move toward the colony's center courtyard. A dozen wells were scattered through the colony, but Kirk figured the one in the center courtyard was the most protected and therefore the most likely to have survived.

He was half right. The pump and structure around the well were gone, but the pressure in the well had kept the water bubbling into a wide concrete-type pool, then running off through the dry earth toward the fields beyond. They were the first to find the well, and all four of them splashed water on their faces and arms before drinking.

Kirk couldn't remember cold water ever feeling so good. It soothed and cooled his skin like nothing he'd ever felt before.

"Drink as much as you can," McCoy said after a few large swallows of his own. "Our bodies need every bit they can get to replace what they've lost. And keep our kidneys from shutting down."

This was one doctor's order that Kirk had no trouble obeying. He let the cold water flow down his throat, almost without swallowing.

After washing as much dirt and grime as he could off his face, head, and arms, and drinking until his stomach rebelled, he straightened up and looked around.

None of the colonists had yet appeared. The ones

left alive obviously thought another attack was coming. And they were probably right. But for the moment they had time to prepare for it.

"All clear," he shouted, his sour, dry throat screaming in pain at the effort.

He took another long drink of cold water, then flipped open his communicator. "Kirk to *Enterprise.*"

"*Enterprise* here, Captain," Mr. Spock's voice came back strong.

"What's your status, Mr. Spock?" He could barely croak out the words. The water had helped, but not entirely.

"All systems operational," he said. "We are standing at red alert."

"Keep an eye on those transports, Mr. Spock. Give us as much warning as you can if there's any movement toward the surface."

"Understood, Captain."

"And, Mr. Spock," Kirk said, "how long until the *Farragut* arrives?"

"Three hours, fifty-two minutes," Spock said.

"Let's hope we can last that long. Kirk out."

He flipped the communicator closed and turned to McCoy, Sulu, and Rathbone. "Enjoying landing party duty, Doctor?" Kirk asked the dirt-caked, heat-baked woman as Dr. McCoy spread burn lotion on her arms and face.

She snorted, then said, "Can't wait until my next one, sir."

Kirk studied her for a moment. He could tell she was half in shock. This experience had been doubly hard on her, since this was her first time in combat.

"Good," Kirk said, smiling at her. "We'll try to make the next one as fun."

McCoy shook his head as he turned to Sulu and began to apply the burn medication.

"We need to signal the all clear to these colonists," Kirk said, "And, Bones, don't let the Klingon doctor stop you from helping this time."

McCoy looked around. "I doubt if he's still alive. But I'll find out. Now stand still so I can apply this."

Kirk did as he was told as McCoy put cool, soothing lotion on his arms and then dabbed at his face and neck. "Rub that around," he said.

Again Kirk did as he was told, letting the lotion cut the sharp sting of the burns. Then he took another long drink and faced his landing party.

"When you hear my call, I want you heading back to the bunker at a full run. Understood? And next time we all take water with us. All right?"

Kirk waited until each nodded their agreement.

"Good," Kirk said. "Let's spread the word. Doctor, you find the Klingon doctor. Rathbone, head north, giving the all clear. Sulu, you go south. I'll see what happened to the disrupter cannons and our men. I want to figure out a way to take some action against these ships."

"And everyone keep drinking," McCoy said.

"So we can boil in our own gravy during the next attack?" Sulu asked.

"Nope," McCoy said, turning and heading off. "So you'll live long enough to see that next attack."

With that sentence hanging in the hot air, Kirk took another long drink from the bubbling well before he headed toward the cannon.

Kerdoch fought to wake from the nightmare.
Heat. Searing heat.

Fever dream.

Flames surrounding him. Trapping him.

Roaring monsters. Stamping the ground, shaking him.

Flames. Heat. Roaring monsters.

Over and over.

A nightmare. A nightmare he'd never had before.

Kerdoch knew it was a nightmare, but he couldn't awake, couldn't fight his way through the flames to get away from the deep blackness crawling at him from all sides. Cool, alluring blackness that he knew was not the right path.

He must fight to wake up. He knew there were important things to be done. He could not think of them, but the feeling of important things to finish edged him forward.

He must fight.

Fight to beat the flames.

Fight to see his family again.

He was a Klingon. Klingons never gave up. Klingons fought. He had important things to do. The blackness must not touch him.

He turned and snarled at the creeping blackness, warning it away.

Again the roaring. Again the ground shook, as if to answer his challenge.

Again the heat.

In his dream he stepped forward, stared at the flames, then ran and dived over them.

He felt as if he were flying in slow motion, his dive taking a lifetime.

He thought of his wife. His children.

He thought of the welcoming coolness of the blackness behind him. Of how easy it would be to give in to it.

But he was a Klingon. Klingons did not surrender.

He ran.

He dived.

Then he passed beyond the flames.

The rumbling of the ground stopped, the heat seemed to ease, and his eyes snapped open.

Again he was awake. And alive.

He could feel his body covered with the salt of his sweat. His throat and nose were parched from the heat, his back and arms seared by the flames.

But he was awake. The darkness had not gotten him this time.

A light weight pushed down on his body and something flat and gray hung just above his face. He moved his arms and pain shot through his shoulders as he broke the burned skin, but he ignored it, pushing himself up.

Suddenly the light of day blinded him. Two prefabricated panels had toppled over and hung above him. Around him were the remains of a colony home and a few feet away was the charred body of a colonist. It was burned so badly he couldn't tell who it was.

He shoved the life-saving panels off and pushed himself to his feet. The world spun for a moment, then slowed as he stood, taking deep, painful breaths of fresh air.

All he could remember was running for the disrupter cannons when the attacks began. He hadn't made it.

He took another deep, scratchy breath, then looked around slowly, letting the pain in his head and back sharpen his focus. The attacks were slowly leveling the colony. More buildings were down now. Clearly there would be more dead.

He was very, very lucky to be alive. He hoped his family had fared as well.

He glanced in the direction of his home, then in the direction of the cannons. His wife knew of his duty to fight. She would either be alive or dead. There would be nothing he could do there. His duty was to the fight.

He picked his way carefully out of the rubble, then staggered toward the disrupter cannon, doing his best to keep his spinning head from knocking him to his knees.

He would fight until they killed him.

McCoy had hoped his caustic statement about the Klingon doctor would turn out to be wrong. But he quickly discovered it wasn't.

The Klingon doctor's makeshift medical building was nothing more than ashes, fireproof panels, and charred bodies. The doctor had been trapped under a panel. The lower half of his body had been cooked in the plasma attacks, boiling and draining away the fluids in the upper half. It had clearly not been a pleasant death. McCoy would have wished it on no one, even an arrogant Klingon.

He did a quick check through the building, looking for survivors. He found none. A Klingon or human would have to have been in good health to survive two hours of firebombing. The injured had no chance, especially when the building came apart.

McCoy moved back into the area between the domes and took a hard look around. A surprising number of domes still stood, charred and black, with nothing left to burn off the outside. Those families inside most likely were alive if they were drinking enough fluids. He didn't know exactly the fluid needs of a Klingon compared to a human, but he doubted it was significant enough to make a difference in these conditions.

"It's all clear for now," he shouted, his voice harsh and dry.

He moved toward another dome and shouted again. Near him he could hear rustling as a Klingon colonist stuck his head out of a door. In his hand was a weapon of some sort.

"The attack has stopped for the moment," McCoy said. "Get water for yourself and your family and drink it."

The Klingon stared at him for a moment, then nodded.

McCoy turned and moved back in the direction Jim had gone. He would be needed more at the point of fighting. And he felt better keeping watch over the captain. Sometimes the captain just didn't know when to take care of himself.

On either side of the colony he could hear Sulu and Rathbone giving the all clear.

He went back to the center area and took another long drink of water. In all his years he had never remembered water simply tasting so good.

He made sure his canteen was brimming full, and then, after one more large drink, headed toward the cannon on the western corner.

On the way he met Sulu and Rathbone headed for exactly the same place.

Chapter Nine

KIRK SHOUTED "All clear!" as he passed two domes that looked mostly intact, then worked his way around others that were nothing more than piles of prefabricated panels. The heat had been so intense and so long-lasting that nothing was left to burn. It was as if the attackers were trying to sterilize this area of the planet. And *if* the Klingon colony domes hadn't been fireproof, they would already have succeeded.

Kirk wondered what they were going to do next. Whatever it was, he planned on at least having something here to fight back with. Hiding in a hole just wasn't his style, even though it had saved his life and the lives of part of his land party.

Two Klingon colonists slowly climbed out of a shallow bunker near the disrupter cannon. They looked dazed and badly burned, but at least they were alive. Better than the two piles of charred bones ten paces from the guns.

The colonists watched him approach, saying nothing. Kirk doubted they could speak.

"It's clear for now," he said. "The well in the center court is working. You need water."

They nodded and shuffled in that direction. Kirk had never seen Klingons shuffle, only swagger. It was an odd sight.

Behind them Kirk saw one of Kor's men stand up from the bunker and stare down at something at his feet.

Kirk jumped up on the gun and looked down.

Kor! And sitting next to him, looking shocked, was Ensign Adaro.

"Are you all right?" Kirk asked, jumping down into the bunker beside the Klingon commander.

The warrior managed a hoarse yes.

Adaro just nodded.

It was clear to Kirk, without being a doctor, that Kor wasn't alive by much. Kirk flipped open his communication handset. "Dr. McCoy, I need you at the western disrupter cannon."

"I'm already on my way," McCoy said.

Kirk stood up and glanced around. McCoy, Sulu, and Dr. Rathbone were no more than twenty paces away. McCoy ran when he saw the captain and a moment later was kneeling beside Kor.

"The other doctor?" Kirk asked.

"Dead," McCoy said as he scanned Kor. He quickly dug into his medical kit, gave the Klingon a quick injection, then he scanned him again.

"How is he?" Kirk asked.

"Badly burned, and, like all of us, dehydrated. He's also got a number of broken bones." McCoy uncapped his canteen and forced a solid flow of water into Kor's mouth. The commander swallowed some, then choked.

McCoy shrugged and let some more water dribble into Kor's mouth.

Kirk turned to Sulu and Dr. Rathbone, who were watching from the cannon platform. "Sulu, take Ensign Adaro and this man to the well." He pointed to the warrior who still stood above Kor, looking dazed. "Force them to drink, if you have to."

Sulu nodded.

Kirk turned to Dr. Rathbone. "I need you to head for the other disrupter cannon to look for Ensign Chop."

"On my way, sir," she said, and quickly hurried off.

"Sulu," Kirk said, "after you get them to drink, I want you and Adaro to carry water back here, as much as you can. We're going to need it."

For an instant he didn't think the warrior would go with Sulu. Kirk looked him right in the eye. "I want you back here beside Kor, refreshed and ready to fight in ten minutes. Understood?"

The warrior nodded and turned to accept Sulu's helping hand. Ensign Adaro stood, his hand on the cannon platform beside him. For a moment Kirk didn't think the young man would be able to walk, but he seemed to gather his strength as he climbed from the bunker.

Behind Sulu, Kirk saw Kerdoch stagger into the open, then fall to his knees in the dirt. The man staggered to his feet and came forward some more.

"Bones, is Kor stable for the moment?" Kirk asked.

"He's as stable as I can get him," McCoy said. "Damned Klingon blood systems, anyhow."

"Then I've got another patient for you," Kirk said.

McCoy took one look at the staggering Kerdoch and grabbed his canteen. A moment later at the foot of the disrupter cannon platform, Kerdoch was drinking while McCoy applied burn cream to his arms and back.

While McCoy worked, Kirk looked around at what they were facing. From what he could tell, the disrupter cannon was still armed and ready to fire. The two piles of burned bones must have been the poor souls who tried to man the gun in the first attack. One of them must have been one of Kor's warriors.

The cannon was anchored to the top of a square concrete-type platform sitting out in the open.

"We need more protection," Kirk said to himself.

The bunker where Kor lay had been dug on the western edge of the platform. The alien craft had come on too fast to be fired upon directly and to have allowed the operator to get to safety, but the alien attack craft could have been hit while they were moving away from the colony after they'd made a run.

They needed a fireproof shelter around the cannon on three sides. Something to protect the gun operators until the craft moved past.

Kirk looked around. Somehow they had to build something out of fireproof panels that would withstand an attack.

Sulu and Ensign Adaro appeared from behind a dome carrying three pans of water each. Kirk watched as the young ensign stopped at McCoy and Kerdoch and handed the Klingon colonist a pan. Kerdoch drank almost all of the water before stopping, and McCoy patted his shoulder.

Sulu climbed up beside Kirk, set down two pans, and handed one to him without a word. Kirk drank the cold water with relish, wondering if there would ever be a time again when he wouldn't be thirsty.

"Kirk," a faint voice came from behind them.

Kirk turned as Kor tried to sit up and failed.

"Bones!" Kirk yelled and jumped down beside Kor.

"Drink this," he said, holding the water to Kor's mouth and pouring, not giving the Klingon a choice. This time Kor managed three good swallows before he choked and coughed.

"Go easy," Kirk said.

Kor only nodded as McCoy jumped down beside him and scanned him. "You shouldn't be moving," McCoy said. "You've got two shattered ribs, either one of which might puncture a lung. And in these conditions, you wouldn't last ten minutes if that happens. I've got the ribs mending, but you'll have to give them some time."

Kor nodded. "You order well, Doctor."

"Just don't cross me, Commander," McCoy said. "Or I'll give you a sedative that will make you sleep for a full month."

Kor only nodded, but Kirk could tell he was laughing at McCoy. And was glad the doctor was here.

Kerdoch and Kor's second-in-command were standing above the bunker. Kirk stood and looked at those around him. "It's time to get to work," he said. "We've got to build a cover for this bunker and a shelter for that gun. We can use those fireproof panels. Think we can do it?"

Sulu nodded.

Ensign Adaro glanced around, still looking confused.

Both Kerdoch and the warrior looked down at Kor.

Kor laughed softly. "Kirk, you are a strange one. Fighting for a planet you do not possess." Then Kor nodded to his two men. "Do as he says. His word is as mine."

Both nodded.

Kirk turned to Kerdoch. "We need more help. Round up as many men as you can find. And bring more water back with you, along with any tools that might help build a shelter out of those exterior dome panels."

Kerdoch nodded and without a word headed off.

"The rest of us need to start gathering panels from the destroyed shelters." Kirk said. "Take only whole ones. We need as many of those as we can get. We have to get this bunker covered first."

He leaned down and patted McCoy on the shoulder where he knelt above Kor. "Stay with your patient. I don't want him dying before the fight."

Kor coughed and frowned at Kirk. "I will live to the day we fight, Kirk. It will be a glorious day."

"I look forward to that," Kirk said, laughing.

And actually, at that moment he did.

Rathbone moved quickly away from the captain, heading through the burned domes of the Klingon colony. She was having a hard time grasping what was happening around her. She felt somehow detached from her burned and aching body. And the heat seemed to wrap itself around her like a blanket, smothering the sounds.

Too much had happened to her too fast and with no preparation. One moment it seemed she had been peacefully working in her lab on the *Enterprise;* the next moment she was trying to survive intense heat and seeing dead bodies everywhere. Starfleet had taught her procedures to use in emergencies and on planetary missions, but nothing could have prepared her for this.

She forced herself to slow her walk and conserve energy. But it still seemed like only a few seconds before she reached the other disrupter cannon.

There was no doubt that it would take hours or maybe even days of repair before it would fire again. It lay on its side, its barrel smashed down into the hard ground. In front of the concrete base platform were two burnt bodies, the clothes and skin completely gone, the bones blackened. All the blood and bodily fluids had long since boiled away, leaving only a red powder in the dust around the remains.

She was almost afraid to look, but hearing the captain's orders again inside her head, she moved up close to the remains.

Then she saw what she'd been afraid she'd find. Standing on end, seeming to stick out of one pile, was a charred Starfleet insignia, blackened by the heat but still recognizable. Ensign Chop, the cute brown-haired kid from Arizona.

"Oh, no," she said, holding her hand over her mouth and forcing herself to breathe deep gulps of the hot air. The water she'd drunk threatened to force its way back up her throat, but she held it down.

After two more long, deep breaths, she reached down and plucked the scrap of cloth from the pile of bones. She shuddered as she did so. How did people get used to this kind of duty? She took a deep breath of the hot, fetid air. *Calm,* she told herself. *Calm.* Then, grasping the singed insignia tightly in her hand, she turned and headed back for Captain Kirk.

Crossing the colony should have taken longer. She wondered if she blanked out as she walked. She knew that between the heat, the burns, and the stress, she wasn't thinking as clearly as she should have been.

One moment she had been standing near Ensign Chop; the next, she was beside Captain Kirk. When she saw him, she handed him the insignia.

He gazed at it a moment, then closed his fist over it. "Damn," he said softly.

And then he turned away, standing alone, facing the burned Klingon fields.

McCoy came up to her.

Nothing was said.

Nothing could be said.

Captain Bogle stood in front of his chair, facing the image of Commander Spock on the main screen. As far as possible, Bogle had his ship and his crew ready for any upcoming fight. His engineer, Projeff, said the *Farragut* hadn't been in such good shape since it left spacedock the first time. Every system had been checked and double-checked. And for the last hour Projeff had been working long-distance with the chief engineer of the *Enterprise,* Mr. Scott, on a method of strengthening the shields against the enemy weapons.

"Your estimated time of arrival, Captain?" Spock asked.

"Forty-one minutes," Bogle said.

Spock nodded, his Vulcan face unreadable. "Captain Kirk and the landing party are still trapped on the surface, along with Commander Kor and his team. Subcommander Korath reports his ship is repaired and standing by. Two more Klingon battle cruisers have been dispatched but will not arrive for twelve hours."

"All right," Bogle said as he processed the information. "Are the alien ships still holding position?"

"Yes, sir," Spock said.

"Have there been further attacks on the colony?"

"No," Spock said.

Bogle nodded. That was as he had hoped it would be. "Commander Spock, do you have a suggestion as to our course of action?"

Spock nodded. "I do, sir," he said. "When you arrive we should endeavor to find out exactly why these invaders are attacking the Klingon colony."

Bogle stared at the Vulcan for a moment, then stifled a laugh. "And how would you suggest we do that, Commander?" he asked.

Spock shook his head, his serious expression unchanged. "I do not know, sir. But logic leads us to believe that the reason for this attack is the path to the solution."

Bogle had never understood exactly how Kirk managed to function with a Vulcan at his side, even though Spock was becoming well know as the best first officer in the fleet, and most likely in line for the captain's chair. But at times like this Bogle wondered how Spock's logic didn't drive Kirk nuts. It would him.

"I would agree with you, Mr. Spock," Bogle said, "but there does not seem to be a direct course of action implied in your suggestion."

Spock nodded. "I agree. Therefore, if the situation

remains the same, the course of action I would suggest is negotiation."

"Negotiation," Bogle said dryly. "Do we even know who these aliens are?"

"Clearly, we do not," Spock said in that infuriatingly calm tone. "We have no record of these ships, nor have we identified their makers. They do not answer our hails."

"Then how do you suggest we negotiate?"

"Obviously they want something from the planet," Spock said. "We must determine what that is."

"They want the colonists off it," Bogle said. "It seems fairly simple to me."

"Forgive me, Captain, but it does not seem simple to me. These ships may carry a life-form so alien that it does not recognize the life signs below."

"You'd think it'd recognize that the ships above are filled with life-forms," Bogle said.

"They did not obliterate our ships," Spock said. "They are attempting to obliterate the colony."

"Do the Klingons recognize these ships?" Bogle asked.

"They claim they do not," Spock said.

"Sounds like you don't believe them," Bogle said.

"I do not have any evidence to believe or disbelieve the Klingons, Captain. I merely report their statements. They claim they do not know."

"But you reserve the possibility that they do."

"The attack is directed at a Klingon colony," Spock said. "Perhaps there is enmity between the aliens and the Klingons. We are not the Klingons' allies. They may not believe we need to know who their enemies are."

Bogle nodded. For once, Spock's maddening logic

made sense. The Klingons wouldn't want the Federation to know who their enemies were. Thought of in Klingon terms, the Federation might ally itself with the enemies to wipe out the Klingon Empire.

There was nothing more they could accomplish through such speculation. "Thank you for your insights, Mr. Spock," Bogle said. "Keep me informed if the situation changes. *Farragut* out."

The image of Commander Spock was replaced by the view of stars flashing past in warp.

Behind Bogle, Science Officer Richard Lee said, "Fascinating."

Captain Bogle could only sit and stare at the stars and wonder just what exactly he was rushing into.

Kerdoch ran at his full pace, even though his head still pounded and he felt weak. Within a few moments he was at the well in the central area of the colony. Dozens of women and men were filling pans and bottles from the bubbling pool. It was good to see that so many had survived.

He stopped at the well and allowed himself the extra few seconds to dip his face into the water and drink fully. Then he let the cool water run down over his hot arms and neck. The medication that the human doctor had spread on his burns had helped a great deal, but the water still felt wonderful.

"Attention," he said, his voice harsh and sore as he tried to force volume from it. "Commander Kor and the human captain need help defending the colony on the west side."

Around him three of the men nodded. "We will be there," Katanin said.

Kerdoch nodded. "Bring weapons and tools to work on the dome panels. Also bring water."

He turned and at a run headed deeper into the colony in the direction of his home. He had tools and water jugs there, and he had to make sure his wife and children had survived.

Relief swept over him as he discovered that his home was again one of the ones standing. His wife and eldest son were outside, doing what they could to cover a hole in the paneling with other panels.

She saw him coming, and her face lit up.

Such a look he would always remember.

Such a look would keep him fighting for his home and family until he could no longer stand or even crawl to the battle.

She hugged him, and he returned the hug. Then he slapped the back of his very excited oldest son. "Have you got water?" he asked.

"We have been to the central well twice since the all-clear signal," she said. "Will the enemy craft return?"

"Yes," he said. "And this time we will knock them from the sky."

She nodded but said nothing.

He turned to his son. "Bring me my tool belt. Quickly."

His son ducked inside their home. While he waited, Kerdoch held his wife by the shoulders, wanting to have her remain there. They had both survived the last attack. He hoped they continued to be so lucky. Many of his friends had not been.

A moment later his son appeared carrying a heavy tool belt and a canteen. Kerdoch nodded and took both. "You think clearly, son. Help your mother prepare for the next attack. Take extra panels inside and form a second line of paneling over the furniture."

The son nodded.

"He is my right hand," she said.

"You are both my heart," Kerdoch said. Then with a light squeeze of his wife's arm, he turned and jogged toward the disrupter cannon, the heavy tool belt and full canteen a comfort in his hands.

On the way he recruited three more colonists.

Chapter Ten

KIRK, SULU, RATHBONE, Ensign Adaro, and Kahaq, Kor's officer, worked as best they could gathering the fireproof panels. Within a few minutes after Kerdoch left, three more colonists arrived with tools. Kor, from his place in the bottom of the bunker, told them to follow Kirk's orders, and within minutes Kirk had them digging Kor's bunker deeper and placing a double layer of panels over the top.

There was no way Kirk was going to let Kor get killed if he could help it. Building the bunkers big enough and deep enough for all of them to survive another attack was the first priority. The last thing he wanted was for all of them to end up as Ensign Chop had done.

Ten minutes later, Kerdoch and three more colonists returned and, also at Kor's command, set to work following Kirk's plan. Seven colonists, Sulu,

Kahaq, Ensign Adaro, and Rathbone made the work go extremely fast.

Kirk could tell that Sulu and McCoy, who still sat next to the Klingon commander, didn't much care for the fact that Kor had to give his okay, but Kirk didn't care at all. As long as the bunkers got built and the protection over the gun was up and ready for the next attack, it didn't matter at all to him who gave the orders. What was important was stopping the attacks, and then maybe figuring out why they were happening.

The group, at Kirk's direction, next dug cross-bunkers on either end of the first bunker and covered them with panels. The newly dug bunkers ran up the two sides of the concrete platform for the disrupter cannon. At four places along the three bunkers an opening was left so that a person could dive from the concrete slab into the bunker for protection. As fast as the alien ships attacked, Kirk knew such an escape might be necessary.

As the group began to build the shelter over the disrupter cannon, Kirk flipped open his communicator. "Kirk to *Enterprise*."

"Spock here, Captain."

"Has the *Farragut* arrived yet?"

"It is due in twelve minutes," Spock said.

"Is there any movement from our alien friends?"

"No, Captain. We have continued to hail them and have received no response."

"Don't take them on unless you need to, Spock."

"Captain, it would not be logical to 'take on' a larger force. We shall do what we have to."

"I expect nothing more. Kirk out."

He snapped the handset shut and glanced around. The shelter over the disrupter cannon was going up quicker than he had thought. Now he just hoped Spock and Captain Bogle could figure out a way of stopping the aliens before they launched another attack on the colony.

After handing a panel to a colonist on the gun platform, Kirk watched Rathbone stop and wipe the sweat from her face. She and McCoy both looked beat. Sulu had taken off his shirt, and his body glistened with sweat. The twin suns were clearly sapping the strength out of everyone, almost as quickly as the heat from the attackers' plasma beams.

"Doctors," Kirk said. He motioned for McCoy and Rathbone to join him beside the bunker for a moment.

"Hot enough to bake a fish," McCoy muttered as he climbed up to where Kirk stood.

"I thought the saying was 'fry an egg'?" Kirk said.

"Not where I'm from," McCoy said.

"Well," Dr. Rathbone said, "I'm from the British Isles, and we don't have any saying at all for this kind of heat, because it *never* gets this hot."

McCoy only snorted, but Kirk laughed.

"I need you both, and Ensign Adaro, to go for more water," he said. "Carry as much as you can, but get back as quick as you can. I don't want you trapped outside these bunkers if another attack starts."

McCoy shook his head. "After watching you people work this hard to build them, I damn well plan to be in them."

"I'm with you, Dr. McCoy," Rathbone said.

Both of them turned to gather up the empty and

half-empty water containers. Then they rounded up the ensign from his work on the shelter and headed into the colony center.

Kirk moved to the shelter that had gone up around three sides of the cannon. The colonists had actually braced the bottoms of the panels against the concrete base of the gun, and used the same dome skeleton structures to support the upper ones. Then they had added a second layer of panels.

As Kirk finished his quick inspection, the six colonists were connecting in a third overlapping layer, forming a very strong wall. Kirk had no doubt it would withstand an attack on three sides. But if the aliens broke their pattern and attacked from the opposite direction, anyone inside without protection would be baked like a potato almost instantly.

"What do you think, Captain?" Sulu asked as he fixed a panel in place near the front opening.

"I think I'll have to trust my life on it," Kirk said.

Sulu nodded. "You'll need a second on that gun."

Kirk glanced at the sweaty face of Sulu. "Yes, I will."

"I would be honored, sir," Sulu said.

"I would be honored to have your assistance, Lieutenant," Kirk said.

Suddenly the beep of his communicator he'd been fearing filled the hot air. Inside the bunker Kirk could hear the deep tone of Kor's communicator.

That was not a good sign. Not at all.

Kirk flipped his handset open. "Kirk here."

"Captain," Spock said, "the small ships are leaving the two transports. They will arrive at your location in five minutes and seven seconds."

"Where is the *Farragut,* Spock?"

"It is dropping out of warp now, Captain."

"Stop as many of those small ships as you can, Spock. And good luck."

"Luck will have nothing to do with it, Captain. *Enterprise* out."

Kirk flipped his communicator closed and glanced at Sulu's worried face. "Let's hope that's not the last time we hear those words."

"It won't be, Captain," Sulu said.

Kirk could tell Sulu was as worried as he was. But there was no time for that now. Only action.

"The ships are on their way, people," Kirk said, turning to face his work crew. The colonists had all stopped and were watching him.

He pointed to Kahaq. "Get down below with your commander and stay with him. Take any water left up here below as you go."

Kahaq nodded and jumped toward the bunker.

Kirk turned to the colonists. "The ships will be here in five minutes. Spread out through the colony and warn everyone to take cover. Then do the same yourselves. Don't come out until someone sounds the all clear."

This time the colonists didn't need Kor's permission to move. As a unit they jumped from the platform and ran toward the remaining domes, shouting the warning as they went.

Only Kerdoch held his ground. "I am here to fight," he said. "I will help you with the gun."

Kirk looked at the Klingon colonist's stern expression for a moment, then nodded. "Take some water inside the shelter."

Kerdoch jumped into action without so much as a nod.

"Mr. Sulu, ready the gun." Kirk glanced at the bare chest of his officer and remembered the coming heat. "And you might want to put a shirt on to protect your skin."

Sulu nodded and sprang into action.

Kirk grabbed another sheet of paneling. He tossed it in on the floor of the shelter near the gun. Then he did the same with two more. It wasn't much, but they might serve as one man shields in case the ships came in from another direction.

It wasn't until he jumped back up on the concrete platform and moved inside the gun shelter that it dawned on him that McCoy, Rathbone, and Adaro hadn't returned yet.

He glanced in the direction of the colony. No sign of them yet. They had less than two minutes. Surely they must have heard the warnings from the colonists.

As the seconds ticked past, Kirk's stomach twisted with the realization that his friend McCoy wasn't returning.

With one minute left, Kirk moved to the edge of the concrete platform, turned his back on the colony, and began scanning the skies on the western horizon for the ships.

McCoy was smart. He and the others would find shelter. They'd make it.

Somehow.

McCoy knew the moment he, Rathbone, and the young ensign entered the main colony square near the well that something was wrong. A large Klingon woman was sprawled on the edge of the pool, one hand dangling in the water. A boy, not more than two years old, lay with his head against her stomach. A baby in a basket moved slightly.

McCoy ran up to her, dropping the water containers and pulling the medical scanner from his belt. The woman was almost dead. It was amazing she had made it this far, she was so dehydrated.

Since the baby moved, he scanned it first. It was alive and dehydrated, but not as bad as the woman. The boy was also alive.

"Get the children water," he said to Rathbone. Then he quickly gave the woman an injection of fluids, hoping to pull her away from death enough to get water into her the natural way.

She didn't move.

"Damn," McCoy said under his breath.

"Is she going to make it?" Rathbone asked, taking the baby into her arms and patting the child's dry lips with a wet part of her uniform. Ensign Adaro put his arms around the small boy and lifted him. The child moaned. Adaro held the boy near the fountain, and he drank as though he had never had water in his life.

"I don't know if she's going to make it," McCoy said. He knew he should have studied the Federation's limited records on Klingon physiology on the way here instead of checking the medical supplies. "We need to get her out of this heat somehow, and pour water down her."

Rathbone stood with the child and looked quickly around the square. "There is no help in sight," she said, sounding perplexed.

No help in sight. He didn't like the sound of that, but he didn't have time to think about it.

He scanned the woman's vital signs. No change at

all. And he didn't really know if he was doing the right thing by giving her fluids directly. For all he knew, what worked for a human might be deadly for a Klingon. It had never occurred to him to study the fluid needs of Klingons in high heat. In his worst nightmare he had never imagined he'd need to know such a detail.

Suddenly three of the colonists who had been working with the captain came running into the square. "The ships!" they shouted. "Take cover."

"Wonderful timing," McCoy said to himself. He stood and shouted at the running colonists. "We need help here!" He pointed to the woman and children.

One of the colonists veered his way while the others went on giving the warning. "My home is close," he said.

"Fine," McCoy said. "Take her anywhere. Ensign, help him."

Ensign Adaro set the small boy down and came to McCoy's side. Together he and the colonist picked up the large, unconscious woman.

"We'll follow with the children and water," McCoy said.

The Klingon who had offered his home only nodded.

McCoy quickly grabbed three pans and filled them, then took the little boy by the hand and headed after the two men. Rathbone, with full bottles of water and the baby, was right behind him.

As they ducked behind the two men inside one of the domed homes on the edge of the central courtyard, McCoy's own words about making it back to the bunker came back to him. They weren't going to be back, at least not until this attack was over.

He hoped the captain made it through the attack.

Then the woman moaned as the two men laid her on a cotlike bed, and McCoy became too busy to think about his captain.

Until the first blast shook the domed structure and the heat filled the room so fast he could hardly breathe.

"So much for deciding what to do," Captain Bogle said to himself as the *Farragut* dropped out of warp. "Battle stations everyone!"

The alarms blared and the lights dimmed slightly as his ship smoothly went to alert.

Bogle forced himself to take a deep breath and focus on the events going on in front of him. They'd been in fights before. This was just another. Even though it was five against three. And each of the five ships against them was twice the size of the *Farragut*. It was still just another fight.

On the main screen two of the five huge alien ships were opening their large rear sections. Small, thin, wedgelike craft were pouring from both ships and turning toward the planet's atmosphere, obviously heading into another attack run at the Klingon colony.

Both the *Enterprise* and the Klingon battle cruiser had turned and were moving in, firing phaser beams at the smaller ships scattered behind the larger ones. It looked as if they were firing at a swarm of large flies buzzing a cow.

"Ensign Summer, bring us in over the planet," Bogle said.

He moved up and put his hand firmly on Lieutenant Michael Book's shoulder. "Lieutenant, target any of the smaller ships you can lock on to and fire when in range."

"Yes, sir," Book said.

Bogle let go of the lieutenant's shoulder and stepped back next to his captain's chair.

The next few seconds went by slowly as the *Farragut* moved into range. Then the phaser fired three times as one of the larger alien craft turned and moved toward them, firing as it came. Two of the targeted smaller craft exploded.

"Got them," Lieutenant Book said.

"Keep firing, mister," Bogle said.

The *Enterprise* had destroyed three of the atmosphere fighters, and the battle cruiser had taken out two. But at least fifteen of the smaller craft were still dropping toward the planet's surface.

The *Farragut* rocked with the impact of phaser fire from the large alien ship.

"Shields holding," First Officer Lee said.

"Continue targeting the smaller ships!" Bogle ordered. "They'll be out of range soon."

More phaser fire shot from his ship and took out two more of the smaller craft in small balls of orange and red flame.

The larger alien ship fired its phasers again and again, all direct hits against the *Farragut*'s screens.

The *Farragut* rocked so violently Bogle was tossed to the deck.

Annoyed at himself for not being in his chair, he rolled with his fall and came up on one knee holding on to the rail.

Somehow Lieutenant Book had managed to stay in his seat, but everyone else was down on the deck, scrambling to get back to their stations.

"Arm torpedoes," Bogle yelled. "Target the large ship and fire when ready."

A moment later the *Farragut* rocked as four torpedoes were fired, all exploding in direct hits on the alien's screens.

"Evasive action," he said as Ensign Summer scrambled back to his chair.

The ship swung high and to the left of the huge alien ship, but not fast enough to avoid three more direct hits on the screens. This time Bogle remained in a kneeling position, his eyes on the screen, as the *Farragut* shook and rumbled at the impacts.

After the rocking calmed he quickly climbed back to his feet and dropped into his chair.

"Screens at forty percent," Lee said. "Damage on decks eight and ten."

"The *Enterprise?*" Bogle asked.

"Under heavy fire," Lee said, "but still returning fire. The Klingon battle cruiser is pinned between two of the big ships. One of the alien transports seems to be standing off and watching."

Bogle nodded. Lucky break there.

"The Klingons will have to take care of themselves for a moment," he said, more to himself than any of the crew. Then to Ensign Summer he said, "Take us right at the ship the *Enterprise* is firing at. Ignore the one that's after us."

The main viewscreen shifted around to show the fight between the *Enterprise* and the much larger alien ship. Even from here Bogle could see the *Enterprise* rocking with the impact of the alien phasers.

"Lieutenant Sandy, open an audio channel to the *Enterprise.*"

"Open, sir," Sandy said almost instantly.

"Spock, this is Bogle." The captain didn't wait for a reply. "Target their right wing section. On my mark."

Then he turned his attention to his crew. "We're going to do the same," he said. "On the same mark. All right, Lieutenant?"

"Ready, sir," Book said.

"Now!" Bogle said to him and Spock.

The phaser beams from both starships pulsed on the alien's right wing screens for a long moment, then broke through, cutting into the skin of the ship underneath.

Then the *Farragut* rocked like a bad ride in an amusement park as the alien ship behind them hit them with a series of full, direct hits, one right after another.

Bogle managed to stay in his chair this time, but not by much.

"Aft screens failing," Lee shouted.

"Turn us around," Bogle ordered. "Return fire!"

More direct hits rocked them.

Behind them the *Enterprise* was firing over the *Farragut*'s bow, going after the ship that was attacking the *Farragut*.

"You got it, Mr. Spock," Bogle said through his teeth as his ship rocked again. "We've got a chance if we gang up on these giants."

"Shields failing," Lee shouted.

"Full fire," Bogle said. "All weapons. Now!"

If they were going to die, Bogle figured, they were at least going to put a dent in the ship that killed them, maybe give the *Enterprise* a fighting chance.

Bogle noted the *Enterprise* was also firing with all weapons at the alien ship when everything on the screen and around him suddenly exploded.

He was tossed sideways from his chair like a doll thrown by an angry child.

He cleared the handrail in the air, rolled once, and smashed shoulder and head first into the turbolift doors.

The last thing he heard was the whoosh of the lift's doors opening before the blackness took him away.

Chapter Eleven

KIRK STOOD at the opening of the shelter over the disrupter cannon. He gripped the edge of the three-layer-thick material, and studied the horizon. Both suns were lower in the sky, and the light seemed to shimmer in the heat waves across the flat, blackened farmland.

Then, just at the exact time Spock had predicted, the ships appeared, thin silver lines against the sky. They were staging their run from the exact same direction as the first attacks. Whoever these aliens were, they certainly were patient, as well as creatures of habit. That fact might come in very handy in face to face meetings, if he lived long enough to get to that point.

Kirk counted seven ships in the first wave. At least three less than last run. Maybe Spock and Bogle had managed to make a dent in their numbers.

"Get ready," Kirk shouted, both to Sulu and Kerdoch behind him, and to Kor and his first officer in the bunker.

Kirk ducked back inside the shelter and took up a position near Sulu, who had the targeting controls for the cannon.

"The moment they're past us, target and fire," Kirk said. "You might have time to get two shots off before they're out of range."

Sulu nodded.

Kirk picked up a panel and slid it to Kerdoch on the other side of Sulu. Then he picked up a second. "Hold these up in front of us to slow down any heat backwash," Kirk said. "But be careful to not block Sulu's aim."

Kerdoch nodded and got the first sheet into position just as the world exploded around them.

The structure over them shook, and the heat washed over Kirk like a full-force blast furnace. The world seemed to go red, the ground trembled, wind whipped the hot air through the shelter at almost hurricane force.

Kirk barely managed to hang on to the sheet he was holding, and only then because it was braced and it had smashed back against his chest.

Kerdoch stood no chance of holding his panel. It blasted out of his hands and the shelter like it had been shot from some strange gun. It swirled in the air like a feather from a passing bird.

Somehow, the shelter the colonists had built over the gun withstood the plasma attack.

Almost instantly the ships were beyond the edge of the colony.

Sulu fired.

The report of the disrupter cannon discharging in the confined space of the shelter was more like a bomb going off inside a small room. The concussion filled the air and rocked the shelter.

Kirk's ears rang, and he hoped his eardrums hadn't been damaged.

Just beyond the edge of the colony the third alien craft from the right exploded in a ball of orange flame.

Sulu fired again.

Kirk had managed in the short instant between shots to cover his ears. The sound of the discharge still increased the ringing in his head to a painful level.

The second craft on the right exploded.

"Great shooting, Mr. Sulu," he shouted over the ringing in his head, then scrambled to the front edge of the shelter. If the alien ships stayed on the same pattern as the morning attacks, there would be almost a full sixty seconds before the next wave.

He slowly poked his head around the corner to stare through the heat waves to the west.

He was right. No ships had yet appeared for an attack run, and the remaining five ships from the first run were long out of sight.

"Get ready," Kirk said. Sulu and Kerdoch nodded as they checked over the gun.

Kirk stepped farther out on the concrete platform to get a better view of the surrounding blackened farmland. He scanned all sides once, just to make sure. Then he saw the new wave of attack ships forming in the same location.

He glanced in the other directions again. Nothing but the one wave forming in the exact same place as before. Seven ships again. If nothing else, they were consistent. That would be their downfall.

He ducked back into the shelter. "Next wave in about fifteen seconds."

"Should I try for three?" Sulu asked.

"Do you have time?"

"No way of telling exactly," Sulu said.

"His second shot," Kerdoch said, "was well within the range of this cannon."

Kirk nodded to the Klingon, then faced Sulu. "Why not? I think my ears can take it. Brace yourselves."

As the last word came from his mouth the shelter again seemed to explode in a whirlwind of heat, thundering sound, and shaking ground.

Then Sulu fired.

The concussion from the gun pounded Kirk into the side of the shelter, but he managed to keep his feet under him.

The center ship exploded.

Sulu fired again.

The next ship to the right exploded.

Sulu fired a third time.

The next ship down the line exploded.

Three down, four to go in this wave.

"Great work," Kirk shouted over the deafening ringing in his ears. He was convinced that all three of them were going to have their hearing damaged, but that was a small price to pay for staying alive.

Kerdoch laughed and slapped Sulu on the back.

Sulu patted the handholds on the gun. "We got to get us one of these," he said. "That felt good. But I might never hear again."

Kirk had to agree with his officer. Fighting back did

feel good. Much better than hiding in a bunker. And he too was amazed by the ability of the Klingon disrupter cannon. A very impressive weapon.

Kirk looked around for water. Two of the pans had been knocked over by the high winds, but a large jug still looked full. He picked it up and handed it to Sulu.

"If the aliens are as consistent as I think they are," Kirk said, "we've got four minutes until the next attack."

"My ears might almost recover by then," Sulu said as he took the jug from Kirk and took a long drink. Then he handed it to Kerdoch, who did the same and passed it back over the end of the gun to Kirk.

Kirk let the warm water almost pour down his throat. Every inch of his skin was coated in sweat, and even the hot afternoon wind felt cool compared to the furnacelike temperatures caused by the enemy plasma beams.

He handed the jug back to Sulu and moved out to take his watch post. No ships in sight at all. In any direction. It would be a few minutes, if they stayed on pattern.

He moved to the end of the platform above the bunker and inspected the panels. Like the shelter, every panel had stayed in place.

"Kahaq? Kerdoch?" Kor shouted. "Are you okay?"

"We live," Kahaq's voice came back strong and defiant from inside the bunker.

"We downed five of their ships," Kirk said. "Another attack should be coming in a few minutes."

"We will join you," Kor's voice came back, much weaker than that of his officer.

"There is no more room in the shelter," Kirk said.

"If we are killed, you must take our place. Until then, stay where you are. Rest and prepare for the fight."

"Kirk," Kor said, "you sometimes know us too well. We will remain here."

Suddenly Kirk's communicator beeped for attention. Kor's did not this time. The *Enterprise* still existed, but did this mean the battle cruiser did not?

Kirk flipped open his communicator. "Kirk here."

"Captain," Spock said, "nine of the small attack ships have returned. Five are unaccounted for."

"Mr. Sulu accounted for those five, Mr. Spock. How's the *Enterprise?*"

"We sustained heavy damage on seven decks. Mr. Scott has returned the screens to eighty percent. All weapons are now back on-line."

"Good," Kirk said, feeling very relieved that the *Enterprise* had made it through the fight. "The other ships?"

"The *Farragut* sustained heavy damage and casualties. Their warp, weapons systems, and screens are off-line, but Mr. Projeff, their chief engineer, informs me that the screens should be back up within two minutes. Weapons may take a little longer. Captain Bogle was injured. He is unconscious but alive."

Kirk didn't like the sound of his friend Bogle being injured, but there was nothing he could do for him at the moment. "The battle cruiser?"

"Also heavily damaged but still weapons-and warp-capable. One of the enemy ships was completely destroyed, another heavily damaged. The remaining alien ships are holding a position between the *Enterprise* and the planet, keeping us out of transporter range."

"Good work, Spock," Kirk said. "Hold your position and keep me informed. Kirk out."

Kirk flipped his communicator closed and let out a deep sigh. For the moment, at least, the attack was over. Now it was time to give the all clear.

He looked around at the blackened structures and the fields beyond. Somehow this colony still survived, holding on and fighting back.

Now it was time to see if McCoy and Rathbone had made it through the attack.

Crouched on the floor beside the Klingon cot, McCoy did his best to protect his face and the face of his unconscious patient as the second attack smashed into the colony dome, shaking it and sending waves of intense heat swirling inside.

During the first attack the dome had shaken and a blast of burning air had filled the room, twisting the interior around like a Kansas tornado had been turned loose inside the building. McCoy had felt the heat burning his face and hands and other areas of unprotected skin. He had managed to bury his face quickly against his shirtsleeve. Most likely he'd only have a sunburn level burn from this attack.

Rathbone, with the Klingon baby in her arms, had managed to protect both her face and the baby by bending over the child and pushing her face into its blanket. Between attacks the child cried, but McCoy could tell it was a healthy cry.

Ensign Adaro had managed to hide his face and arms under the blanket near the woman's feet as he sat on the floor.

The family who lived in this dome had built a protective fort of furniture near one wall, and the young boy and the family were all in there. Only McCoy, Rathbone, Ensign Adaro, the sick Klingon woman, and the baby remained in the main room.

When the second attack rocked the dome, McCoy managed to protect both his face against his shirt and the unconscious mother's face and arms with a blanket held tight over her. The last thing she needed was more heat damage.

After a few short seconds the heat eased, and McCoy quickly scanned the mother. She was still alive, still breathing, but under these attack conditions, she wouldn't be for long. Outside three explosions echoed between the colony domes.

"Let's hope that's Jim," McCoy said to Rathbone.

She nodded, then swallowed, not saying a word. Her face was red and covered with sweat. Her eyes had the look of a person nearing shock. McCoy had seen that same look a number of times in crewmen inexperienced in sudden violence. There was no doubt Dr. Rathbone had never experienced this sort of thing before. She'd have had no reason to. Considering that, combined with her finding Ensign Chop's body, she was doing better than could be expected. But now he needed to get her moving, doing something.

He glanced around. The two colonists who had carried the woman into the hut were emerging from a pile of furniture. Inside the pile McCoy could hear a child sobbing softly.

"Everyone all right in there?" McCoy asked the colonist.

"We live," he said.

"Good. Everyone needs to drink," McCoy ordered, putting as much force behind his voice as he could manage. "Now. Before the next attack. Rathbone, drink some water and then get some into that baby."

She looked at him with a blank stare for a moment, then her eyes cleared and she nodded and turned for the water.

McCoy pointed to Adaro. "Ensign, help me move this woman under this cot. We've got to keep her protected from the damn heat as much as we can."

McCoy stood, pulled out his medical scanner, and checked her again. As he was doing so, she took one large shuddering breath and died.

She just died. Before they could move her. And there wasn't a damn thing he could do to stop it.

Nothing.

"Damn, damn, damn," he said softly. He did another scan of the large woman hoping to see anything he might do to revive her. Nothing. Besides the heat, he didn't even know why she died. He didn't know enough about Klingon physiology. He knew they could die, but they were so strong that he thought it would take a lot to kill them.

She had gone through a lot, though.

In all his years he had never felt this helpless.

Adaro stood over the woman, waiting for McCoy's instructions to move her.

"Never mind," McCoy said, softly, so the children hiding in the pile of furniture wouldn't hear. "She's dead."

Ensign Adaro stared at her for a moment, then turned his back. It was clear to McCoy that the kid hadn't seen much death, either.

"Oh, no," Rathbone said. She looked down at the baby in her arms, then back up at McCoy, a questioning look on her face. What would become of the woman's children?

He didn't know what to do. It was a Klingon baby. What could he do?

The Klingon man who owned the dome came calmly around the cot and took the baby gently from Dr. Rathbone. "We will take care of the children," he said.

Without another word he took the child to the shelter of furniture and ducked inside. The other child of the dead woman was already in there.

McCoy was impressed. He'd always heard that family was very important to the Klingons, but the man's actions, as if it were expected, made McCoy feel good for the future of the woman's children. Assuming, of course, that they all survived the rest of the day.

"We need to get ready for the next attack," McCoy said. He pulled Dr. Rathbone gently by the sleeve into the area near the head of the dead woman, and they both sat down on the floor, getting ready to shelter their faces and hands at the first rumble of the coming attack.

"Ensign," McCoy ordered. "Get down and cover your head and arms."

The ensign nodded, sat down on the floor, and put his head down.

Three minutes later they heard Kerdoch outside the dome calling the all clear.

McCoy didn't even look at the woman's body as he stood and pulled Rathbone to her feet. "Come," he said to her and the ensign. "We need to get some water and then get back to the Captain."

He gently shoved her toward the door of the dome. It felt like he was pushing a zombie. They emerged into the cooler temperatures of the evening air.

Ensign Adaro followed slowly behind.

They had survived another attack.

Barely.

Chapter Twelve

BRIGHT WHITE LIGHT flooded through his closed eyelids. Captain Bogle ached. He didn't open his eyes. The light was too bright. Where was he? He couldn't remember. He felt as if he should remember, but he couldn't. The inside of his head felt as if a dozen pins were being stuck into it at the same moment. All he could hear was a faint buzzing, and he wasn't sure if the buzzing was inside or outside his head.

Blue, orange, and red sparkling stars floated in the bright white light in front of his eyes. As they swirled around and around he began to remember: the attack on the alien ships, trying to stop the attack on the colony.

His shields failing.

The ship lurching as everything around him seemed to explode.

Maybe this was what it was like being dead.

The thought crossed his mind and he forced his eyes open.

The pain of the bright overhead light snapped them closed again. But one glimpse had been enough. Sick bay. He was in the *Farragut*'s sick bay. He could feel the relief flooding through his system.

Holding his head very still, he cleared his throat. "Is the ship still in one piece?"

Dr. Grayhawk, his chief medical officer, laughed, the sound coming from off to Bogle's right. He forced his eyes open again as the rugged face of Grayhawk blocked the light over him.

"It is," Grayhawk said in his thick, deep voice, "thanks to Commander Lee and Commander Spock. From what I understand, after you were knocked out all our shields failed."

"As I was knocked out," Bogle said, managing to get the words out between the waves of pain surging through his head. "I remember."

Above him Grayhawk laughed again, his voice deep and full, as it always was. Grayhawk was the kind of man who could find humor in just about any situation. He always seemed to be laughing at something. Yet when shoved, the man was as hard as a desert rock and one of the best doctors in the Federation.

"Good. Either way, the shields got knocked out," Grayhawk said. "That Vulcan managed to get the *Enterprise* and her screens between the enemy craft and our ship." Grayhawk continued scanning Bogle's head as he talked, and Bogle could feel the pain ease by a degree or two. "And Commander Lee, with almost no power, somehow kept the *Farragut* in the narrow protected area behind the *Enterprise* during the last few minutes of the fight. It was an amazing show of control, if you want my opinion."

So after the rush to come help the *Enterprise,* it's Kirk's ship that ended up saving the *Farragut.* It figured it would end up that way.

"I need to get back to the bridge," Bogle said, moving to sit up.

Stupid idea.

The sharp pains in his head suddenly became major bolts of lightning, and he slumped backwards, the blackness easing in around the edges of his vision.

"You'll go back to the bridge when I say so," Grayhawk said, his voice very serious. No sign of laughter at all. "You ever heard of an aneurysm? Don't nod; just say yes or no."

"Yes," Bogle said softly, being very careful to not move his head at all. The blackness was slowly moving back away from the spinning stars and Grayhawk's face, but Bogle had no desire to test it again.

"That blow you suffered to the top of your head," Grayhawk said, again scanning Bogle's hairline, "caused a single blood vessel to explode. Basically you had a stroke. I fixed the damage, but only a few hours will tell if you'll have more problems. Even one more stroke, if it happened in the wrong place, or the wrong time, could be fatal, or so bad that I wouldn't be able to repair the cells. So no movement. Understand? Don't even nod."

"Yes, Doctor," Bogle said. "But could you do me a favor?"

"I won't call First Officer Lee down here, if that's what you want. He and Projeff are doing their best to get the ship back up and running, and they don't need to be bothered running in and out of here."

"No," Bogle said, "not that."

"Then what?" Grayhawk asked.

"Could you turn off that damn light?"

Now Grayhawk really laughed. And a moment later the light vanished, leaving Captain Bogle with pain swirling in his head along with the stars as he wondered just how much damage one stroke had caused.

He knew one thing. He didn't want a second.

Kerdoch finished giving the all clear around the colony, then checked on his wife and children. Again they had made it through the shortened attack. He made sure they had water, then told them to stay prepared and went back to the well in the center courtyard. There he drank his fill, refilled a bottle his wife had given him, and turned to head back for the disrupter cannon.

In front of him was the human doctor, the young human, and the human woman moving slowly toward the well. The doctor seemed almost to be supporting the woman.

"Your captain worried over your welfare," Kerdoch said.

McCoy nodded. "Good. I always worry about his. Help me get her some water."

McCoy steered the slowly walking woman toward the well as Kerdoch went around to her other side. He carefully grasped her arm and held her. She was walking, but she did not seem to be well. Neither did the other.

"Was she injured?" he asked.

"In a way," McCoy said, holding her on the edge of the pool and trying to lift handfuls of water to her mouth.

"Use this," Kerdoch said, handing the doctor his bottle. "I filled it a moment ago."

McCoy looked at Kerdoch as if seeing him for the first time, then nodded. "Thank you."

Kerdoch understood the look the doctor had just given him. He had always thought of the humans as enemies, but today with Kirk and Sulu he had discovered they had honor, just like Klingons. He had given Kirk the same look for the first time that McCoy had just given him. As with any day of battle, it was also a day of learning. For both Klingons and humans.

After a few long drinks of water the human woman's eyes seemed to clear. Kerdoch watched as the doctor used a scanning instrument to check her.

"Can you walk?" McCoy asked her as he snapped the instrument closed.

"I think so," she said.

McCoy nodded and gave her another drink from Kerdoch's bottle. Then he took a very long drink himself, refilled the bottle from the well, and handed it back to Kerdoch with a nod of thanks.

Kerdoch put the bottle in his belt and helped the human woman to her feet, steadying her on her left while the doctor stayed on her right.

"Ensign," the human doctor asked the younger man, "can you make it?"

"I can, sir," he said.

"Good," the human doctor said.

They all slowly started toward the disrupter cannon.

"How much light do we have?" the doctor asked after a few steps, glancing at the suns low in the sky.

"One hour," Kerdoch said. "It will get very cold then."

McCoy nodded. "I was afraid of that. We're going to need fires, but I doubt there's much left to burn."

Kerdoch agreed. Almost everything was already burned. Only the fuel stored inside the surviving domes would be usable. Kerdoch looked ahead at the shelter over the disrupter cannon.

The doctor was correct. It would be a long, cold night.

Kirk was kneeling in the dim light of the bunker beside Kor. Kahaq was on the commander's other side, and Kirk could tell he was as worried as Kirk was. Kor seemed to be sleeping, but it clearly wasn't a healthy sleep.

"Captain," Sulu called out from above the bunker.

"Stay with Kor," Kirk said softly to Kahaq. "I hope the doctor will be back shortly."

Kahaq nodded, saying nothing.

Kirk scooted quickly on his hands and knees out of the bunker and then stood. The evening air was cooler now as the suns neared the horizon. Sulu had kept his shirt on while working to secure the shelter over the gun.

Sulu pointed toward the colony's center. McCoy, Dr. Rathbone, Ensign Adaro, and Kerdoch were walking toward him. It seemed that McCoy and Kerdoch were helping Rathbone along.

He moved out to meet them. "Are you all right, Doctor?" he asked Rathbone, glancing at McCoy.

"I'm fine," she said. "Just a little weak and dizzy is all."

"She's in a mild shock," McCoy said, "but she'll be fine in a few hours."

Kirk nodded. "There's room in the bunker with Kor for her to lie down."

McCoy and Kerdoch helped Rathbone up and into the bunker as Kirk watched. Then Kerdoch turned and came back the few paces to Kirk, his firm steps kicking up small clouds of black ash and dust.

"Captain Kirk," Kerdoch said. "The night will be cold. We need to prepare."

Kirk nodded. He was afraid that might be the case in this area of the planet. Long, hot, dry days with fairly short but intensely cold nights. After all the heat punishment they had withstood today, the night would seem even colder.

"Do you have suggestions?" Kirk asked Kerdoch.

The Klingon pointed to one colony dome that still stood about fifty steps from the gun. "There is a heating unit inside with enough emergency fuel for one night, maybe two."

"Can we bring the unit out here?" Kirk asked.

"No," Kerdoch said. "It is too heavy. But the building is now empty. The owner was killed during the first attack."

Kirk stared at the dome and the distance between it and the disrupter cannon. There would be more than enough time to get back to the gun if Spock warned them, but if they only had their tricorders to warn them of a coming attack, it would be close. But close was better than freezing to death out in the open. He and Mr. Sulu could take turns standing guard on the gun just in case.

"Would you prepare the dome?" Kirk asked. "Water, heat, and any food you might be able to find. We'll move Kor and Rathbone at sunset."

"I will inform you when the dome is heated and ready," Kerdoch said.

He turned and strode off.

Kirk watched him go. This time there was no question from the Klingon that Kirk was in command. He wasn't sure what had changed, but something had.

Kirk flipped open his communicator. "Kirk to *Enterprise*."

"Spock here."

"What's going on up there, Mr. Spock?"

"Mr. Scott has the ship fully operational, Captain. The enemy ships are still holding their positions. The *Farragut* has restored full shields, phasers, and impulse power. Their engineer reports they will have full warp power within an hour."

"And the Klingons?"

"The Klingon battle cruiser is also making repairs," Spock said. "They claim to be ready to fight again."

"They'd make that claim with the ship exploding around them."

"I understand that, sir," Spock said.

"I'm sure you do," Kirk said. Then he asked the question he was afraid to hear the answer to. "And Captain Bogle?"

"Still in the *Farragut* sick bay. First Officer Lee reports he is out of immediate danger."

"Good," Kirk said. He could feel the relief easing muscles in his back and shoulders.

"Do you have any idea, Mr. Spock, as to just who we're fighting?"

"I do not, Captain," Spock said. "Or any indication as to motive. This situation is very illogical and puzzling."

"And very deadly," Kirk said, thinking about Ensign Chop. "I assume you are still hailing them without success."

"That is correct, Captain."

"Well, keep an eye on them. I want to know the moment any ships are headed this way that you and the *Farragut* can't stop."

"Understood, Captain," Spock said.

"And, Mr. Spock, you mentioned something about the Klingons sending more help."

"Two battle cruisers will arrive in twelve hours and seven minutes. There is no Federation ship within twenty-six hours of our location."

"Twelve hours, huh?" Kirk said. "Who knows how many more alien ships might arrive in that time."

"I have no way of estimating that, sir," Spock said, "since we know nothing of their origin."

"I understand, Mr. Spock. Kirk out."

Kirk looked around the burned-out Klingon colony in the fading light of the evening. The colony had withstood almost thirty hours of siege. It might not survive another twelve. But then again, it just might. If the aliens didn't change their tactics.

"But if they change . . ." Kirk said aloud to himself.

"If who changes, Captain?" Sulu said.

Kirk glanced at his officer. "Just talking to myself, Mr. Sulu." Then he frowned. Sometimes thinking aloud was good. "Do you think the aliens will change their attack pattern the next time?"

Sulu shrugged, glancing at the horizon where one of the two suns was just touching the top edge of the mountains. "I would have thought they would change before now. And continuing an attack with wide-focus plasma beams makes no sense at all."

"Ah, but it does," Kirk said, finally grabbing on to what was bothering him. "It does if this enemy is interested only in clearing and sterilizing the land."

"I'm not following you, sir," Sulu said.

Kirk pointed out at the burnt fields. "In the first attacks they were clearing crops and Klingons. Didn't matter which was in the way of their beams. But you and that disrupter cannon there gave them a wake-up call. Sort of like being in a garden pulling weeds and one of the weeds suddenly pulls back. Things will change now."

"That sounds likely, sir," Sulu said. "But if they do change, we need to figure out what they are going to do."

Kirk looked over the colony domes at the expanse of blackened, burned-out fields. Then he realized what would happen. They had been using a scorched earth policy. It was classic military strategy. So classic that all pre-warp cultures had used it at one time or another. "Classic military strategy," he muttered.

That was it. That was the key.

"Sir?" Sulu asked.

"Military strategy, Mr. Sulu. They'll change from a cleanup operation to a military operation. After you soften up the targets with air attacks, what comes next?"

"Ground assault," Sulu said. He quickly looked

around, trying to guess where the assault would come from.

Beside him Kirk did the same thing. A ground assault was coming, most likely at sunrise. Kirk knew it. He could feel it. He would have bet his life on it.

Now the big questions: how to prepare? And what, exactly, should they prepare for?

Chapter Thirteen

SCOTTY SAT at his console. His hair was mussed and his uniform was covered with dirt, equipment casings, and small metal bits that he hadn't had time to identify. His sleeve was still ripped, even though the wound was healed. In all the confusion, he hadn't had time to change his shirt.

He was performing several difficult mathematical equations with one hand while monitoring the computer with the other. It bothered him that the alien ships could affect the shields so quickly. They were doing something—something that he hadn't been able to pinpoint.

Several of his staff were working on the shield problem. Others were maintaining the weaponry, and the rest were keeping an eye on the matter-antimatter container, making certain everything was running normally. These aliens were difficult in ways the

Klingons were not: At least Scotty knew what to expect from Klingons. He didn't even know what these creatures looked like.

Then Uhura's voice echoed through engineering. "Mr. Scott, I have a communication from the engineer of the *Farragut*. Will you take it?"

"Aye, lass." He positioned himself in front of his small video screen. It flickered on. Projeff seemed to be sitting in the equivalent location aboard the *Farragut*. His dark hair was tousled, and his warm eyes had deep shadows beneath him. He looked like a man who'd been working for days with no sleep—and he probably had.

"I got a question for you," Projeff said.

"All right," Scotty said.

"Remember that experiment we were doing on Starbase Eleven?"

"I'm not likely to forget it, lad. We still haven't settled all of the technical issues. But we don't have time to play such games at the moment."

Projeff ran a hand through his hair. "I'm not interested in games. It's just that the alien ships seem to have a knack for destroying the effectiveness of our shields and—"

"Ya noticed that too, have ya? I'm doin' some calculations on it now."

"I was thinking perhaps we could work together on this."

"Laddie, you and I canna work well together," Scotty said with a grin. "We're only effective in competition with each other."

Projeff grinned. "That's really what I had in mind," he said.

"All right," Scotty said. "Let's hear what you've got."

"You first," Projeff said.

Then they both laughed with the pleasure of working with another mind so similar. They were considered the best engineers in the fleet, and were known to work miracles.

They would share, and they both knew it. And together they would come up with something.

"Here's what I have," Scotty said. "Their weapons seem to be doin' something to the shields that we're not protected against."

"Something new," Projeff said.

Scotty looked at the small screen image with fondness. "You're a young one, laddie," he said. "'Tis something old."

"Old?" Projeff said.

"Aye. Look into your computer files. We used to have weaponry similar to this. Our new shields were designed with the new technology in mind, not the old technology."

Projeff grew excited as memory clearly kicked in. "Because the designers figured the shields would be adequate enough to handle older weapons."

"And they believed that these starships could conquer any ship with older weaponry."

"They didn't expect the older weaponry to be mixed up with alien technology," Projeff said.

"Right, lad." Scotty smiled. "Now we're gettin' somewhere."

Projeff grinned. "So it's a race then, a race to see which of us can modify the shields properly."

Scotty got suddenly serious. "I don't think a race is quite the right term, lad. I think we need to share information when we have it. We're in a serious conflict here—"

"I know that," Projeff said. "But that can't stop us from seeing who makes the right adjustment first."

"Ah, that's decided aforehand," Scotty said. "It'll be the *Enterprise*. It always is."

Then he signed off, smiling, despite the seriousness of the operation. As he had said earlier, they did better when they were competing with each other. He liked defending the honor of the *Enterprise*. But both engineers knew they were working together. The competition just helped them work faster, harder, and more effectively.

And he knew, deep down inside, that they needed all the help they could get.

Rathbone eased herself up onto one elbow and looked around at the interior of the dirt bunker. The light coming from the open ends of the bunker was getting dimmer, and for the first time in what seemed like an eternity, she felt chilled. Goose bumps covered the red, burned skin on her arms.

Dr. McCoy crouched over Kor, running a medical scanner slowly over him. After a moment McCoy sighed, sat back in the dirt, and flipped the tricorder closed, looking very upset and confused.

Kahaq, Kor's officer, glared at McCoy through the dark. "Will he live?"

McCoy sighed again, then said, "I don't really know. His broken ribs are healing fine. But Klingon burns and dehydration are not really my specialty, as I've said a half dozen times during this hellish day."

"He will live," Kahaq said, answering his own question with the answer he obviously wanted.

McCoy just shook his head in disgust at his own powerlessness and didn't move.

Rathbone was impressed at the loyalty Kor received from Kahaq. Kirk on the *Enterprise* also got that "ignore facts, follow Kirk" loyalty from his crew. And after seeing the captain in action here, she was starting to see why. And feel the same way. At this moment she trusted him totally with her life.

McCoy glanced over at her. Through the faint light she could see him smile.

"Feeling better?" he asked.

She nodded. "Much."

In reality she was. She had distant memories of the last attack, Ensign Chop's body, the intense heat, the Klingon mother dying and McCoy and Kerdoch leading her back here. But the memories felt like they had happened to someone else, as if she'd watched them on a monitor while sitting in her room.

"Good," McCoy said. He scooted over beside her on his hands and knees and pulled out his medical scanner again. After a moment he snapped it closed, smiling. "Better, but you need to keep pouring down the water."

"All right, Doctor."

"I've got to get out of this rathole," McCoy said, patting her shoulder and moving toward the open end of the bunker. "You up for a walk?"

"Yes." She followed him out and straightened up carefully, letting the cool evening air fill her lungs and calm her slightly spinning head. After a moment she followed McCoy up onto the concrete platform holding the shelter and the disrupter cannon. Kirk and Sulu were digging through the remains of a colony dome about thirty paces away. There was no one else in sight.

Beside her, McCoy took a long, deep breath. She did the same thing, looking out beyond the colony into the blackened fields. And then her gaze moved beyond the remains of the Klingon crops to the natural vegetation. The aliens had been careful not to destroy anything that was native to the planet. And something about that fact nagged at her.

"Are you all right?" McCoy asked, touching her elbow.

"I'm feeling better, Doctor," she said, then realized that he sensed her distraction. "I'm just wondering why the aliens are focusing only on the Klingon crops without touching the planet's native vegetation. That seems like such a precise attack. They must be doing that for a reason."

"I've been wondering the same thing." Kirk said.

Kirk's voice startled her, and she spun around. Kirk and Sulu had returned to the edge of the cannon platform with more fireproof panels while she'd been staring out at the fields.

"It does seem odd," McCoy said. "They must really hate the Klingons."

"Maybe there's more to it than that," Kirk said. "Nothing about this attack makes sense."

"Not much about this planet makes sense," Sulu said.

Kirk looked out at the blackened fields, then back to Rathbone. "Are you feeling well enough for a short mission?"

"Put me to work," she said. And she meant it. So far it felt as if she'd been a burden to the landing party. She wanted to carry her own weight.

"Good," Kirk said. "I want you and Mr. Sulu to make another trip into those fields, looking for anything that might give us any clues as to why they're being destroyed while the native vegetation isn't. It is just too odd an occurrence to let pass. And at this point any clues we can get might help."

"I agree. We'll find something, Captain," Sulu said. He moved forward and slipped on his tricorder.

"If something's there," Vivian said with a scientist's caution.

McCoy handed her his tricorder. "Drink some water before you go."

"Yes, Doctor," she said, smiling. She quickly moved to the edge of the shelter, retrieved a full water bottle, and took a long drink in front of the doctor. Then she passed the bottle to Sulu, and he did the same thing.

"Mr. Sulu," Kirk said, "I don't want you to go any farther from this shelter than a two-minute fast run. Is that understood?"

"Yes, sir," Sulu said.

Sulu turned and, motioning for her to follow, led her toward the edge of the burnt fields. She could feel her heart racing slightly again, but it felt good to be doing something to help.

Behind her she heard Captain Kirk say, "Bones, fill me in on Kor's condition. Can he be moved?"

Ahead of her, Sulu ducked past the edge of a ruined dome and moved out at a good pace. She increased her stride to keep up.

In front of her were the burnt fields and the dry, brown natural vegetation beyond them. Again the nagging feeling that the answer was out here overwhelmed her.

The problem was she had to find it. And do it very quickly.

Kerdoch finished lighting the dome's emergency heater, then surveyed the rest of the interior. This had been Kablanti's home. Kerdoch could feel the man's presence. His essence was with this home still. Far past the age restrictions, Kablanti had managed to get on this planet simply because he had done a favor for one of the members of the High Council. As it turned out, he had been a valued member, a good fighter, and a good singer. His presence would be missed.

Kerdoch checked the water supply. Enough. More would be needed tomorrow. Colony food supplies filled one cabinet, more than sufficient for one night.

Kerdoch finished his inspection with a quick check for weapons or anything that might be useful to the fight. Nothing. Old Kablanti had died with his weapon in his hand, outside defending his fields during the first attack. A proud death.

An honorable death.

Kerdoch picked up a stein engraved with Kablanti's family crest. He held it up in a silent toast to his dead friend. Then he said, "Thank you, Kablanti, for the use of your home to shelter our commander."

Kerdoch placed the stein on a high shelf. The dome would welcome the commander.

He ducked back out the emergency exit of the dome and started across the short distance to the disrupter cannon. Ahead, Kirk talked to the human doctor. In the field beyond the colony Sulu and the woman were walking away from the gun at a fast pace. Obviously they had a mission. Kerdoch had no idea what the human captain was thinking. Nothing existed in that direction except Kablanti's burnt fields and natural weeds.

But Kirk was a crafty one. He had a very real reason, Kerdoch would wager.

Kirk saw him coming. "Is the dome ready?" he asked. He had clipped command style that was as close to Klingon as humans seemed to get.

"It is prepared," Kerdoch said.

"Good," Kirk said. "We need to move Kor now while we still have light."

"And before the next attack," the doctor said.

"Possibly," Kirk said. "But I doubt the next attack will come before morning."

"Why would you think that?" Kerdoch asked. "Their first attack was at dusk. They returned many times during the night with their evil fire."

Kirk looked at Kerdoch, holding his gaze. Kerdoch was amazed. This human did not back down or even look away. In the few humans that Kerdoch had met, that was not the case.

"Because," Kirk said, "I'm betting the next attack will come on the ground. They won't risk another ship to this cannon. And the logical time for a ground attack would be at sunrise. And it will come from the same direction the planes attacked from."

Kerdoch stared at the captain for a moment, then said, "If you are correct, do you have a plan as to how we will stop them?"

Kirk smiled at Kerdoch. "Not yet." He turned and headed for the bunker. "Let's get Kor moved."

The human doctor laughed and whispered to Kerdoch, "Don't worry. He always does his best work without a plan."

Kerdoch stood on the edge of the cannon platform

and watched the two humans stride toward the end of the bunker. He had always thought of humans as enemies of the Empire. Yet they fought to defend a Klingon colony, and worked to save the life of a Klingon commander. If humans were enemies, this enemy had much honor.

He followed the two, wondering why all Klingons were not informed of such facts.

Kirk found it interesting that neither he nor McCoy was allowed to help carry Kor to the dome. Kerdoch and Kahaq dragged Kor out of the bunker, then picked the Commander up and supported him, as if he were actually awake and walking between them. They ended up half dragging him, half carrying him, and the toes of Kor's boots left parallel trails in the dust leading from the bunker to the dome.

McCoy protested the unusual carry position, but not loudly. He didn't know enough about Klingon physiology to be certain that the lift would harm Kor. All he knew was that it would hurt a human in Kor's condition.

The Klingons ignored him, and Kirk let them. They had customs that were based on things he did not understand. Often such customs had more than a symbolic significance. Often they were created with real physical reasons behind them.

McCoy knew that too. That was probably why his protest wasn't too loud.

McCoy paced ahead of the Klingons, and Kirk walked a few paces behind them, using his boot to smooth out the tracks Kor left. If there was a ground assault, there would be no point in leaving a direct trail from the gun to the dome for an attacker to follow. Of course, if the attackers got this far, most likely what Kirk was doing would make absolutely no difference. But he brushed out the trail anyway. It made him feel better.

After Kor was settled on the cot near a center wall of the dome, Kirk ducked back outside and stepped up on the cannon platform. The air now had a cold bite to it, and the burns on his arms and face stung. Above him the stars were starting to appear.

Sulu and Rathbone were faint figures in the fading light as the second sun dropped below the horizon. From what Kirk could tell, they were working along the edge of the burned Klingon crops and the remaining natural plants. He hoped they'd found something that would lend a clue to what was happening here. Anything at this point would help.

He turned in the direction of where the ships had attacked. Nothing but flat, burnt-out fields for a thousand or more paces. Most likely the ships would land out of range of the disrupter cannon, near the edge of those low hills. Then the ground troops would start toward the colony. They would be shielded in some fashion, but he was fairly certain they wouldn't have enough shielding to stop a disrupter cannon shot.

Kirk moved around behind the shelter over the cannon and studied it for a moment. If a ground attack did start, they'd have to find a way to turn the gun around and get it aimed at the attacking forces. Ideally in such a way that they would be able to get the shelter back in place. That might be asking too much of such a make-shift building. When Sulu returned, they'd see what they could figure out.

In the fading light he studied the perimeter of the

colony. Five of the domes along the edge were destroyed. Those ruins would be a logical place to try to stand off ground troops marching across the fields, if he could get enough colonists to help.

He walked to the edge of one dome and looked out over the open, black field. He hoped it never came to an attack across this field, because if it did, they'd all die for sure.

Unless Spock could find a way to get them off this planet in time.

He flipped open his communicator. "Kirk to *Enterprise.*"

"Spock here."

"Any change, Mr. Spock?"

"None, Captain."

"Any chance you can get close enough to beam us out of here?"

"Not without attacking the alien ships directly, Captain. I've run seventeen possible scenarios and all of them end in complete failure."

"Keep working on it, Mr. Spock."

"I will, Captain."

"And Spock, I expect a ground attack on the colony at dawn. Stand ready."

"We will, sir," Spock said. "We will endeavor to stop the attack in orbit."

"And get us out of here at the same time," Kirk said.

"Of course, Captain," Spock said.

For a moment Kirk thought he heard the slightest hint in Spock's voice that his feelings were hurt by such a comment. Then Kirk realized he was just imagining it.

"Thank you, Spock. Kirk out."

He slapped the communicator closed, and headed back to the dome where Kor slept.

Inside the warm room, Kerdoch stood over the Klingon commander as if on guard. Kahaq sat beside him, and McCoy sat at a large steel table about three paces away. It looked like a deathwatch to Kirk, and he didn't want it to continue. They had too much work to do.

"Kerdoch," Kirk said, "I could use your help."

Kerdoch nodded to Kahaq and turned. "Yes, Captain."

"If our enemies attack at dawn, as I think they might, I'd like to have a line of defense set up for the colony."

Kerdoch bowed his head in acknowledgment. "What would you suggest?"

Kirk had hoped that was what the colonist would ask. He indicated that Kerdoch follow him out into the fading light.

A few steps from the dome Kirk stopped and pointed to the five destroyed domes along the perimeter of the colony. "We'll set up defensive positions in there, using the rubble for protection."

Kerdoch stared at the domes for a moment, then turned to the captain. "How many more defenders do we need?"

"As many as have guns," Kirk said. "If a ground force makes it past that line, we're all dead anyway. We might as well make our last stand there."

Kerdoch nodded. "If there are no further air attacks this night, then I will assume you are correct about the ground troops. Every colonist who can move and fire a weapon will be here."

"Have them assemble one hour before dawn," Kirk said, "so we'll have time to dig in and prepare."

"One hour," Kerdoch said.

Without a glance at Kirk, or at the door leading back to Kor, Kerdoch turned and strode off toward the center of the colony, his head high, his pace long and solid.

Kirk watched him go, glad that Kerdoch was helping. Farmers in any culture tended to be the strong, sturdy, reliable people, proud of their work and their lifestyle. It had never occurred to Kirk before that Klingon farmers would also be skilled, fearless fighters.

They were certainly not to be trifled with, as the aliens were quickly discovering. It was a lesson the Federation might want to take to heart in the future.

Chapter Fourteen

IT WAS GETTING too dark to work, and the cold was starting to numb Vivian's fingers.

She slowly climbed to her feet and tried to brush the black soot off her aching knees and hands. She switched the tricorder to her left hand and put her right hand in her armpit, trying to warm it. She had no memory of ever feeling this cold, this dirty, this tired, before.

Sulu was on his knees about ten paces from her, studying readings on his tricorder in the faint light.

Neither of them really knew exactly what they were looking for. They were just hoping to find any clue to solve what was happening. Were the Klingons doing something with their crops that might cause another race to attack them? It had sounded far-fetched to her when they came out into the field, and now it seemed even more so. But both the captain and Sulu thought it likely enough to investigate, so she had tried.

Tried looking for something that didn't exist.

"Any luck?" Sulu asked, standing and moving over beside her, blowing on his hands to warm them as he came.

"I've found nothing new," she said.

"Me either," he said. "We should report to the captain, unless you think we should stay out here longer."

"What is there to report?" she asked. "Or find, for that matter."

She glanced around one last time, hoping to find anything that might help, as if it might be sitting out in the open. But there was nothing but the stubble and ashes of burned crops.

She hated failure, and this planet seemed to constantly want to hand her failure after failure. She could remember being so happy the day she got the assignment to the colony on Signi Beta. Now she wished she'd never heard of this miserable place.

"Let's go back," she said.

Quickly, through near-darkness made even blacker by the burned crops, they moved toward the colony. Once in a while a light would flash ahead of them in the colony, then disappear again.

Otherwise they were alone in the dark, under the stars. Stars she very much wished she were traveling between, instead of walking under.

It felt as if they had to go forever. Her steps seemed to merge into one another. Beside her Sulu became nothing more than a faint ghost walking silently in the dark. For a moment she thought she was having a nightmare and she would awake at any moment in her warm bed on the *Enterprise*. It would only be one of many nightmares about Signi Beta that she'd had.

Then she found herself stepping past some debris from a ruined dome and following Sulu up to a figure standing in the dark near the big Klingon gun.

"Captain?" Sulu said.

"Did you find anything?" Kirk asked, his familiar voice bringing her back to reality. This wasn't just a dream. This was very, very real. Again the image of Ensign Chop's body flashed in her mind. She focused on the captain, pushing the memory away.

"We found nothing new, sir," Sulu said.

"I was afraid of that," Kirk said.

Rathbone could tell he was tired. His voice didn't have the force it had just this morning.

"Commander?"

"I'm afraid I can only confirm what Sulu said, Captain," Vivian said, doing her best to make her voice sound firm. "All the Klingon plants I found were just their standard tIqKa SuD. It's a form of hybrid, a blend of the Klingon Doctuq and the natural grain found growing here."

"What I still find interesting," Sulu said, "is the hybrid nature of the natural plants. It's as if they'd been blended with other plants years before."

"The Federation colony botanists found the same thing interesting," she said. "We spent five years studying it and we had no more explanation for it at the end as the first day."

Kirk seemed to shift, turning to face them, most likely to see them better in the dark. "The original plants are hybrids?" he asked. "How long ago did that happen?"

"At least eight hundred years ago," Sulu said. "Maybe up to a thousand."

"The colony pinned it closer to nine hundred," she said. "And not so much as hybrids, as genetically shifted. All the records of the research are available in the Federation data banks, Captain."

She watched as he seemed to be thinking, staring off into the dark. Granted, this area was fascinating, but she had no idea how it might be important to stopping the alien attacks.

"Mr. Sulu," the Captain said. "Have Spock look over the colony records as quickly as possible. Also have him scan as best he can from his position for any previous civilizations on this planet."

"We did that, Captain," Rathbone said. "And so did the original survey team. No trace of any previous culture even visiting this planet, let alone living here."

"Except for hybrid plants," he said.

"Captain," she said, "there could be a hundred natural causes for such a genetic shifting. Asteroid collision could have caused it. So could intense solar flares. And those are only two examples. It could—"

Even in the deepening dark she could see him hold up his hand and smile. "Just checking everything. None of this makes sense. I just hate to leave anything unchecked while we have time to investigate."

Rathbone felt the heat of embarrassment crawl up her neck. "I'm sorry, Captain. I'm frustrated we didn't find more."

His smile faded. "You might have found just enough. Only time will tell." He put his hand on her shoulder and propelled her toward the shelter. "Now both of you need to get inside and get warm. I'll take the first watch near the gun. Mr. Sulu, you relieve me after you call Spock and when you get warm."

"Yes, sir," he said.

Without knowing what else to say, Vivian turned and followed Sulu through the dark to the dome and the warmth it held. Suddenly it was very clear why Captain Kirk was such a good captain. He never overlooked anything. He had the ability to step outside a situation and see it clearly.

Once again the young captain had impressed her. She wouldn't question him again.

Dr. Grayhawk, chief medical officer of the *Farragut*, huffed, then turned his back on Captain Bogle, working with something on a medical table. Bogle smiled, knowing exactly what that action meant. Grayhawk couldn't hold him in sick bay any longer even though he hated letting any patient out in anything short of perfect health.

"So," Bogle said, "am I going to live?" He reached up and gently felt the top of his head. The intense pain was gone, but the area was still very sensitive.

"You land on your head again anytime soon and I won't guarantee it," Grayhawk said. "But for now I'm returning you to duty, Captain."

Bogle eased himself down off the medical table and straightened his tunic. "Thank you, Doctor."

"Next time strap yourself into that captain's chair," Grayhawk said.

"I'll take that under consideration," Bogle said, and laughed. Both he and the doctor knew there were no seat belts on a starship.

He turned and headed for the sick bay door, moving slowly at first. As he reached the hall he was moving at a good pace again. By the time he stepped back on the bridge the dull ache in his head was forgotten as he focused on the situation at hand.

Communications Officer Sandy nodded at him and smiled. "Welcome back, sir."

"Glad to see you feeling better," Lieutenant Michael Book said from Navigation.

First Officer Lee stood at his science scope, face buried in it. Lee obviously heard and raised his head, smiling at Bogle.

"Good job, people," Bogle said as he moved to stand beside his captain's chair. It felt damn good to be back, he had to admit. And he was very proud of his crew, especially Mr. Lee, for saving the ship so that he had a bridge to return to. He would put in for commendations for his bridge crew if they survived this.

He took a deep breath, stepped down to a position beside his chair and looked forward. On the main viewscreen was an amazing sight: Five alien ships hovered in a fairly tight group over the planet. The Klingon battle cruiser was to the *Farragut*'s left, the *Enterprise* to the right—a three-against-five stand-off.

"Mr. Lee," Bogle said, "what's the ship's status?"

"Warp has been restored. Our screens are at ninety percent, and Projeff reports he'll have them back to one hundred percent in ten minutes. All weapons systems are on-line and ready."

"Good job," Bogle said. "The other ships?"

"The *Enterprise* is at one hundred percent," Lee said. "It's hard to tell with the Klingons. They took a bad beating in that last fight, just as we did, but they should be getting the repairs done by now."

"How about the enemy?"

Lee moved down and stood beside Bogle. "The transport ship farthest to the right took the most damage from us and the *Enterprise*. It's amazing it still exists. Its shields failed, and we pierced its hull in a dozen places."

"Enlarge the image of that ship," Bogle said. Almost instantly the ship filled the viewscreen. Bogle could see that it had suffered extensive damage. It floated at a slight angle that indicated it was nearly dead in space. Debris drifted close to it, indicating that no gravity fields remained on inside the hulk.

"One of the other ships used a tractor beam to get the crippled vessel to that position," Lee said. "It shows no signs of life and has no screens. It's just a hunk of useless metal."

"So that leaves four mother ships," Bogle said. He would never consider that ship again in his thinking.

The main viewscreen switched back to the scene of all the enemy ships.

"The remaining four are fully functional, from what we can tell," Lee said. "We punished one of them, but not enough to get through their screens."

"What about the *Enterprise* and Klingon landing parties?"

"Holding out," Lee said. "Kor is seriously injured, but still alive. Captain Kirk thinks the next attack on the colony will be a ground assault at sunrise, four hours from now. They're preparing for that possibility as best they can."

"Do we have help on the way?"

"Starfleet has been informed of the situation," Lee said, "but we have no starships close by. However, the Klingons have sent for reinforcements. We were told that two battle cruisers are on the way, but they won't arrive for another nine hours."

"By then, who knows how many enemy ships will be here," Bogle said.

"We're doing continuous long-range scans, sir," Book said, "watching for just that possibility."

"Good," Bogle said. He stood staring at the planet beyond the alien ships. "So if Kirk's right, it's up to us to stop the transport ships before they get to the atmosphere," Bogle said, more to himself than First Officer Lee.

"If we can," Lee said, softly.

Bogle only continued to stare at the alien ships, wondering just why they were even fighting this fight.

Kirk blew on his hands to warm them. The night had turned bitter cold, a stark contrast to the intense heat they'd survived during the day. He wondered how much of the cold he was feeling was because of that heat and the burns he'd received during the attacks. If he thought about it, he would ask Bones, just out of curiosity.

Kirk nodded to Sulu in the faint light as the lieutenant came up through the dark and relieved him of guard duty on the Klingon disrupter cannon.

Each of them had stood three shifts of guard duty. Nothing had changed. He'd checked in with Spock four times, and everything in orbit also remained unchanged. They were at a standoff, with neither side talking to the other. Actually, only the aliens refused to talk. The *Enterprise* had kept up a constant hail on all frequencies. But if the other side didn't want to talk, there was no talking.

Kirk headed back to the warmth of the dome, walking slowly to make sure he didn't trip in the extreme darkness.

Just over an hour until sunrise. It was time to start gathering the defense forces. He was convinced the next attack would be on the ground, especially since there had been no other air attacks during the last few hours. Only a ground attack made sense, if anything about this situation made sense.

Inside the dome the warm arm washed over him, taking the sharp edge off the chill. He could feel his arm and back muscles relaxing as they warmed.

Near the right wall Kahaq and McCoy watched over Commander Kor, who was stretched out on a cot. The colonist Kerdoch sat alone at a steel dining table, and Rathbone was dozing in a large chair, her head back, her mouth slightly open. Ensign Adaro had fallen asleep leaning against a wall.

He moved across the room to where McCoy sat beside Kor. Kirk could never remember McCoy looking so tired and dejected. His old friend was clearly not happy with the Klingon commander's condition and somehow blaming himself for not being able to do more.

Kirk knelt beside the Commander as McCoy shook his head slowly as a report on Kor's status. Obviously Kor remained unconscious and unchanged. Kirk very much wished his old enemy would recover. At this point the more help they all had, the better chances of surviving this.

Besides—and this was something he'd admit only in the dark of night, and only to himself—he found Kor a worthy adversary. The idea of facing the Klingon Empire without Kor simply wasn't as challenging.

Kirk patted McCoy's knee. "Stay with him, Bones."

McCoy nodded without looking up.

Kirk turned and moved over to where Kerdoch sat at the table. The Klingon colonist looked as determined and as angry as he had the first moment Kirk saw him aboard the battle cruiser.

"Time to prepare?" Kerdoch asked.

Kirk dropped down into a chair across from the colonist. "I'm afraid it is."

"What do you need?" Kerdoch asked, being as blunt as most of the Klingons Kirk knew.

"Any colonist who can fire a weapon. Most likely this fight will be our last defense, if the attackers get this far."

"They should be stopped in orbit," Kerdoch said, his tone matter-of-fact.

"I agree," Kirk said. "Kor's ship and our two Federation ships will do everything possible to stop whatever is heading our way. But they didn't manage to stop them last time, so we need to be ready, in case they fail again."

"Agreed," Kerdoch said. He put his hands flat on the table and pushed himself up, taking a deep breath, obviously preparing himself. "I will gather warriors near the cannon."

The captain watched as the Klingon farmer turned and strode out of the dome, leaving Kirk sitting alone

at the table. There had to be a way to stop this fight—
if they only knew the cause, or even who their
attackers were.

Kirk felt as helpless as McCoy felt with Kor. He
knew there must be something he could do.

But what?

Chapter Fifteen

"THAT'S IT!" Scotty said, banging his fist on the console. "That's it, lads."

The engineering staff looked at him and smiled. It didn't matter that half the staff was female: when he was excited, he tended to call them all lads.

And he was excited now. He'd figured out the shield modifications, and he hadn't even looked at the figures Projeff had sent. Projeff, in the meantime, had apparently not found anything, or he would have contacted Scotty to brag—

And to share.

"It's so simple," he said to the ensign beside him. She had long black hair and the look of his mother— at least until she turned, revealing eyes a color not normally found in human beings. "We create ghost shields, harmonic echoes that— Ach, just do it." He slid the calculations to her, and the others crowded around.

Then he hit the comm button. "Mr. Scott to the bridge."

"Spock here." Spock's responses were always prompt and always dry.

"Mr. Spock, I've figured out the problem with the shields."

"I had not realized we had a problem with the shields, Mr. Scott."

Scotty blinked. Usually Spock was on top of these things. But he had a lot to think about, what with the captain on the surface and all. "You dinna notice how quickly they affected the shields' power and with such old-fashioned weapons at that?"

"Well," Spock said, "now that you mention it, I do recall thinking that the shields went down quickly, but it did not strike me as all that unusual."

"All that unusual? All that unusual! Mr. Spock, this ship can protect us against Klingon firepower, against Romulan treachery, against—"

"I take it you've solved the problem, Mr. Scott," Spock said, his voice sounding drier than usual.

"Of course I have, man. And a slight hair before young Projeff of the *Farragut.*"

"I'm sure the captain will be pleased. How long will modifications take?"

"It may be an hour or two, Mr. Spock," Scotty said.

"I would prefer a more precise estimate," Spock said.

"That is precise," Scotty said.

"I may need the shields sooner," Spock said.

"When you need them," Scotty said, "let me know. We'll be working as fast as we can."

Scotty signed off, then asked Uhura to contact Projeff.

When the visual came on the screen, Projeff was bent over his console, his hair sticking out in all directions, a smudge of dirt under one eye.

"We've found the solution, laddie," Scotty said, with more than a bit of pride, "and we're sending it to you now."

"I hope you're not talking about turning up the harmonics," Projeff said. "We've tried that and—"

"No, lad. It's an elegant solution." Scotty grinned. "Courtesy of the *Enterprise.*"

Spock noted the time.

It had been an hour since he spoke to Mr. Scott. There was still no word on the shield modifications.

If the Captain was correct that a ground attack would be launched against the colony at the colonies sunrise, adding the appropriate amount of time for a landing force to reach the surface from orbit, within the next sixty-two seconds the enemy should be deploying forces.

He pressed the comm button. "Mr. Scott, how is your work on the shields progressing?"

"We're finishing the last of it now."

"Good," Spock said. "As I believe we will need them within the next sixty seconds."

"You *believe?*"

Spock couldn't very well say that he knew. "Using the captain's calculations and my own—"

"I was merely teasing, Mr. Spock," Scotty said. "You'll have your shields. Mind you, we need to test them first—"

"We shall do so any second now," Spock said, ending the communication.

On the screen the five enemy ships remained in position. Nothing seemed to have changed, but Spock agreed with the captain. Under these circumstances, the next logical move for the attacking force would be a ground attack.

And it would happen soon.

"Red alert," Spock said as he moved down from his science station and stood beside the captain's chair, his hand gripping the back padding.

Around him the red lights snapped on, the siren filled the air of the bridge with a shrilling background sound.

"Ensign Haru, arm photon torpedoes," Spock said to the young ensign at the weapons panel.

"Yes, sir," Haru said.

Spock turned toward the screen. "Mr. Chekov, cut the distance between the *Enterprise* and the enemy ships by exactly fifty percent."

"Aye, sir," Chekov said.

"Do so slowly, Ensign," Spock said. "At one-tenth impulse."

"Aye, sir," Chekov said without looking away from his console.

On the main viewscreen the five enemy ships got gradually larger.

"The *Farragut* is hailing us, sir," Lieutenant Uhura said.

"On audio only," Spock said. "And scramble the communication, Lieutenant."

He wanted to make sure he didn't lose sight of the ships in front of him. He had worked out a possible line of attack and a point of weakness in the ships. At the moment of deployment of the ground ships, the mother ships would have their docking-bay doors open. They would be less maneuverable and more vulnerable. He planned to take advantage of that weakness, but the *Enterprise* had to be in position first.

"Spock," Captain Bogle said, his voice booming with authority, "what are you doing?"

"Preparing, sir," Spock said.

"Preparing for what?" Bogle asked. "To get us all killed?"

"To stop the coming attack on the ground colony, sir. Spock out."

On the screen a line suddenly appeared across the rear section of two of the wing-shaped enemy ships. The docking bays were opening. Captain Kirk had been correct about the timing of the attack.

"Mr. Haru," Spock said, never taking his gaze from the opening bay doors. He had studied the video from the last deployment, and he knew exactly what he was looking at. "Target the center of both those openings. Fire torpedoes."

The *Enterprise* rocked slightly as four torpedoes sped toward their targets, two at one ship, two at the other.

"Lieutenant Uhura, inform the captain of the situation."

"Yes, sir," she said.

"Continue firing on your targets, Mr. Haru," Spock said as the closest attacker opened up its weapons on the *Enterprise*.

The ship rocked slightly at the direct hits, but the stabilizers kept it level.

Spock could tell that the hits had done little damage. Obviously Mr. Scott's modifications to the screens had proved worthwhile. At least for the moment.

"Screens at ninety-six percent and holding," Chekov said.

Spock watched as the *Farragut* opened up full phaser fire on the ship attacking the *Enterprise,* distracting them for a moment, but doing little damage.

The Klingon battle cruiser jumped into the battle, running a standard attack pass above the closest alien ship, firing with full disrupters.

The two docking bays across the backs of the alien ships continued opening.

Mr. Haru fired two more torpedoes at each ship. All four torpedoes disappeared through the docking openings in the sides of the ships. Inside, the bays lit up with orange and yellow explosions.

A moment later Mr. Haru followed the first two torpedoes with two more. They also found their targets.

Both enemy ships seemed to rock in space as their docking bays were filled with bright orange and red fire.

Mr. Spock had theorized that the weakest area of the attacking ships would be inside the docking bays. It looked as if he might have been right. "Continue firing," he ordered.

The *Enterprise* rocked with direct hits against the screens. Spock gripped the back of the captain's chair and maintained his balance.

Four more torpedoes streaked from the *Enterprise* at the same moment the enemy hit with direct phaser fire.

Out of the flames and explosions of the alien

docking bays two large transport ships appeared. Both were ten times larger than the small attack ships deployed before.

"Shields at sixty-percent," Chekov shouted over the rumbling sounds of phaser fire hitting the screens.

"Target the transports, Mr. Haru," Spock ordered. "Fire phasers."

Instantly phasers licked out from the *Enterprise,* making direct hits on one of the transports. Its shield instantly flared to life as an orange ball around the transport.

At that moment the *Farragut* also targeted the same transport with full phasers.

The small ship's orange shields flared to bright red, then into blue and disappeared with an explosion.

"Got him," Chekov said.

"But the other has gotten away," Spock said as the other transport quickly dropped into the atmosphere and out of range.

The *Enterprise* again rocked with the impact of more direct phaser hits. Spock managed to hang on, never taking his gaze from the screen.

"Screens at thirty percent," Chekov said.

"Return fire, Mr. Haru," Spock ordered. "Mr. Chekov, evasive maneuvers. Look for any possible course that would take us into transporter range of the captain."

"Yes, sir," Chekov said.

"Sir, we have a message from the *Farragut,*" Lieutenant Uhura said. "Their shields are almost down. They are pulling back."

Spock noted that the Klingon battle cruiser was also standing off.

"Mr. Chekov. Move to a position flanking the *Farragut* and hold there."

"But sir," Chekov said. "The captain—"

"I want you to continue looking for that course, ensign," Spock said. "Until then, move us beside the *Farragut.*"

"Aye, sir," Chekov said.

Spock moved over and stood by the captain's chair studying the alien ships re-forming into a group and standing off.

The attack had destroyed one transport and had damaged two of the larger ships. But that was not enough to change the odds in this battle. At this point the only hope the *Enterprise* and *Farragut* had of survival was to wait for the Klingon reinforcements in six hours and seven minutes.

But would the captain be able to withstand a ground assault for six hours? The odds were too long to even calculate.

"Mr. Spock," Lieutenant Uhura said, "Captain Bogle said to tell you nice work."

Spock nodded. His timing had been correct. But he had made an error: he had underestimated the defenses of the enemy ships. He would not make that mistake again.

"Lieutenant, have you informed Captain Kirk of the transport's arrival time?"

"Yes, sir," Lieutenant Uhura said.

"Good. Have Mr. Scott come to the bridge." Spock had a theory he needed to work out. And if it worked, he might be able to get within transport distance long enough to get the captain and his party off the surface.

"Mr. Spock," Chekov said. "We have company."

"Company, Mr. Chekov?" Spock asked as he

looked at the screen. Three more large alien ships moved into position near the others.

"They have been on the other side of the planet," Chekov said. "It blocked our scans."

"Let's hope those Klingons can get here quickly," Sulu said.

Spock said nothing. He had just done a quick calculation of the odds of rescuing the captain now. They were odds that not even the captain would go against.

Rathbone stood in the faint morning light outside the dome, her hands tucked into her armpits trying to keep warm. Her breath formed silver crystals in front of her. She knew that in a few hours, if she lived that long, she'd be wishing for this cold again. But that thought didn't help warm her now. Just as it had seemed she'd never be cool again during the day, tonight she had felt as if she would never be warm again. If any planet was hell for her, it was this one.

Klingon colonists were starting to gather near the disrupter cannon—men, women, young adults, even children around the age of ten. All of them carried weapons of one sort or another; all ready and willing to fight for their homes.

In that respect, Klingons were just like humans and most other races she was acquainted with. They fought for their homes. But she hated to see the children carrying weapons. There seemed something very wrong with that.

Captain Kirk and Lieutenant Sulu stepped down off the disrupter cannon platform and strode toward her. Watching them come, intent purpose obviously in mind, twisted her stomach into a little knot.

She took a deep breath of the cold air and told herself to get a grip on her fear. She was an official member of a Starfleet landing party. She was trained to do what needed to be done. And she would do it.

Captain Kirk said, "Feeling better?"

"Much," she said.

"Good," he said. He glanced around at the gathering Klingons. "I'm going to send the children back to their domes. If we get overrun by the aliens, we can hope they'll spare the children."

"Good decision," she said. Inside she breathed a sigh of relief that the captain felt the same way she did.

He smiled at her. "Now I've got a job for you."

Again her stomach twisted, but she managed to say, "Anything, sir."

"If we're attacked," the captain said, "I need you and Sulu to try to get into a flanking position off to the right of the colony, dig out a little area for yourselves in a ditch or something. Some sort of cover where you'll end up behind their lines."

"Who's going to man the disrupter cannon?" Sulu asked.

Kirk smiled at him. "I was a good shot in my day. Kerdoch will help."

At that moment the captain's communicator beeped. Vivian watched as he snapped it open with practiced ease and said, "Kirk here."

"Captain," Lieutenant Uhura said, her voice coming through very clearly. "The docking bay doors of two of the alien ships are starting to open. "Mr. Spock is now staging an attack on the ships, focusing on the bay doors."

Kirk nodded. "Good thinking. Keep me posted if any ships get through to the atmosphere."

He snapped his communicator closed. "The fight's going on above us. Get to positions. We need to assume Spock and Captain Bogle can't stop them."

"Yes, Captain," Sulu said. "This way, Commander."

Sulu turned and headed off in the faint light, for the second time moving toward the edge of the colony.

For a moment Rathbone couldn't get her feet to move.

"Go ahead," Kirk said. The look in his eyes was one of understanding. "I've got children to get out of the line of fire."

"Understood, Captain," she said. With her numb fingers over her phaser, she nodded to the captain and headed after Mr. Sulu.

A few moments later she once again stepped out into the blackened fields. This time it wasn't to study plants. This time she was to hide behind enemy lines to defend a planet she hated, and a colony of Klingons who had defeated her and her work.

Sometimes life was just a little too strange.

It had taken Kirk only a minute to convince Kerdoch that the children did not belong on the front lines. And that the best possible way for the young children to survive was to be in the domes, without weapons.

At first Kerdoch had argued that it was the Klingon way, but the argument had a token sound to it. After a short exchange, Kerdoch had agreed, and very shortly only adults and teenagers remained near the disrupter cannon.

Kirk stood, watching in the faint morning light as the Klingon colonists took up positions along the edge of the colony. All of them carried panels of dome-coverings in case of an air attack with plasma beams again.

Kirk blew on his hands in a vain attempt to warm them. He so much wanted to be aboard the *Enterprise,* in the middle of the fight up there. But instead he was here, with almost no weapons. And very little chance of winning.

His communicator beeped. He flipped it open. "Go ahead."

"Captain," Spock's voice came back clear and strong. At that moment Kirk realized that he had been worried about his ship and his crew. Very worried. He was just too busy to think about them.

"Two large transport ships attempted to leave the alien craft. We destroyed one, but the other managed to get into the atmosphere. It should be on the surface in twelve minutes and ten seconds."

"Acknowledged," he said.

They were coming, as he had feared. There had to be a way to stop them.

"What's the status of the *Enterprise?*"

"The *Enterprise* and the *Farragut* came through this fight without damage, Captain. Mr. Scott is working on continuing to strengthen our shields against their weapons."

"The other ships?"

"We have had no report from the Klingon battle cruiser *Klothos.* Three more enemy craft have joined the attack force. They now have seven working ships and one hulk in orbit."

"You've pulled back, I take it," he said.

"For the moment," Spock said. "We had no choice."

Kirk knew that. Still, it was startling to hear Spock say so. "How long until the extra Klingon battle cruisers arrive?"

"Four hours, one minute, sir," Spock said.

Even then, Kirk knew it would not be an even fight. Obviously one of the alien craft at least matched the power of a starship or battle cruiser. Seven against five usually won. Not always, but more than not.

"Let me know if you come up with anything, Mr. Spock. Kirk out."

He flipped his communicator closed and started toward Kerdoch and the disrupter cannon. Unless he could think of something quickly, this was going to be a very long day. And it might be his last.

Chapter Sixteen

KERDOCH STOOD on the disrupter cannon platform, inside the shelter of dome panels, staring out over the blackened fields in the orange light of sunrise. Fields that had been growing and a healthy blue and green only a few days before. Now, finally, he was about to meet, face to face, those responsible for the destruction of his crops, the death of his friends.

The enemy ship had landed. Just before the sun K'Tuj touched the lower edge of the sky.

Along the rims of the colony his neighbors lined up, weapons at the ready. Today they would all die defending their homes. It was an honorable way to die.

Beside him in the shelter the human Kirk stood, one hand on the disrupter cannon, also ready to fight and die for this planet, this colony. Kerdoch had spent the night wondering about such actions. Humans had always been described as cowards, butchers, animals with no honor. Yet here was a captain who had honor. He and his people could have hidden in the distant hills. He did not have to stay to defend Klingon homes. Yet he did. Without complaint. And with great courage.

This human captain had honor.

In the distance Kerdoch could see the cowards' ship standing tall and bright on the natural vegetation beyond the black crops. A line of forms had stretched out from the ship, facing the colony. Soldiers, lining up for the attack.

They stood upright on two limbs, as Klingons did.

"How many would you estimate?" the human captain asked.

"Three hundred," Kerdoch said. "They wear armor."

As Kerdoch spoke, the line started moving toward the colony.

The human captain flipped open his communicator device. "Spock, they're coming. Anything you can do?"

Kerdoch clearly heard the reply from the human ship. "No, Captain. They are holding us out of range."

"Understood. Kirk out."

The human captain flipped his communicator closed and grasped the two handles of the disrupter cannon firmly with both hands.

"The cannon fire will extend to the edge of the fields," Kerdoch told the human captain. "It was a consideration on shaping our fields."

"Good thinking," the human said. "I'll wait until they cross over the line before opening fire."

Kerdoch said nothing. He slowly drew his disrupter and checked it one more time. It was charged and ready. He would take many of the enemy with him. The cowards approaching him deserved to die for attacking his home and his family. Revenge would be sweet this day.

He glanced down the line of defenders. His wife and eldest son were tucked behind a sheet of dome paneling. Both had weapons in their hands and were staring at the coming enemy. He could feel pride filling his chest.

The line of enemy forms crossed into the blackened fields, their shining blue armor reflecting the early rays of the sun.

The human captain waited.

Kerdoch turned to him. Had he frozen from fear? No, he seemed to be studying the entire scene, his look cold and intent. This human was not one to freeze in battle.

"Okay," the human said. Then he shouted, "Now!"

With that, Kirk fired the disrupter cannon, the sound deafening inside the shelter.

Then he fired again.

And again.

And again.

Kerdoch stood, ignoring the pain in his ears as the human's first shot cut out two soldiers in the center of the line. The force of the blast also knocked others backward.

His second shot had moved to the right ten figures. Again his shot was accurate.

His third shot moved ten more to the right and did not miss.

The enemy troops continued forward.

Kirk continued firing, knocking large holes in the enemy lines to both the left and the right.

Suddenly, before the enemy soldiers could get within phaser range of the colony, the line stopped. As a unit they turned and, at the same trudging pace, moved back toward their ship.

Instantly the human captain stopped firing, even though he could have shot many of them in the back as they retreated.

Kerdoch nodded his agreement. It took no honor to shoot an enemy in the back. Humans truly did have honor in battle. It was something he would always remember.

"You fire a disrupter cannon well," Kerdoch said.

The human captain nodded as he rubbed his ears. "Thanks. But you folks really should put mufflers on these things."

"Mufflers?" Kerdoch asked. He had never heard such a term.

"Never mind," Kirk said as the line of enemy crossed back into the natural vegetation, leaving many shining armored bodies laying in the blackened fields.

Kerdoch felt the surge of revenge coursing through his blood as he stared at those bodies. It was good the enemy died in the fields they had destroyed. It felt right. Only their death at his bare hands would have felt better.

Rathbone lay face down in a deep ditch, trying her best to press her body even farther into the hard dirt. A fine black ash covered everything in the ditch, including her. Her blackened hands held her phaser in front of her. They shook, and she tried to tell herself it was from the cold. But there was no kidding herself.

She was afraid. Very afraid.

During all the practice on the firing ranges in her youth, she had always wondered what being in a real fight would be like. It looked as if she would soon find out.

Facing her, Lieutenant Sulu also lay flat in the ditch, his tricorder tucked under his chin. He had been studying it for the last five minutes, but to her it had seemed like at least an hour.

"They're moving," Sulu whispered. "They should pass to our right in about sixty seconds."

She only nodded, far too afraid to trust her voice to speak. How the captain, Sulu, the other members of landing parties ever got used to this kind of danger was beyond her. It had her stomach clamped down into a knot and she had no idea how she was going to move if she had to fight.

She took a deep, shuddering breath and grasped the solid, reassuring feel of the phaser. Even being able to hit a pinpoint from fifty paces didn't comfort her at the moment. She had heard that some people froze in life-and-death situations while others managed to overcome their fear and fight. She hoped she was the type who overcame, but she feared even more than dying that she was the type who froze.

Now it looked as if she might find out very soon.

Suddenly the ground shook from an explosion.

She jumped, but Sulu put his hand on her arm. "Disrupter cannon fire," he said as another explosion shook the ground under her stomach, seeming much closer.

"The captain?" she whispered.

He nodded, not taking his gaze from his tricorder.

A third explosion, then a fourth, rocked the ground under her. Then more and more, one right after another.

The ground seemed to shake continuously under her, as if the explosions were linked.

Then, just as suddenly, it was silent.

Unnaturally silent.

Had the captain been killed?

Had the troops already reached the colony? She wanted to jump up and look, but she remained in the dirt, almost too afraid to breathe.

"They're retreating," Sulu whispered. He looked up at her, smiling through the black soot that covered his face. "The captain turned them with the cannon."

Suddenly she felt heavier, as if the weight of her body would punch a hole through the dirt under her.

"Thank heavens," she managed to say. Then she took the first true breath in what seemed like an eternity, let it out slowly, then took another.

It pleased her to see that Sulu was doing the exact same thing.

Kirk stood beside Kerdoch on the edge of the cannon platform, staring out at the bodies of the attackers littering the blackened fields. There must have been at least fifty of them, and he doubted that all of them were dead; many of them were probably only injured.

What would the attackers do now? Would they return for their injured? Would they attack again?

And why had they retreated? If they wanted to overrun the colony, why hadn't they simply continued forward? They were taking casualties, but nowhere near enough to prevent the success of their mission.

Yet under the type of fire he had been hitting them with, he would have pulled back too, if they had been his troops. Maybe that was the key to all this. He had guessed correctly about the ground attack. And their retreat was what he would have done. Maybe their thinking wasn't that far from human military thinking.

He flipped open his communicator. "Mr. Sulu, where are you?"

"In a ditch just to the right of where their line stopped advancing."

Kirk looked in that direction. One of his shots had knocked down four of the enemy right near Sulu's position. Maybe he could exchange their wounded for an opportunity to talk.

"Mr. Sulu, you and Rathbone check out the enemy casualties near your position. If you find a wounded soldier, bring him to me."

"Understood," Sulu said.

Kirk punched his communicator. "McCoy, I need you at the cannon at once."

"On my way," McCoy said.

Out in the blackened field two forms rose from a ditch and moved in a crouch toward a fallen enemy soldier.

"Why do you worry over the dead?" Kerdoch said. "They fell in battle. They have their honor."

"Because, like your commander in the dome there, they may not be dead."

"But they are the enemy," Kerdoch said, as if that were enough for Kirk to understand his meaning.

"Yes, they are," Kirk said. And he added silently, *So are you.*

At the captain's order, Rathbone had managed to push herself to her feet and climb out of the ditch beside Lieutenant Sulu. The second sun was starting to break above the horizon, and she could already feel the heat of the day coming, knocking back the cold that had filled her body.

Twenty paces in front of her, lying face down in the black soot, was a blue-armored soldier, the light reflecting off his armor like it was a mirror.

She glanced around. To her right were the enemy troops and the enemy ship; to her left was the colony. She felt as if she were walking naked onto a stage in front of the entire world. Even with Sulu beside her, she had never felt so exposed and vulnerable.

They both moved in a crouch, not really sneaking, but making sure they both stayed low until they reached the fallen alien who lay on his side, his back to them. Slowly, without touching the armor, they moved around in front of him.

The face inside the helmet was humanoid, with long black hair framing its face. It also had thick black eyebrows and ridges of thick hair running across its forehead. The nose lay flat against his face, giving him the look of a lion.

The soldier was also clearly dead.

Sulu picked up the enemy's rifle-looking weapon and moved to the next body. This soldier had less hair on his face, and was clearly younger. He was also very much alive, his eyes glowing green as he looked at them.

Those eyes startled her. For some reason she had

not put real live creatures behind the thought of the enemy. Before now the enemy had only been fast moving ships spraying waves of deadly heat. But now the enemy had eyes and a face.

When Sulu pulled the weapon from his hand, the soldier didn't move an inch to stop him.

Then Sulu studied the alien with his tricorder. "It looks as if he's broken both legs," Sulu said to her.

She could have guessed as much. The soldier's legs were twisted underneath him at very odd angles. "Can he be moved?"

"I don't know," Sulu said. He glanced around, then leaned over the soldier. "Can you hear me?"

Behind the face plate of his helmet the alien nodded yes. His gaze darted from Sulu to Vivian, then back again.

"Are you in pain?" she asked. "Bleeding?"

He shook his head. "The medical function of my suit has stopped the bleeding, killed my pain."

She was amazed at the richness of the alien's voice. Likely it was only the suit's speakers that made it sound like that.

"Good," she said. "What race are you?"

"We are Narr," he said.

"We're going to get you help," Sulu said.

The Narr soldier shook his head. "You will not move me," he said, his voice coming through the faceplate clearly.

"Why not?" she asked. "You need medical help."

"My suit cannot be moved by you."

"Will it destruct?" Sulu asked.

Once again the alien shook his head. "It is heavy. The gravity units were damaged in the battle."

Sulu sat back, looking at the fallen soldier, nodding

his head. "Your legs were broken when the antigravity units in your suit failed and the suit crushed your legs."

"That is correct," the soldier said.

She couldn't believe what she was hearing. "You mean," she said, "that these soldiers wear suits so heavy that if the suit fails they can't stand up?"

Sulu nodded. "We've seen it before."

She stared down into the green eyes of the wounded soldier, then gently touched the sleeve of his suit near his wrist. It felt solid.

Carefully she tried to pick up the arm. It was like pulling on a solid steel wall—not even a fraction of an inch of movement. "Unbelievable," she said.

"Standard for some cultures," Sulu said. "It also stops their enemies from taking prisoners."

The alien nodded behind his faceplate. "I will be rescued after the battle has been won. Until then I wait."

"Let's hope there is no more battle," Sulu said. He snapped open his communicator. "Captain?"

"Kirk here."

For some reason being reminded that the captain was so close made Vivian relax a little.

"Captain, we have a live casualty inside damaged mobile armor. It's far too heavy for us to move."

"I was afraid of that," Kirk said.

She glanced around at the open field and the other very still armored figures littering the blackness. How many of them were alive inside those heavy shells?

"Return to the colony. Kirk out."

"But what about this soldier?" she asked, shocked. How could Captain Kirk simply ignore an injured person, enemy or not?

187

Sulu stood. "There's nothing we can do for him at the moment. Come on." He turned and started toward the colony.

She remained beside the Narr, staring at his green eyes. Finally he smiled at her. "Follow your orders, soldier," he said. "You can do nothing to help me."

She nodded slowly.

"Rathbone," Sulu called to her.

She looked one more time into the deep green eyes of the Narr soldier. "Good luck."

"And to you," the soldier said.

Feeling as if her entire body was numb, she pushed herself to her feet and, without looking back, stumbled after Sulu toward the colony.

Chapter Seventeen

SCOTTY LOOKED AT the young ensign. She was slender, her dark hair falling out of its neat bun. She had been working non-stop in engineering since they left Starbase Eleven, probably the longest shift she had ever pulled.

"What I meant," she stammered, "is that I doubt we could improve them."

She was referring to the shields. Scotty's modification had worked, but not as well as he would have liked. Shield strength had still gone down, but not as rapidly as before. There was an element to the enemies' weapons that he had not yet discovered—and he had told Mr. Spock that in their brief meeting on the bridge.

"You doubt, lass?" Scotty said softly. The more established members of Engineering stepped back. They knew what was coming. They had worked with

189

Scotty long enough to know that when he spoke softly, they had best watch out.

"Yes, sir," she said. "I have double-checked your calculations."

"You double-checked *my* calculations?" His voice got even softer.

"You asked me to, sir," she said, oblivious of his tone, "and I found nothing wrong."

"You found nothing wrong," he said.

"No," she said.

"Did you expect to, lass?"

Someone guffawed behind him. Scotty turned and, with a look, silenced the laugher.

The ensign finally got the idea that something might be wrong. She flushed. "Well, sir, you did ask me to check your figures, and I assumed that meant you thought there might be errors."

"You assumed," Scotty said.

"Yes, sir," she said.

He nodded thoughtfully. "And did you not assume that maybe I was asking you to see if you could spot a different modification?"

"Sir?"

"Did you not know, lass, that engineering is not a science of mathematics?"

She blinked those extraordinary eyes at him. "But of course it involves math," she said. "The calculations—"

"Mean nothing without creativity behind them," Scotty said, his voice rising. "Lass, the engineers on this ship are second only to the captain in their creative abilities. In fact, the ability to think on your feet and to come up with solutions not in the guidebooks is the hallmark of a chief engineer."

"But I'm not a chief engineer," she said quietly.

"Aye, you're not, and you're not likely to be, either." He picked up the small padd she had used and slammed it on the console. Then he raised his voice even more. "The *computer* can check my math. It cannot check my creative thinking, now, can it?"

"No, sir." She glanced at the others for help, but they didn't look at her. They had all been in this situation before. It was one way that Scotty trained his assistants. He had to work the rigidity out of their systems—the rigidity drilled into them by well-meaning Academy instructors. "B-b-but I'm just an ensign, sir."

"And do you think I magically became chief engineer? Do you think I was not once an ensign?" Scotty asked.

"Ah, I, ah, had not given it any thought," she said, then added, "sir."

He was about to show her how to approach the new problem when Uhura hailed him. "What is it, Lieutenant?" he snapped, forgetting for a moment that he wasn't training her.

"Projeff of the *Farragut*," she said. "Shall I tell him you're busy?"

"No, put him through." Scotty pointed at the ensign. "Be creative," he said, handing her the padd. "And try again."

She nodded, obviously relieved to no longer be the center of attention.

Scotty looked at the screen. Projeff was grinning at him.

"Picking on children again?" Projeff asked.

" 'Tis the reason I get more work from my staff than you get from yours," Scotty said.

Projeff shook his head slightly. "The modifications worked, but not well enough, I think."

The ensign beside Scotty stiffened, obviously expecting an outburst. But Scotty knew the truth of Projeff's statement.

"I agree," Scotty said. "We're working on more improvements here, but so far we haven't found much."

"I think there's a third element to the enemy weaponry that your calculations didn't catch," Projeff said.

"And what's that?"

"Harmonics."

"You said that before, lad, but you had no evidence."

"I do now," Projeff said. "Your modifications took care of the new and the old versions of the weapons systems, but these weapons also use a harmonics sequence that is out of the range of our systems. It is, I think—"

"What makes them truly alien," Scotty said, suddenly understanding. "You're right, lad, it's worth checking out. Send me your information."

"I will," Projeff said, "and my ideas for solving the problem." Then he grinned. "Courtesy of the *Farragut.*"

Captain Bogle paced back and forth in front of his chair, his hands tucked behind his back, his gaze watching the alien ships on the main screen. Now at least the enemy had a name.

Narr.

Over the last century there had been rumors of a race called the Narr, but there was no actual record of any contact with them, and no one had any idea where their homeworld was or what they looked like. Nothing. Just rumors.

Until now.

Now seven of their wing-shaped ships formed an effective blockade of the planet below—the planet the Narr were attacking for some unknown reason.

Behind the Narr ships, on the planet's surface, Bogle knew the colony was moving into the heat of the morning. Kirk and the colonists had managed to hold off the Narr ground troops for one attack, but Bogle doubted they could do it again.

"They're moving again," Mr. Lee said.

"Red alert," Bogle said.

Around him the lights dimmed and the sirens went off.

On the main screen the two Narr ships that had released the transports were moving, shifting to a position closer to the *Enterprise* and the *Farragut.*

At the same time the three new arrivals were shifting to positions closer to the planet, more protected from the Federation ships, with their transport bays turned away.

Instantly Bogle knew what they were planning to do. More transports would be heading to the surface from the new ships any moment, reinforcements to make sure the colony didn't survive another attack.

"Arm torpedoes," he said. "Lieutenant Book, take us above the Narr ships. I want to be able to see exactly what comes out of those transport bays."

"Yes, sir," Book said.

"The *Enterprise* is moving under them, sir," Lee said. "And the two new Klingon battle cruisers are entering the system."

"Here we go, people," Bogle said as he dropped down into his captain's chair. "Stay sharp."

The two front Narr ships suddenly opened fire, their phaser beams striking out against the *Farragut* and the *Enterprise* as the two Federation ships tried to move above them, trying for a better angle on the three new ships.

The *Farragut*'s shields flared bright white and the ship rocked slightly.

"Shields holding," Lee said. "The modifications seem to be working."

Bogle nodded to himself. The changes Projeff and Engineer Scott had made on the shields were keeping the ship in much better shape than in the first encounter. And would give him more room to try to save those on the planet.

"Hold your fire until you see a transport," Bogle said.

He stared at the edges of the three Narr ships as if trying to see what was happening on the other side. He would bet money that their docking bays were opening.

Again the *Farragut* rocked from phaser impacts against the shields.

"Shields still holding," Lee said.

The two new Klingon battle cruisers dropped out of warp and instantly joined the other battle cruiser facing the Narr ships. All three opened up on the big Narr ships almost simultaneously.

The Narr shields flared from orange to red.

"Transports," Lee said at the exact moment Bogle saw the nose of one transport poking out of the docking bay of a Narr ship, then another from the second ship. All three new ships were releasing transports, just as he'd feared.

"Target transports and fire," Bogle said. "Don't let them get to the atmosphere."

Photon torpedo after photon torpedo sped from the *Farragut,* blasting the shields of the transports with direct hit after direct hit.

From the other side, the *Enterprise* was doing the same, as if Mr. Spock was mirroring Bogle's actions.

Again the *Farragut* rocked as two direct phaser hits flared against the shields.

Bogle held on.

"Shields still at ninety-six percent," Lee shouted over the rumbling noise.

"Keep firing," Bogle shouted.

On the screen the shields of one of the transports flared bright red, faded into blue, and then vanished. In the next instant a huge flash of light signaled the end of that ship.

"Target the ship that's closest to the atmosphere," Bogle said. "Fire!"

Again the *Enterprise* simultaneously mirrored his actions.

The *Farragut* sustained another direct hit, rocking Bogle almost out of his chair. He held on, his gaze never leaving the transport they were firing at.

With the full force of both Federation ships pounding it, the transport's shields flared through the spectrum and disappeared. An instant later the ship exploded like a small sun going nova.

"The third transport has already reached the atmosphere," Lee said.

"Damn," Bogle said, pounding his fist into the arm

of his chair. Normally he managed to control his anger, but this failure made him angry.

He sat and watched the Narr transport, which looked like a streak of light as it cut through the upper layer of the atmosphere. It was now beyond his reach.

Again the ship rocked with more direct hits.

"Mr. Book, take us back to our previous position."

"The *Enterprise* is also withdrawing," Lee said. "And the Klingons have broken off their attack."

Bogle stared at the image of the planet on the screen. With another transport ship heading to the surface, Kirk and the colonists would have no chance of holding off a ground attack.

"Sorry, Jim," Bogle said softly to himself. "For a moment there I thought we were going to win that round."

"Excuse me, sir?" Lee said.

"Nothing, Commander," Bogle said.

Then he spoke louder to get everyone's attention. "I need ideas, people. We have to figure out a way to get Kirk and those colonists out of danger. Think, people. Think."

Bogle managed not to smile at the shocked looks he got from his crew. He almost never asked for their opinions; now he was asking for their help.

He sat back in his chair, staring at the Narr ships and the planet beyond as the silence on his bridge became almost deafening. If he had anything to say about it, his friend Jim Kirk would not die in such an awful place.

And if that meant asking for help, so be it.

Kirk flipped his communicator closed and sat down on the edge of the cannon platform. Another transport ship had made it past the *Enterprise* and the *Farragut*.

Now what? He hadn't felt this tired and discouraged in years.

Sulu, Dr. McCoy, Ensign Adaro, and Rathbone stood near him, Rathbone and McCoy both in the shade of the cannon shelter. They had all heard the news.

Kirk wiped the sweat from his forehead. Only two hours into the day and already the heat was stifling. Freezing at night, cooking during the day. What a wonderful planet to die defending.

"Dammit, Jim," McCoy said, "there's got to be something we can do. We should negotiate."

"That's hard to do, Bones, with a race that won't talk."

"That young soldier talked to us," Rathbone said. "He answered every one of our questions."

Kirk looked at her, then back out over the blackened field where the armored soldiers lay. He hoped their armor had an air supply and a cooling system. The ones out there who were still alive were going to need it.

Suddenly Dr. Rathbone's words sank in. The Narr had talked. The problem was getting them to do so.

"You have a point, Dr. Rathbone," Kirk said. "Maybe there is a way to get them to talk."

He stood. Removed the sweat-drenched shirt. He had an idea, and the only way to make it work was to show to the Narr he was no threat.

"What are you planning, Jim?" McCoy asked.

Kirk could already hear the skepticism in McCoy's voice.

"I'm going to do a little peace talking," he said.

He sat back down on the edge of the cannon platform, reached for his boots, and took them off. Then he stood again, dropped his trousers, and slipped them off, handing them to the startled doctor. Now he wore only standard Starfleet-issue shorts. The dirt-covered and burned red skin on his arms and face were a sharp contrast to the pale skin on his legs. He wagered he looked damned funny.

He slipped his boots back on quickly.

Rathbone choked back a laugh, and Kirk looked at her. Both she and Sulu had their hands over their mouths. He had been right.

"Dr. Rathbone," Kirk said, keeping his face serious while he faced her, "it doesn't do a man's ego much good to have a woman laugh at him when he takes off his clothes."

She had enough sense to blush under her dirty and sunburned skin, but her laughter didn't disappear far below the surface of her eyes.

"I'd be laughing too," McCoy said, his voice angry, "if I didn't know you were damn serious."

"That I am, Bones," Kirk said. He turned to Mr. Sulu. "Inform Mr. Spock that I'm trying to talk to the Narr. If I don't return, give them your best fight."

"Aye, Captain," Sulu said, all the laughter gone out of his eyes.

Kirk glanced at McCoy. "Bones, keep Kor alive."

"It looks at the moment as if he's going to outlive you," McCoy said.

Kirk laughed, then turned and headed out toward the blackened field and the fallen Narr. In the distance he could see the enemy transport ship. In a few minutes it would be joined by another. The time for talking was now or never.

"Jim?" McCoy called out behind him.

Kirk stopped and turned around. The three of them remained at the edge of the disrupter cannon.

"Do you know how silly you look?" McCoy asked, a grin slowly crossing his sunburned face.

"Yes, Doctor, I do," Kirk said. "I'm counting on it, in fact."

"Well," McCoy said, "for heaven's sake keep your shorts on. You don't want them laughing *too* hard when you try to talk to them."

Beside McCoy, both Rathbone and Sulu almost managed not to laugh.

"I owe you, Bones," Kirk said. Then with a smile at his old friend he turned and strode out into the blackened field, heading straight for the Narr transport ships, his hands above his head in the traditional sign of surrender.

For a moment Kerdoch could not believe his vision. The human captain, with almost no clothes on, walking directly at the Narr ships. What was he thinking? He had not seemed to be a fool in the first battles. Had the heat gotten to him?

A number of colonists stood near their shelters, pointing and laughing. It was a humorous sight, but not one that Kerdoch would laugh at until later.

Kerdoch moved quickly along the edge of the colony until he reached the other three humans near the disrupter cannon.

"Your captain," Kerdoch said. "He has gone insane?"

"It would appear that way," the human doctor said. "But he thinks he can get the Narr to talk this way.

I'm not sure why he thinks that, but I gave up years ago trying to figure James Kirk out."

"Talk?" Kerdoch asked. "For what purpose?"

The human doctor looked at him. Kerdoch could tell that he was very, very angry.

"To save your stupid, ungrateful life, that's what purpose," the doctor said.

"Doctor," the one named Sulu said.

Kerdoch looked at the doctor. He felt no anger at the insult; he was only puzzled. "We are prepared to fight," he said. "It would be an honorable death to die defending our homes."

The human doctor shook his head. "Honor can be gained in more ways than fighting and dying."

"He's at the edge of the field," the human woman said.

Kerdoch turned from the doctor and watched as the human captain stopped, his hands high in the air.

Six minutes later when the other Narr transport landed beside the first, he was still standing there.

Chapter Eighteen

KIRK HAD STOOD NOW for one hour at the edge of the black field in the hot sun, watching the Narr transports. The sweat ran down the sides of his face and off his back. He knew if he stayed much longer he might not have the strength to stand, let alone walk back to the colony.

Every few minutes during the hour he'd lowered his arms and let the blood flow back into them. But as time went along, he was having more and more problems holding his arms above his head for even thirty seconds. Yet he kept trying.

Finally, what he hoped for happened.

Three Narr in full battle armor strode toward him from the transports. Somehow he managed to keep his hands in the air until they stopped ten paces in front of him.

"You are human," the Narr soldier in the center said.

"Yes," Kirk said, letting his arms drop to his sides. "I'm Captain James T. Kirk of the Federation Starship *Enterprise.*"

The one in the center nodded slightly.

Kirk could tell no difference between the one who spoke and the others. Inside their faceplates, they all had long black hair, flat noses, and lines of hair on their foreheads. In an odd way they were almost catlike in appearance, but still very humanoid.

"Do humans have a claim on this planet?"

"No," Kirk said.

"Then why do you fight for it?"

"We fight because we were asked to help. This planet belongs to the Klingons."

"This planet is ours," the Narr soldier said. "We have kept it for years, preparing it. We want you and the ones called Klingons to leave."

"I'm afraid Klingons don't normally give up a planet they claim just by asking."

"Nor do we," the Narr said. "We will reclaim the planet at sunset."

With that all three turned their backs on him.

"Wait!" he shouted.

They stopped and slowly turned around.

"Your wounded," Kirk said, pointing to the armored soldiers lying in the field. "If you want to retrieve them, we will not fire on you."

The one in the center nodded. "We shall do so."

Again they turned their backs on him.

Kirk stood there, watching them lumber away in their heavy armor. The only thing he could think of was sunset and the coming attack. At least they had the sense not to attack during the heat of the day.

And that gave him until dusk to come up with a plan.

Dr. Rathbone stood with McCoy, Sulu, and Kerdoch at the edge of the colony, watching the captain talk to the Narr. The sun was beating down on Vivian, and she could feel the back of her uniform growing wet with sweat, but she didn't move into the shade. There was no way she was going to leave the others watching the captain. She wished she could hear what was being said, listen in to the negotiations going on at the edge of the black Klingon field.

Then suddenly the talks were over. The Narr turned and moved slowly over the natural plants in the direction of their transports.

After a moment Captain Kirk turned and started toward the colony. She could see that his skin was now bright red from the sun. He was clearly having problems. Finally, when he stumbled and fell, they all started out across the field toward him.

While Kerdoch stood watching, she sat down next to the captain and held his head.

Sulu helped him gulp down water mixed with nutrients specially prepared by McCoy.

McCoy scanned him with the medical tricorder, then grunted.

"Will I live?" Kirk asked, smiling up at McCoy.

"Another half hour and you'd have ended up beside Kor in that dome," McCoy said. "Now lie still."

As Kirk relaxed a little, his head became heavier in Vivian's hands. His hair was wet with sweat, and, like her, he was covered with black soot.

McCoy took out a medical spray and gave the captain a shot, then sprayed a fine mist over the bright red skin on his shoulders and arms. Then Vivian helped him sit up, and McCoy sprayed the captain's back and legs.

The captain started to say something, but McCoy interrupted. "Keep drinking. You're not moving until you have two of those bottles of water down you."

Kirk nodded, leaned back against her again, and drank. Then she and Sulu lifted him to his feet.

He leaned against Sulu, and with Kerdoch on his other side they slowly made their way to the shade of the cannon shelter.

The captain dropped down into a sitting position, and Sulu handed him more water.

"You are crazy, you know that?" McCoy said.

The captain started to say something, but McCoy pointed at him. "Drink."

Kirk laughed, but he obeyed. Finally, after the captain had drunk another half a bottle of water, McCoy said, "So tell us what happened."

"Kerdoch," Kirk said, his voice raspy for a moment, then clearing.

The large Klingon colonist knelt beside the seated captain.

"Tell your people not to fire on the Narr," Kirk said. "They will be unarmed and retrieving their wounded from the field very shortly."

Kerdoch nodded. "I will tell them." He stood and moved quickly away from the shelter.

McCoy watched the Klingon go, then glanced at the captain. Rathbone could tell that McCoy understood something she had missed. She wasn't sure what, but she knew that look.

"So what didn't you want to tell him?" McCoy said.

Kirk smiled and took another drink. "The Narr claim they own this planet."

"What?" she found herself asking.

"That's about all they said," the captain said. "That and that they had been preparing the planet for years."

Vivian looked at Sulu, and he glanced at her. It was clear he was thinking what she had been thinking—that it was the Narr who had modified the planet's natural plant life.

"Terraforming," she said.

Sulu nodded.

"What?" McCoy asked, glancing at her.

She took a deep breath. "Captain, remember when we told you the planet's plant life had been genetically changed at some time in the past."

"Very clearly," he said. "Now you know what I'm thinking. The Narr made the changes."

"It's possible," she said. "We've never had an explanation for that change." Her stomach told her this was the right answer. An answer to a question that had bothered her for almost five years. Everything fit. The Narr had changed the planet for their own use, just as the humans and Klingons had been doing.

"I assumed that was the problem," the captain said. "It would explain why they're so angry at the Klingons."

"And why they're destroying only Klingon crops," Sulu said.

"And why they attacked in the first place," McCoy said.

"Good point," she said, glancing at the blackened

fields. "Obviously they don't like what the Klingons planted."

"Or they never bothered even to test it," Sulu said.

"So what do we do now?" McCoy asked.

Kirk took another drink of water, then glanced up at McCoy. "Doctor, if I knew that, I wouldn't still be sitting here."

"Think the Klingons will just give the planet back to them?" she asked.

The captain laughed. "Would you, if the Federation colony had won and the Narr were attacking your home?"

"Probably not," she said slowly. She hated to admit that, but it was how she felt. It was always easy to tell others to give up their homes, but she *had* been told to leave this planet, which had once been her home. She knew how it felt. She didn't like it.

The captain took another long drink, then sighed. "People, at the moment our plan is to help the Klingons defend this colony from the coming attack at sunset."

"Until a better plan comes along?" McCoy asked.

Kirk smiled. "Until a better plan comes along."

Spock stood on the bridge and listened as the captain finished relaying the conversation he'd had with the Narr to him and Captain Bogle on the *Farragut*.

"It is logical," Spock said, staring at the image of the planet on the main viewscreen.

"What's logical, Mr. Spock?" the captain asked.

"The Narr claim to this planet. They are obviously telling the truth."

"Do you have clear evidence of that, Mr. Spock?" Captain Bogle asked.

"Give me a moment, sir," Spock said. "I will run a molecular scan of the derelict Narr ship, then compare it to the data I have on the structure of the native planetary growth."

"Good idea, Spock," Kirk said. "We'll wait."

Spock moved to his science station and keyed in the commands for running a scan of the Narr ship.

"Computer," he said. "Compare molecular structure of the Narr ships with the structure of the plant samples I have selected."

"Comparison complete," the computer voice said after only a second.

Again staring at the planet and the Narr ships on the main viewscreen, Spock asked, "Is there a statistical possibility that the plant and the scanned metal came from the same planetary system?"

"Yes," the computer said.

"What is that percentage?" he asked.

"Eighty-six percent," the computer said.

"Well," Captain Kirk said, his voice filling the bridge almost as if he were there, "that settles that."

"I guess it does," Captain Bogle said.

"It would seem that way," Spock said.

"So, Mr. Spock," the captain said, "how do we convince the Klingons that they really don't own this planet?"

"How is a Klingon convinced of anything?" Bogle asked.

"By fighting," Spock said calmly.

There was a moment of silence on the bridge.

Finally Captain Kirk's voice again filled the bridge.

"Mr. Spock, relay this information to the Klingon ships."

"I shall do so immediately, Captain," Spock said.

"Then, gentlemen, I hope you can find a way to get us off this oven of a planet before the fighting starts."

"We'll do our best, Jim," Bogle said.

"I know you will. Thanks. Kirk out."

Mr. Spock turned to Lieutenant Uhura. "Relay the molecular information and comparisons to the three Klingon battle cruisers. Include a transcript of what the captain said occurred in his conversation with the Narr."

"Yes, sir," Uhura said.

Spock moved back to his science station. The first half of the captain's order had been carried out. It was the second half that would pose more of a problem. Much more.

Chapter Nineteen

KIRK SAT in the relative coolness of the dome, sipping water and watching McCoy work on Kor. It had been two hours since Kirk had talked to the Narr, and he was finally starting to regain some strength. It was lucky the Narr had showed up when they did.

At the moment Sulu stood guard at the disrupter cannon, but Kirk knew it was pointless duty. The Narr would come at sundown and not one minute sooner.

Kerdoch stood near the door while Kahaq, the only surviving member of Kor's landing party sat beside his commander.

Rathbone stood at McCoy's shoulder. Her brown hair was matted back on her head, and as with all of them, her face was badly sunburned and very dirty.

Kor moaned and moved his head slightly.

Both Kerdoch and Kirk moved quickly to the Commander's side.

"Can you wake him, Bones?" Kirk asked.

Bones nodded. "I think he's finally stabilized. And his ribs are mostly healed. Damned if I know if I did anything to help anything else, but I think I can wake him up."

"Do it," Kirk said. He needed Kor awake and in command of the Klingons when the colonists were told the news about the Narr claim on the planet. There was no guarantee that Kor would react in any positive way, but at least it would be one reaction instead of six different options with the leaderless colonists.

McCoy injected Kor and then sat back as the Klingon commander moaned again, then slowly opened his eyes and looked at McCoy.

"I am having a nightmare," he said and closed his eyes again.

Kirk laughed and Bones gave him a frozen look, which made Kirk laugh even more, and after a moment Rathbone joined in.

"The next time you need sunburn spray, remember that you thought this was funny," McCoy threatened.

Kirk laughed, nudged McCoy aside, and knelt near the commander. "Kor, we need to talk."

The Klingon commander slowly opened his eyes again. "This is not a nightmare, then?"

"Oh, it's a nightmare all right," Kirk said. "But I'm afraid it's a real one."

Kor groaned and tried to sit up.

"Not yet," McCoy said.

Kirk put a hand on the Klingon's chest and held

him on his back. "You were seriously injured. Give yourself a little more time to recover."

Kor looked from Kirk to McCoy. McCoy nodded to confirm Kirk's words.

"I would like water," Kor said. It was as close as a Klingon came to asking for help.

Rathbone handed the commander a bottle and he drank deeply, then sighed and seemed to relax a little.

"Are you able to talk?" Kirk asked.

Kor nodded. "What has happened?"

Kirk spent the next few minutes bringing the Klingon commander up to date on their situation, right to the moment he had talked to the Narr.

Kor took a long drink, finished the bottle Rathbone had given him, then looked Kirk in the eye. "You do not like what the Narr told you," he said. "I can tell."

Kirk nodded. "They claim to own the planet."

Kor laughed. "How can that be? The planet was awarded to the Klingon Empire by the Organians."

"I know," Kirk said. "But ask your colonists about how eight or nine hundred years ago the natural plants on this planet were biologically altered."

"Is this true?" Kor asked Kerdoch.

The colonist stepped forward. "It is true," he said. "We found no explanation for the alteration and assumed it had been caused by a natural event."

Kor nodded. "So the Narr claim they were forming the planet to their needs."

"They did not claim it exactly," Kirk said. "But they did say they had been preparing it."

"And you expect us to just give up the planet on that basis?"

Kirk shook his head. He had expected, and hoped, the conversation would get to this point.

"Kor, tests run on both the altered plants here and the materials in the Narr ships show a biological match. The natural plants on this planet were combined with Narr plants hundreds of years ago. The data has been given to your ship."

Kirk watched as Kor kept his expression blank. There was no way to tell what the commander was thinking. Finally he said, "Captain Kirk, do you have a solution to this standoff?"

Kirk did not expect that question. "I do not."

Kor nodded and closed his eyes. "How much time until the suns set?" His voice was weak and tired.

"Six hours," Kirk said.

"Then I have time to rest before I must fight," Kor said. He let out a deep sigh and seemed to fall asleep.

McCoy did a quick medical scan of Kor, then nodded to Kirk that the commander would be all right after a little rest.

"We all need the rest," Kirk said. He stood and moved back over to the table where he sat down.

No one, including Kerdoch, said a word as they settled into positions scattered around the dome. It would be a long, hot afternoon waiting to fight, and waiting, most likely, to die.

Unless Kirk could come up with some way of stopping the fight.

"Mr. Spock," Captain Bogle said to the Vulcan on the main Farragut screen in front of him, "have you gone crazy?"

"I assure you, Captain," Spock said, his expression never changing. "I am quite sane. I simply offer a possible means of rescuing Captain Kirk and the landing party."

"Have you checked with Kirk?" Bogle asked.

"I have not," Spock said.

Bogle shook his head. "Give me a moment to consider your plan."

"Certainly," Spock said and cut the transmission.

Immediately the Narr ships returned to the main screen, orbiting seemingly peacefully over the blue-green planet.

Bogle dropped down into his chair and stared at the screen, thinking about Commander Spock's plan. Actually, the idea was typically logical. There were seven working Narr ships facing two Federation and three Klingon ships. All ships on both sides seemed to be fairly matched, although with the shield modulations against Narr weapons, Bogle would now give the *Farragut* and the *Enterprise* a slight advantage. But not a two ship advantage.

Spock's idea was for the *Farragut* and the *Enterprise* to simultaneously launch unmanned shuttles in high orbits over the planet, in opposite directions. Each shuttle, logically, would draw one Narr ship into pursuit, temporarily pulling it away from the main blockade, leveling the odds. At that moment the Federation and Klingon ships would attack, with the two Federation ships working to get into a position within transporter range long enough to drop shields and get the landing party off the planet.

Bogle shook his head. It was a logical, but foolhardy plan. It risked the lives of all the members of the *Farragut* crew, as well as all the members of the *Enterprise* crew in an attempt to save four other crew members. And that was not logical in any fashion.

Spock should know better than to use an entire crew to rescue a handful of people.

But he was Kirk's first officer, working on assumptions Kirk would make. Perhaps when Spock had his own starship, he would act differently. But now, he had to second-guess his creative captain.

He seemed to do it pretty well.

It sounded like a Kirk plan.

Bogle sighed. And because of that, it might work.

If the shields on the shuttles could be modulated to withstand the Narr phasers for at least a minute, that would be long enough.

Another idea popped into his head. The shuttles could be programmed to land near the colony if they survived long enough to get into the atmosphere; that would give the landing party yet another chance.

Then still another idea struck him: they could use Spock's same idea, only not endanger the crews of the starships.

He quickly punched his ship intercom button on the arm of his captain's chair.

"Projeff?"

"Yes, Captain," Projeff answered at once.

"Can both shuttles' shields be modified to withstand the Narr weapons long enough to get to the atmosphere?"

There was a pause, then Projeff said slowly, "They can be modified, sir. But I wouldn't wager a man's life that they would hold under full Narr attack all the way to the atmosphere."

"But is there a chance that one, or maybe both, would make it?"

"There is a chance, sir," Projeff said. "With the modifications Mr. Scott and I have come up with, it would take a full Narr attack lasting twenty-six seconds for the shields to fail."

"Thanks, Projeff," Bogle said. "Stand by."

He clicked off the intercom, then turned to Lieutenant Sandy. "Hail the *Enterprise,* and make sure the transmission is scrambled. Then raise Captain Kirk and patch him into the conversation."

"Yes, sir," Sandy said.

Bogle stood and faced the screen as Mr. Spock's image appeared.

"Captain Bogle," the Vulcan said, nodding slightly.

"Kirk here."

At the sound of Kirk's voice Spock raised one eyebrow, but did not change his expression.

"Kirk," Bogle said, "your first officer has come up with an idea of using shuttlecraft to decoy away a few Narr ships long enough for us to get you out of there."

There was a pause, then Kirk said, "At this point I'll listen to anything."

Bogle laughed. In Kirk's situation he'd have said the same thing. He quickly explained to Kirk Mr. Spock's idea. "Did I get that right, Mr. Spock?" he asked after he finished.

"That is a correct outline of what I proposed," Spock said.

"Good," Bogle said, "because I like your idea, Mr. Spock. But I don't like endangering the entire crews of the *Enterprise* and *Farragut* to rescue four crew members. Do you agree, Captain?"

"I do," Kirk said. "The numbers would be even for only a short time, then would turn bad again as the other Narr ships returned. I'm not sure it would work."

Spock said nothing.

"Hold on a moment, Jim," Bogle said. "I think Mr.

Spock's idea can be modified slightly to help the landing party escape on its own."

Again one of Mr. Spock's eyebrows lifted, but no other expression crossed his face. "That would be interesting," Spock said. "Please continue, Captain Bogle."

"You got my attention, Kelly," Kirk said.

"Instead of sending out two shuttles as decoys, then trying to fight our way into position to beam out the landing party, we send out four unmanned shuttles, in four different directions, all programmed to land at the edge of the colony."

"Do you think the Narr would chase four shuttles?" Kirk asked.

"I honestly don't know," Bogle said. "If they did, it would then be three of them against five of us, for at least a minute. We can do a lot in one minute with those odds."

"And if they don't," Kirk said, "you don't attack and we have at least one or more shuttles here to help us defend the colony, and maybe get off the planet."

"Exactly," Bogle said.

"Great idea, Kelly," Kirk said. "I think it just might work."

"Thanks," Bogle said, "but it was Mr. Spock's idea. I just modified it."

"To a much better plan, sir," Spock said.

Bogle nodded to Spock. "Thank you."

"I have two modifications of my own," Kirk said. "Kelly, Spock, I'm sending up the data from Mr. Sulu's tricorder, as well as my scans of the Narr armor. Let Scott and Mr. Projeff see if they can come up with a weapon that will slow that armor down. Or better yet short out its antigravity units."

"We'll come up with something," Bogle said. "And we'll put it and other weapons in every shuttle."

"Great," Kirk said.

"Captain," Spock said, "you said you had two modifications."

"Thank you, Mr. Spock. I was just getting to the other one." He almost sounded as if he were smiling.

"Second," Kirk said, "we need to get the Klingons involved in this. I know their battle cruisers carry at least one shuttle-sized craft. Have them launch at the same time, with weapons enclosed. That will pretty much guarantee that some of the shuttles make it down here. If you have trouble convincing them, have them talk to Kor."

"Good thinking on both counts," Bogle said. For the first time since this entire mission started, he was starting to feel there was a possibility of coming out alive.

"You gentlemen sure know how to make a fella feel wanted," Kirk said. "Let me know when you're ready to launch."

"My pleasure," Bogle said, laughing.

Spock remained expressionless as Bogle cut the connection.

"I can't do it," Scotty said. He was sitting at his console, talking to Spock, who was on the bridge. "You want me to modify the shuttle shields and come up with a weapon to short-circuit an antigravity unit I haven't even seen, all within the space of a few hours. You're asking the impossible, Mr. Spock."

"Mr. Scott," Spock said calmly. "I have heard you make this protestation before and still you have done what you call 'the impossible.' I believe this is merely a ruse to make it seem as if your talents are greater than they truly are."

"Do you, Mr. Spock?" Scotty felt heat rush to his cheeks. At times he did exaggerate, but usually it worked: he would get extra time from the captain. "A ruse, you say?"

"Yes, Mr. Scott, a ruse."

"You're a hard-nosed Vulcan, Mr. Spock. It's not logical to give a man an impossible order and then tell him that he lies when he protests."

"I simply mean, Mr. Scott, that to paraphrase your William Shakespeare, methinks you doth protest too much."

"Ah, you thinks, do you?" Scotty said.

"If you would like," Spock said with infinite calm, "I will see if I can assist you."

That offended Scotty even more. "You have your own job on the bridge, Mr. Spock. I don't need your assistance."

And then he signed off.

"Sir?" The young ensign he had upbraided stood beside him. "We could modify the shuttle's shields. I believe they're the same as the *Enterprise*'s. All we have to do is follow your instructions from the last time."

Scotty looked at her. "Is this your creative solution, lass?"

She swallowed. "Yes," she said. "None of us are as skilled at jury-rigging as you are, sir. That's why you're chief engineer."

He grinned at her. "You have a bit of the Celtic in you, lass."

"The Celtic?" she asked.

"The Irish call it blarney, but I'll take it," Scotty

said. "But realize I'll be there to check your work shortly. Lives depend on your accuracy."

She swallowed again. "Aye, sir." And then she led a group from Engineering to the shuttle bays.

"Now, it's me and you," he whispered to the schematic of the various weapons on board the *Enterprise*.

At that moment, Uhura hailed him with a message from Projeff.

"All right," Scotty grumbled. "Nothing could be worse than the last few moments I've had."

Projeff appeared on the screen, grinning so wide that it looked as if his face had split in half. "I assume you heard about the modifications we were to make to the weapons," he said.

"Aye," Scotty said mournfully.

"Well, have I got a modification for you," Projeff said. "Courtesy of the *Farragut*."

Scotty's eyes narrowed. How had Projeff solved this problem when Scotty hadn't even had a chance to work on it? The honor of the *Enterprise* had been at stake, and he hadn't even had a chance to try.

He swallowed his pride and asked, "What have you got?"

Chapter Twenty

KIRK SNAPPED his communicator closed and stood. Even in the heat of the afternoon, finally having some sort of a plan gave him energy.

He paced back and forth, thinking. There was a great chance that at least two, if not three or four shuttles were going to be landing near the colony in about an hour. Having the firepower of the shuttles, as well as the shields and extra armament they would bring, would level the field a little. Not all the way, but enough to keep the battle from being a slaughter.

"Rathbone, would you have Lieutenant Sulu join us?"

She nodded, stood and quickly ducked out the door, letting in a hot, dry wind.

"McCoy," Kirk said, sitting down next to Kor, "can you wake your patient?"

"I am awake," Kor said. "I heard your communication with your ships."

"Good," Kirk said. "Do you think the plan will work?"

"It is a sound plan," Kor said. "It has only one drawback that I can see."

"And that is?" Kirk asked. Kor had always annoyed him in the past, and he was doing his best not to let the Klingon commander do so now.

"The Narr transports," he said.

Kirk sat back, thinking. Kor had a point.

"I have not seen the transports," Kor said. "But I assume they are considerably larger, and likely more powerful, than your tiny Federation shuttles?"

"They are," Kirk said. Kor was right and he knew it. The transports were undoubtedly armed and well shielded.

"And they will have time to launch and engage the shuttles above the colony. Correct?"

"You are very correct," Kirk said.

"Then we must have a plan," Kor said, sitting up slowly and facing Kirk, "to keep the Narr transports on the ground while our shuttles land."

Kirk nodded. "Good thinking, Commander." He turned to Kerdoch. "Can we get to that small ridge of mountains behind the transport landing sites without being seen?"

Kerdoch thought for a moment, then, with a glance at Kor, he answered Kirk's question. "It would be possible to go north into the foothills and circle west behind the Narr transports. It would take at least an hour."

Kirk turned back to Kor. "The Narr shuttles are wing-shaped, and landed standing upward."

Kor nodded. "I see what you are thinking," he said. "They might have some sort of support legs holding them in that position."

"Exactly," Kirk said. "And the transports wouldn't be shielded on the ground. All we have to do is knock a leg out from under them."

"It would certainly slow down their take-off," McCoy said.

"It would, Doctor," Kor said, dropping back on the cot and closing his eyes with a sigh. "It most certainly would."

Rathbone stood in the small sliver of shade offered by the edge of the shelter over the disrupter cannon. It was still five hours to sundown, and the heat seemed to smother her, baking every inch of her. She'd been sipping water almost continuously since sunrise, but she still felt constantly thirsty and dry. She didn't remember having the heat be this oppressive when she was here with the Federation colony. In fact, she remembered enjoying the heat and the cool evenings. Amazing how a little time could change a person's perspective.

She took another long drink of warm water from the bottle she carried. More than anything else she wanted a cool shower to take off the caked salt and black ash, followed by a long cool bath to soothe her burned skin. At this moment that would be heaven.

Just getting off this planet would be heaven.

At the front of the cannon platform Kor and Captain Kirk stood, staring out over the blackened fields at the distant Narr transports.

This was Kor's first time out in the sun, and Dr. McCoy had strenuously objected. But even McCoy's brash manner couldn't stop the Klingon commander. McCoy had managed, to the amusement of the captain, to get Kor to promise to return to the dome at once, and drink water every few minutes while out in the sun.

So far the Klingon commander was willingly complying with the doctor's orders. Kor had to be sicker than he was admitting.

"The plan should work, Commander," Kirk said, turning and finishing a conversation with Kor that Rathbone hadn't been able to fully hear from her position in the shade.

"Mr. Sulu," Kirk said. Lieutenant Sulu stepped up to face Kirk and Kor.

"Kahaq," Kor said. "Kerdoch, the colonist."

Kahaq and Kerdoch stepped up and stood near Sulu.

"You are to disable those transports in any fashion you see fit," Kirk said.

"Disrupter rifle shots to the supporting legs," Kor said. "Focus on only one spot."

"It shall be done," Kahaq said.

"And then we need you back here. Quickly. Before the sunset attack."

"Yes, sir," Sulu said.

Kerdoch and Kahaq glanced at Kor, seemingly uneasy taking too many orders from Kirk.

"At this time we fight beside our enemy against another enemy," Kor said. "It is the nature of war. At this time Captain Kirk's orders are mine."

Kerdoch and Kahaq said nothing, but Rathbone could tell they both understood.

"Okay," Kirk said. "Get moving. And good luck."

Suddenly it dawned on Vivian that Kirk wasn't

planning to send her out with Sulu and the others. For some reason she had just expected him to do so, given her knowledge of this planet. She glanced at the young Ensign Adaro who stood off to one side, then back at the three who had been picked.

"Captain," she said, stepping out of her slice of shade and moving toward him, "I should be included in this mission."

Kirk's hard gaze behind the dirt-smeared face almost froze her in midstride, but she moved right up and faced him and the Klingon commander. "As a former colonist, I know the natural terrain of this planet. Also, there are two transports. There might be a need of four weapons."

Kirk nodded. "Good point. How good a shot are you?"

She glanced at Sulu, uncertain as to how to answer the captain's question. He had clearly not had the time to look at her service record before they left the ship, or he would have known.

"Captain," Sulu said, smiling, "Rathbone is a master-level marksman."

She smiled at Sulu. At least he had read her service record.

"A logical addition," Kor said, letting pass the fact that Kirk didn't know some details about his away team members.

Kirk laughed and patted her on the shoulder. "Make sure you have water."

McCoy handed her a canteenlike water carrier, which she slung over her shoulder, its solid weight a comfort against her hip. She emptied the bottle she'd been carrying with a long, warm drink and handed it to him, then slung the Klingon disrupter rifle over her right shoulder.

"Good luck," Kirk said.

"batlh DaqawLu'taH," Kor said, and nodded slightly to them all.

With that she fell in behind Kerdoch as he headed at a fast pace toward the northern edge and the hills beyond.

Spock figured that the odds were long that the Narr would attack during the hour after the transport attack mission left the colony.

And the project he had in mind could be a valuable asset to the coming attempt to stop the ground attack. So Spock left the bridge and moved straight to sickbay. Commander Scott was busy working with Projeff on a method of cutting off the antigravity units of the Narr soldiers. Therefore, if Spock's idea was to be pursued, he had to be the one to do it.

It took him only a few short minutes to modify a medical imaging device. He reversed its analytical functions and set it to emit a life-form signal where there wasn't one.

It then took him exactly nine minutes and eight seconds to alter the device enough to show ten life-forms from the same signal.

Three minutes and eight seconds more of fine-tuning and mounting the equipment in a small box and he was satisfied. Logically the device would work. But a test was necessary.

He punched the communication panel of sick bay. "Mr. Chekov, please scan sick bay and report how many life-forms are present."

"Yes, sir," Chekov said. After a pause of two seconds he said, "Eleven, sir. But ten are grouped tightly, and the signal is odd. I'm running a check to see why."

Mr. Spock expected as much. The Narr would be scanning through full screens. It would be enough to fool them. He flicked off the medical scanner he had altered.

"Sir," Chekov said, his voice suddenly agitated, "ten life-forms have vanished."

"That is correct, Mr. Chekov. Thank you." He cut the communication. He felt no need to explain his actions to Mr. Chekov at the moment.

He picked up the small box, tucked it under his arm, and left sick bay, headed for Engineering. His theory was that two such boxes on each shuttle should cause the Narr to be a little more cautious on their attack on the colony, thinking there were more soldiers defending the colony than actually existed.

It might also have the secondary function of causing them to break off their blockade and attack more of the shuttles in orbit, allowing the *Enterprise* to move into transporter range—if the captain agreed to the device being used. But Spock was sure he would. Last year in a fight the captain had noted that sometimes the best defense was nothing more than smoke and mirrors. Spock had not understood at the time, but now he was beginning to see the logical principle behind the metaphor.

The little box under his arm would substitute for the mirror in the metaphor.

Captain Kirk would have to provide the smoke, a skill at which he was very talented.

Chapter Twenty-one

KERDOCH SET a fast, but steady pace as he crossed the blackened fields of his neighbors and moved into the rough ground of the small rolling hills. There was no shade, only small scrub brush, ankle-high blue weeds, and rocks. He continued on a northern track until the hills were the height of twenty warriors. Then he stopped.

The human woman had stayed close behind him, as had Sulu, but Kahaq had fallen behind at least fifty paces. He seemed out of breath and flushed when he finally did reach them.

Kerdoch knew the warrior could not make the full distance. The heat would fell him more surely than a phaser blast. But a colonist could not tell a warrior he would fail. So Kerdoch said nothing.

The woman took a quick drink, rinsed the water

around in her mouth, then spit it out. She took another sip, which she swallowed.

Kerdoch was impressed at her actions. They showed clear thinking and practice in this climate. She would have little trouble staying with his pace.

Sulu took a quick sip of water at the same time, recapped his bottle, and seemed ready to move onward. The thin human would also be able to make the journey. That pleased him. Over the last day he had come to respect Sulu. He was a human with strength and honor, much like his captain.

"We follow this valley," Kerdoch said.

He knew the shallow valley wound its way to the east into the slightly higher hills near the Narr transports. They would have to cross over two ridges to get to the transports. But until that point the valley would give them shelter from Narr eyes on the ground. His hope was that the Narr ships in orbit were not scanning the surrounding area in close enough detail to locate them. That was a chance that both Kirk and Kor had thought worth taking.

Kerdoch turned and set his pace, moving with practiced ease through and around the natural brush.

He did not look back.

And he did not stop until he reached a point in the valley beyond the Narr transports. Above, the two suns seemed to have grown in size and energy. He was used to working the day in the sun, but after the last two days of no sleep and little water, he could feel the extreme heat.

He pulled his water bottle and let the warm water fill his mouth and throat. Then he turned around.

He was again surprised to find both the woman and Sulu stopping with him. There was no sign of Kahaq.

"Where is Kahaq?" he asked.

Sulu finished a sip of water, his face bright red and sweating. "He stopped to take a drink quite a long way back. He told me to go on."

"This heat can fell the strongest tree," Kerdoch said.

"How far to the transports?" the human woman asked. She also looked very tired and hot, but she seemed willing to continue without complaint.

Kerdoch pointed over the high ridge to his right. "We should be able to target the transports from the second ridge."

Kerdoch glanced back down the gully in the direction they had come. "We will find Kahaq on our return."

"Lead on," Sulu said.

Kerdoch took another drink, unshouldered his rifle, and began to climb toward the top of the ridge.

To his left Sulu did the same.

To his right the human woman followed.

Kirk stood alone in the slim shade offered by the shelter over the disrupter cannon. Kor, Ensign Adaro, and McCoy had returned to the protection of the dome to rest until the shuttles launched. Rathbone and Sulu were somewhere in the foothills, and the colonists were scattered along the edge of the colony facing the Narr camp. Some were digging trenches; others rested in the shade; many had gone back to their homes to check on their children.

A waiting time. Kirk hated waiting.

Beyond the blackened fields the Narr transports stood, winglike shapes pointing upward as if ready to jump back into the air. And they most likely would do just that when the shuttles were launched, unless Sulu and the others could get them grounded. Otherwise the shuttles would be sitting ducks coming in. They could be programmed to land and do basic maneuvers, but not evade or return enemy fire.

He stared out over the field where the Narr casualties had been. The Narr had used teams of four to retrieve their wounded and dead, floating them between the team members like heavy caskets in a funeral march, as they moved back to their camp. There had been over eighty Narr soldiers in the field at once, and there was no doubt that was only a small part of the force that would be coming against the colony at sunset.

There had to be a way to stop them, to end this fight. Throughout the history of Earth, wars had been fought over disputed ownership of land. Now they were fought over ownership of entire planets. He and the Federation had no real stake in the outcome of this battle, except for the fact that he and his crew were trapped in the middle of it. Somehow there had to be a way to get the two parties who had something to win or lose to talk to each other.

His communicator beeped, and he snapped it open.

"Captain," Sulu said, his voice low, almost whispered. "Kerdoch, Rathbone, and I are in position above and behind the Narr camp. The heat stopped Kahaq along the way."

"How is the camp laid out, Mr. Sulu?" Kirk asked.

"The Narr have four large tentlike structures," Sulu whispered. "Ten guards in armor are outside, posted at the doors. The others must be inside the tents and the transports."

"Can you knock down the transports?" Kirk asked.

"I don't know, Captain," Sulu said. "Like the larger Narr craft, they are wing-shaped, and have landed pointed upward, wing tips on the ground. But there are no support legs of any sort to target."

"None?" Kirk asked.

"None, sir," Sulu said.

He had been afraid that might be the case. The Narr were clearly very good with artificial gravity, and were using it to hold their ships upright.

"Stand by, Mr. Sulu. And keep your head down."

He flicked his communicator closed and at a fast walk covered the fifty paces of hot ground to the dome. Inside, Ensign Adaro sat on the cot, Kor sat at the table, a glass of water in his hand, and McCoy sat across from him. It was clear to Kirk that neither had been talking to the other.

"The team is in place above the Narr camp," Kirk said. "Kahaq is not with them. He had a problem with the heat."

Kor frowned, but said nothing.

Kirk sat down at the table next to McCoy. McCoy slid him a bottle and Kirk drank the lukewarm water gladly, filling his mouth twice. Then he gave Kor the bad news: "There are no support legs holding up the transports."

This time Kor shook his head in disgust. "Antigravity support fields."

"Most likely," Kirk said.

"So this changes the plan," Kor said.

"I know," Kirk said. "What's your idea?"

Kirk asked that way because the ideas he had come up with—finding a way to shut down the anti-gravity devices, for example—weren't possible with the small force he had.

"The shuttles must launch manned, so they can defend themselves. They must have one pilot each."

Kirk had already thought of that option as well. He didn't like it. But endangering one or two crew members to rescue four was far more acceptable than risking the entire *Enterprise*. And with the modified shields and a pilot, the shuttles would have a fighting chance against the Narr transports.

Also with the *Enterprise* and *Farragut* shuttles on the ground, the colony would have a fighting chance against the Narr troops. Kor's plan undoubtedly had a number of other advantages, but there was no way Kirk would sacrifice a pilot in a shuttle to those Narr ships in orbit. The shuttles were to be used as decoys. Nothing more.

He looked Kor directly in the eye. "I will sacrifice four unmanned Federation shuttles to this fight, but no more lives."

Kor laughed and smacked his hand down flat on the table. "Kirk, in your position, I would do the same thing. You are smarter than I gave you credit for."

Kirk sat back, staring at the Klingon commander. He had expected Kor to call him a coward. But instead he had agreed. "You surprise me, Kor."

"'Surprise' puts it mildly," McCoy said. "The sound of my jaw hitting the table could have been heard outside, I'm sure."

Again Kor laughed. Clearly his strength was returning as his voice and laugh were increasing in volume. "Kirk, this is a Klingon planet. Our duty is to defend it. Our shuttles will be manned to engage the Narr transports. Your unmanned shuttles can be used to confuse them and draw their fire. It is a sound plan."

Kirk smiled at Kor. "The team behind the Narr

camp will confuse things even more by firing on the transports."

Kor slapped the table again and stood. "Kirk, someday it will be glorious to fight you. But at the moment working together is also glorious."

Kirk stood also, facing Kor. He flipped open his communicator. "Mr. Spock, are the shuttles loaded and ready to launch?"

"Yes, Captain," Spock said.

"Stand by for my order," Kirk said. He faced Kor. "Commander, we will launch when you give the word."

Kor bowed slightly to Kirk. "It will take five minutes for my pilots to prepare," he said. "Then we shall surprise the Narr."

"That we shall," Kirk said. He sat down beside McCoy as Kor turned away to call his ship.

"Sometimes you really amaze me, Jim," McCoy said as Kirk took another long drink of water.

"How's that?"

"You're more like the Klingons than you think."

Kirk stared at his friend for a moment, then smiled. "I hope that was a compliment, Bones."

McCoy snorted, then said, "I'm afraid, in this instance, it just might have been."

Captain Bogle stood facing the main screen. For the past few hours nothing had changed. The Narr ships had remained in their blockade over the planet, facing the two Federation starships and the three Klingon battle cruisers. But Bogle knew that was about to change. He wasn't sure how, but it would change. Of that he had no doubt.

"Captain," Lieutenant Sandy said, "the *Enterprise* has signaled we should stand by."

"On their signal," Bogle said. He punched his communications button. "Projeff, status of shuttles?"

"Loaded, armed, and ready when you are, Captain," the chief engineer said. "I've patched the automatic launch controls into the bridge."

"Good work, Pro," Bogle said.

"And sir," Projeff said, "we've modified the shields even more. They should hold solidly now."

"Excellent," Bogle said and punched off the comm button.

He sat down in his chair. "Get ready, people. I suspect this is going to get somewhat wild."

Around him the bridge seemed to hum.

No one said a word, but the tension was so thick he could sense it. Lieutenant Michael Book sat on the edge of his chair, his fingers tapping beside his control panel. Science Officer Lee stared into his scope, gripping it firmly with both hands.

"We are receiving a scrambled message from the *Enterprise,*" Lieutenant Sandy said, his voice slightly higher than normal.

"Put it on-screen," Bogle said. He took a deep breath and exhaled as Spock's image appeared.

"Captain," Spock said, "the Klingons will launch their manned shuttles in exactly twenty-six seconds. The *Enterprise* will launch two unmanned shuttles with them."

"Understood, Mr. Spock. We will do so also. Good luck."

Spock nodded, and his image was replaced with the familiar scene of the Narr ships and the blue-green planet beyond.

Nothing more needed to be said. All the details of the directions that the seven different shuttles would take had been worked out almost an hour before between Spock and the Klingons.

Now it was almost time to launch.

"Got the count, Lieutenant Book?" Bogle asked.

"Yes, sir," he said. "Fifteen seconds."

Bogle glanced around the bridge. Everyone was ready. "At two seconds go to red alert," he said.

"Ten seconds."

Bogle took a deep breath. "Stay put," he whispered to the Narr ships facing him. "Just stay put." He desperately hoped they would catch the Narr ships unprepared. At least enough that before they could react the shuttles would be in the atmosphere. He knew he was dreaming, but he could hope.

"Five seconds," Book said. "Four . . . three."

"Red alert!" Bogle said. Around him the lights went to a red hue and the siren blared.

"Two . . . one."

"Launch."

Lieutenant Book's fingers flew over the panel.

On the main screen Bogle could see the two *Enterprise* shuttles emerging from the shuttle bays. One turned and went along the equator of the planet to his right. The other went left.

Bogle knew the two shuttles from the *Farragut* were programmed to head for the planet's poles and drop into the atmosphere there. The three Klingon shuttles were to take courses between the Federation shuttles and, with luck, be near the colony when the Narr transports lifted to meet them.

"We have launch," Book said, his voice clearly excited.

"Captain," Lee said, "the Narr ships. Look!"

Bogle could feel his jaw drop in surprise. Of all the reactions by the Narr that he had expected, this was not it.

None of the big Narr ships moved.

Not a one.

However, two of them were opening docking bays. The same two who had launched the small attack ships.

He couldn't believe it. They were going to send their attack ships after the shuttles, right on down into the atmosphere. How could they have been ready?

"Target those opening bays!" Bogle shouted. "Fire phasers!"

Bright phaser beams struck out of the *Farragut,* right on target, lighting up the insides of the Narr docking bays with intense white light.

At the same instant the *Enterprise* and Kor's ship fired, also targeting the docking bays.

A moment later the remaining two battle cruisers joined in.

Then it seemed to Bogle as if space had gone crazy.

Seven shuttles streaking away from the bigger ships, in seven different directions.

Full fire power aimed at two Narr ships from five other war ships. Then dozens of smaller Narr attack ships suddenly filled the area from the Narr docking bays. They were like bats coming from the mouth of a cave that was on fire, pouring into space.

"How many of those things can they hold?" Book asked.

Bogle had been wondering the same thing.

"Target the Narr attack ships and take them out," Bogle shouted. "Fire at will."

"Captain," Lee said. "To the right."

Bogle had already seen what his first officer was pointing out. One of the larger Narr craft had turned, broken ranks, and was making an attack pass at the *Farragut*. Another was doing the same thing at the *Enterprise*. The other five remained in blockade position.

"Keep after any of the smaller ships," Bogle ordered. "Don't stop firing until I tell you to stop."

Around the larger Narr ships the small craft seemed to swarm. There were far more of them than during the first attacks. How in the world had the Narr had them prepared?

Unless they had planned to run attack missions at the colony before the ground troops attacked at sunset. It would be a logical tactical move. And launching the shuttles had just forced them to launch a little early.

The *Farragut* rocked as the larger Narr ship blasted it with full power.

Bogle hung on to the arms of his chair, studying the screen as the combined focus of the Federation ships blew up one small Narr attack craft after another, like small, silent firecrackers exploding in the night sky.

"Shields holding," Lee said.

"Ignore the big ship," Bogle ordered. "Stay on the attack craft. Knock the stupid little things out of the sky."

"Sir," Book said, "most of the smaller craft are behind the larger Narr ships, dropping toward the atmosphere."

"Take us right at them, Lieutenant," Bogle said. "Follow them to the edge of the atmosphere if you have to."

"But, sir—"

"Do it, Lieutenant!" he ordered, his voice loud and firm. He was more than aware that to follow the small attack craft they must go right through the larger Narr ships' blockade. But the Narr had been holding that blockade long enough. It was time for someone to challenge it.

The *Farragut* turned slightly and accelerated right at an opening between two of the larger Narr ships, firing constantly at the small attack ships as it went.

Then two of the larger Narr ships opened up on the *Farragut,* and the bridge seemed to explode. Sparks flew everywhere. Smoke filled the air around Bogle as something behind him caught fire. The ship rocked as the stabilizers faught to keep the ship level under the pounding it was taking. He held on to both arms of his chair, focusing on the smaller ships.

"Shields at eighty-six percent," Lee shouted.

"Keep firing at those fighters," Bogle ordered.

Another direct hit on the shields again rocked the Farragut.

Then they were past the larger Narr craft and picking off the smaller fighters like darts popping balloons.

"The *Enterprise* is following us in," Lee shouted. "Klingons are also attacking. The Narr blockade has split."

"The shuttles?" Bogle asked.

"Are all still descending through the atmosphere," Lee said. "None of them was even fired on."

"Keep firing on those fighters," Bogle ordered.

Another blast rocked the ship, sending him almost out of his chair.

Then another and another.

"Shields at sixty-five percent," Lee said. "I think we made the Narr mad."

"Good," Bogle said.

"All fighters now too far into the atmosphere to fire upon," Lieutenant Book said.

"How many got through?"

"Twenty, sir," Book said.

"Let's hope the shuttles beat them to the ground," Bogle said.

The ship rocked with another hit.

"Mr. Book," Bogle said. "Target the ship that just fired on us and return fire."

"Yes, sir," Book said.

"And hold this position. If they want to re-form the blockade, they can do so right over the top of us."

Bogle gripped the arms of his chair tightly. He wasn't about to lose this battle.

He'd had enough of the Narr.

Chapter Twenty-two

VIVIAN RATHBONE couldn't believe she had managed to keep up with the Klingon colonist. He had walked with huge strides, seemingly never tiring. At times she had found herself almost running to stay with him through the brush and rocks. And the two short rests hadn't been near enough considering the heat. It had been everything she could do to catch her breath and drink enough water while they walked.

After the second stop, they had crawled over one ridge, hiked down through a shallow valley, and then crawled on their stomachs to the top of the second ridge. In the years of studying the natural plant life of this planet, she had never thought she would end up crawling on her stomach through it, Klingon phaser rifle in hand, desperately trying to keep her head down so she wouldn't be seen.

Sulu was to her right, Kerdoch to her left, when they stopped on the ridge.

She had found a small rock outcropping to hide behind and rest her gun on. Below her, not more than two hundred paces away, was the Narr camp. Large tentlike structures filled the flat area behind the shuttles. She wagered those "tents" were a lot harder than they looked.

The two Narr transports stood in what looked to her to be awkward positions, noses upward. They formed a perfect blockade line between the tents and the colony beyond. The nose of the closest transport was no more than fifty feet below her level. Those craft were huge and very strange looking, as if someone had buried both ends of an old boomerang in the ground.

Beside her, Sulu's communicator beeped. He had it in front of him on the ground. He flipped it open almost without moving or taking his eyes off the camp below.

"Problems," Kirk said. "The shuttles have launched, but the Narr launched their attack ships right after them."

"How many?" Sulu asked. It was the exact same question she wanted to ask.

"At least twenty made it into the atmosphere," Kirk said.

Twenty attack ships with those wide-angle plasma beams. And the three of them were out in the open with no protection. They didn't stand a chance. They'd be cooked alive in one pass.

"What are your orders, Captain?" Sulu asked.

"Is there shelter close by?"

Sulu turned to Kerdoch. "Shelter against plasma beams?"

Kerdoch seemed to think for just a moment, then nodded. "A small rock hollow down the valley behind us. It should be sufficient."

Sulu spoke into the communicator. "Captain, there is a small rock area near."

"Good," Kirk said. "Here's what I want you to do. In exactly eighty seconds, open fire on those transports."

Sulu nodded, and so did Vivian. Eighty short seconds. Her heart pounded so hard it was amazing the Narr couldn't hear it down in the camp.

"See if you can keep at least one transport on the ground. Make a thirty second attack, then run for the shelter. Don't give those transports time to fire back at you."

"Understood, Captain," Sulu said.

"Good luck. Kirk out."

Sulu snapped the communicator closed and reattached it to his belt.

She did a quick check of the Klingon phaser rifle, then made sure her Federation phaser was still on her belt. She tried to dry her sweating hands on her shirt, but only came away with dirt. If she ever got out of this heat she would never complain about cold again. Ever.

"Target the right wing of the closest craft," Sulu said. "See the vent there near the ground? Let's hope it's a thruster vent."

"A good choice," Kerdoch said.

Rathbone nodded to Sulu, then took aim over the rock at the target. It did look oddly like a closed thruster vent. If they were lucky they could blow that thruster and make it too dangerous for the transport to risk a takeoff. But they were going to have to be damn lucky.

"Ten seconds," Sulu said.

Below, a number of armored Narr were moving now, coming out of the tents like slow, lumbering ants. Picking them off would be like shooting slow targets on a training range. But she doubted that the Klingon rifle would do much damage to that heavy armor.

"Five seconds," Sulu said softly.

She took a deep breath of hot, dusty air and let it out slowly. Calm. Focus on the target. Calm.

The years of training came back to her, and her hands calmed on the stock of the rifle.

"Two," Sulu said.

She waited.

"One."

The time between seconds seemed to take forever.

"Fire!"

She pulled the trigger, and the phaser surged in her hands.

The vent area on the side of the Narr transport instantly lit up as the three beams hit it.

Quickly it turned bright red, went to white, then exploded, sending sparks and burning material out over the tents and the armored Narr.

Amazing. She wanted to stand up and cheer.

But she kept firing.

The side of the Narr hull seemed to melt away, and then, just as suddenly as it had exploded, their beams were through the outer shell and cutting into the insides the ship. She couldn't believe it.

She held the trigger down, letting the rifle beam cut into the ship like a scalding hot knife into cold butter.

Kerdoch and Kor did the same thing beside her.

Then she could hear the rumble as something inside the transport started to ignite.

"Target the same area of the other transport!" Sulu yelled over the rumbling.

She swung the rifle into position and fired. Sulu and Kerdoch were only a fraction of a second behind her.

Again the target went red, then white, then another explosion. There must have been small liquid fuel tanks of some sort right behind those vents. The heat from their fire on the surface ignited and blew away the protective outer shell, letting their phasers cut clear inside. They had gotten lucky.

Very, very lucky.

The first transport seemed to be shaking. High-pressure steam was shooting out of the hole they'd made in its side.

For what seemed like forever, they continued firing on the second shuttle until finally they were inside, cutting through the interior metal as if it didn't exist.

Suddenly the ground in front of them erupted, spraying rocks and dirt into a cloud, blocking her vision. One of the Narr soldiers must have started firing at them.

"Let's get out of here," Sulu shouted.

Instantly she had the rifle down and began scrambling on hands and knees away from the top of the ridge. Rocks and brush cut at her hands and knees, but she ignored the pain.

The rock she'd been hiding behind exploded as a shot from the camp below cut it apart.

Sulu and Kerdoch were right beside her as she

gained her feet and ran. Like wild animals stampeding down the hill, they scrambled over, through, and around brush, rocks, and small shrubs.

Twice she lost her balance in loose dirt, but managed to keep her feet under her and the Klingon rifle in her hand.

At the bottom of the gully the world seemed to shake, dirt clouds lifting from the ground as on the other side of the ridge a huge explosion filled the sky with black smoke and debris.

One of the Narr transports must have exploded.

"This way," Kerdoch shouted over the rumbling. He turned toward the colony and started down the gully at a full run.

She managed to stay within ten steps of the big Klingon and keep her feet—until a second explosion shook the ground and sent her sprawling face first into a pile of sand and dirt.

Sulu tumbled beside her, rolled, and regained his feet. He grabbed her arm and yanked her up without a word.

In front of them the Klingon was scrambling up into a pile of large sun-baked boulders.

She followed, breathing hard, spitting sand out of her dry mouth.

The shelter was nothing more than a rock ledge with some loose boulders near the bottom. Large cracks ran up the side of the rock face.

She was about to say there wasn't enough shelter here against the plasma beams when Kerdoch turned sideways, stooped slightly, and slid into a dark opening at the bottom of one of the cracks.

She stopped, leaning against a rock, panting.

Huge clouds of dark smoke billowed up from just

over the ridge, filling the sky with black clouds that cast huge shadows over the nearby hillside.

"Is there room?" Sulu asked.

Kerdoch's faint voice echoed out of the crack. "Yes."

Sulu glanced around, rifle at ready, then indicated she should go first.

Vivian bent down and slid inside. The crack was so narrow the stone rubbed against her chest and back. How had the larger, bulkier Kerdoch made it through?

Then after just two shuffling sideways steps, she was inside a larger area, about the size of a small cabin on the *Enterprise*.

"The children found this," Kerdoch said.

"Lucky for us," Sulu said as he came inside and stepped away from the entrance, letting the light fill the small area.

Vivian took a deep shuddering breath and tried to force her eyes to adjust to the faint natural cave light.

The floor of the cave was the surface of a fairly flat rock. Above her was another streak of light where the cave opened up to the air. Otherwise, the narrow crack they had come through was the only opening, and the cave's only feature.

Sulu flipped open his communicator. "Captain."

"Great work, Sulu," the captain said. "You managed to blow up both transports. Are you in a safe location?"

"I'm not sure about that," Sulu said.

"Where are you? Your transmission's broken up."

"We're in a small cave just down the ravine from

the Narr camp. But one direct hit on the outside of this rock pile will turn this place into an oven."

It took a moment for Kirk to respond, as if he had to decipher Sulu's words. "That's better than being in the open," Kirk said. "Stay put until I give the all clear."

"Aye, sir," Sulu said and snapped his communicator closed.

He glanced at Rathbone and shook his head while leaning his rifle up against the side of the cave.

"Looks like we're on the sidelines for the next part of this battle," she said with more relief than she cared to contemplate.

"Appearances can be wrong." Sulu said. "Stay prepared."

"I will take the watch," Kerdoch said, moving past her to the entrance and squeezing through.

She allowed herself to drop to the floor and pull out her bottle of water. Her hands were starting to shake, but she managed to get one large gulp of water into her mouth before the shaking got so bad she couldn't hold the bottle.

Spock noted what the *Farragut* was doing, jamming right through the Narr to get to the smaller attack ships trying to reach the atmosphere.

"Follow the *Farragut*," Spock ordered. "Target any ship firing at them."

The *Enterprise* rocked as one of the Narr ships opened up at close range.

"I'm not reading any damage," Chekov reported. "The shields are holding, Mr. Spock."

Spock did not reply, but kept his attention on the

Farragut as it fired on and destroyed fighter after fighter. Spock had never realized that Captain Bogle could be so aggressive.

Phaser fire streaked from the *Enterprise*, pounding first into the ship to the right of the *Farragut*, then next to the left.

"Continue firing," Spock ordered. He wanted to cover the *Farragut* as much as possible.

"All Narr fighters, they are out of range," Ensign Chekov said.

The *Farragut* turned and began firing on the larger Narr ships around it.

"The *Farragut* is holding her ground between the Narr ships and the atmosphere," Chekov said.

Spock said nothing. He didn't dare. It was a useless gesture by Bogle. His position was not defensible.

Suddenly it felt as if something large had rammed the *Enterprise*. The entire bridge seemed to tip up on end, then immediately right itself.

Two Narr ships had targeted the *Enterprise* at the same moment, attempting the same attack that the Federation ships had used against them.

"Shields are at eighty-five percent," Chekov said.

"Move in beside the *Farragut*," Spock said. "Continue firing."

The ship rocked again hard left as the *Enterprise* took a position beside its sister ship. Spock managed to hold on to the captain's chair.

The three Klingon battle cruisers continued to run attack passes at the Narr craft, hitting them as they flashed past, then turning and making another run.

No ship, including the Narr, seemed to have suffered any serious damage.

"Continue targeting and firing, Mr. Chekov," Spock said.

"It looks like a standoff, Mr. Spock," Uhura said.

Spock was quite aware of the situation. Three Narr ships had the two Federation ships cornered against the atmosphere. The other four Narr ships had formed a shield against the marauding Klingon battle cruisers.

For the moment Lieutenant Uhura was correct. It was a standoff. But the Narr attacks would wear down the *Farragut* and the *Enterprise* by sheer numbers. Their position at the moment was not defensible.

The ship rocked again slightly.

"The *Farragut* is hailing us, sir," Lieutenant Uhura said.

"Audio only," Spock said.

"Spock," Captain Bogle said, "I think it's time for us to withdraw to our previous positions."

"I concur, Captain," Spock said.

"Right through the center of them again?"

"Agreed," Spock said.

"Ten seconds, on my mark. . . . Now."

"Navigator, lay in a course to our previous position, one half impulse. Mr. Chekov, continue firing at any target." Exactly ten seconds later, Spock said, "Now."

At the same moment both the *Farragut* and the *Enterprise* jumped forward, directly at the Narr ships.

Chekov continued firing beam after beam as the *Enterprise* slipped between two of the enemy ships and beyond.

Suddenly the Narr strikes against the shields stopped.

"Cease fire," Spock said.

The three Klingon battle cruisers pulled away and also took up their previous positions.

"Shields at eighty percent," Chekov said.

Spock hit the comm button. "How soon till we have full shields, Mr. Scott?"

"Ten minutes, Mr. Spock," Scotty said, sounding a bit harried.

"Thank you, Mr. Scott," Spock said, staring out at the seven Narr craft.

"It's as if nothing has changed," Chekov said.

"It only appears that way," Spock said. "The situation is very different than twelve minutes ago."

"Hold your position, Mr. Spock," Kirk said, and snapped his communicator closed. He and his team were still trapped, waiting for the coming attack.

But things were changing quickly.

He and Kor stood on the edge of the disrupter cannon platform, gazing at the smoke billowing from the Narr camp. He had no idea that Sulu's mission would be so successful. From what he could tell both transports had blown up. There was no doubt that would slow the enemy down, but by how much was anyone's guess. Maybe long enough for the *Enterprise* to figure out a way to break through and get them off this planet.

If they survived the coming attack.

"Kirk," Kor said.

Kirk glanced his way, then followed his gaze up into the sky.

Four Federation shuttles were turning on final approach, all coming in for a landing, one right after the other. Kor had rounded up eight of the colonists and they were all standing by to unload the weapons from the shuttles and distribute them among the other colonists.

Since the destruction of the transports, Kirk had decided that the shuttles most likely would be an even match for the small Narr fighters headed their way, not in weapons, perhaps, but in shields. So Ensign Adaro stood in the shade to one side ready to board one.

Kirk would take a second shuttle. The other two would have to stay unmanned until Sulu and Rathbone returned.

The three manned Klingon shuttles swooped in and took up positions on three sides of the colony, hovering silently.

"It sure feels better having them there," Kirk said.

"A slight comfort," Kor said. "I agree."

As the *Galileo* touched down, Kirk stepped off the platform and headed for it. Kor turned and moved inside the disrupter cannon shelter. With the help of a colonist, he would man the weapon. Kirk just hoped he was half the shot Sulu was against the fast Narr fighters.

The other three shuttles touched down within twenty paces of the edge of the colony, one right after the other, kicking up small puffs of dust and black soot.

Behind the *Galileo* was the *Columbus,* followed by the two *Farragut* shuttles. Ensign Adaro had already reached the *Columbus* and was scrambling to open the outer lock. Two of the Klingon colonists already had the *Galileo* door open and were climbing inside.

Kirk reached the *Galileo* a second later.

He quickly helped the colonists unload the weapons, then climbed in and shut the door, slipping into the pilot's seat as if he'd been sitting in one for years.

He quickly powered up all sensors, brought up the shields, and powered up the phasers. The phasers on the shuttles were nowhere near as powerful as the *Enterprise* weapons, but they just might serve the purpose.

The Narr fighters were hovering just beyond the Narr camp, as if waiting for orders.

Kirk took the shuttle up to the same height as the hovering Klingon shuttles and held position, waiting.

Ensign Adaro did the same with the *Columbus.*

Then they waited.

Twenty minutes later they were still waiting.

252

Chapter Twenty-three

KERDOCH LEANED AGAINST one of the large boulders outside the small cave. Smoke billowed from the Narr camp, filling the clear sky with a huge black cloud. Beyond the cloud he could see shiny wings hovering in formation. The Narr fighters had arrived, but were holding position.

The blood coursing through his veins during the attack had calmed, but he still breathed hard from the excitement of it all. Never had he felt so alive. The very truth of being Klingon had faced him, and he had met the challenge. He had avenged the burning of his fields, the killing of his neighbors.

If the Narr attacked again, he would avenge again.

The humans who had fought beside him had also showed great courage and honor.

Today he had learned a great lesson. Enemies have

honor, also. It was a fact he had never considered before.

Sulu squeezed out of the cave mouth, followed by the human woman. He took up a position near Kerdoch while she moved to the right to find shelter behind another large boulder.

"They will wait until sunset to attack," Kerdoch said.

"I think you're right," Sulu said. He flipped open his communicator. "Captain?"

"Go ahead, Mr. Sulu," the human captain said.

"The Narr attack ships are hovering beyond the colony. Kerdoch and I believe the attack against the colony will be coming at sunset, just as the Narr told you."

"I'm starting to think you're right, Mr. Sulu. Can you make it back to camp? I don't want to risk taking a shuttle that close to their camp."

Sulu turned to the woman, who nodded. Then he looked at Kerdoch.

Kerdoch laughed softly.

"How long?" Sulu asked.

Kerdoch glanced at the woman, then at Sulu. He knew they were both tired. Two rest stops would be needed, but this valley was easier than the one they had come down one ridgeline over. However, the warrior Kahaq was in that other valley.

"We should locate Kahaq," Kerdoch said. "One hour to do so and return."

Sulu nodded, then spoke into the instrument in his hand. "Captain, we'll move over one valley to the north to search for Kahaq. We should be back in the colony in one hour."

"The first sun sets in two hours," Kirk said. "If we

see any of the fighters moving, we will notify you. Then take cover. We'll be there to help. Kirk out."

Sulu snapped his communicator back on his belt.

"Your captain is a man of great common sense," Kerdoch said. "Now drink."

He lifted his own canteen and took two large swallows, letting the water fill his stomach and calm him even more.

Both Sulu and the woman opened their bottles and drank deeply with him.

When they had recapped their bottles, Kerdoch swept his rifle up over his shoulder, turned his back on the humans, and climbed up on the nearest rock, looking for a path to the top of the ridge.

Kirk set the *Galileo* down gently inside the colony, twenty paces from the disrupter cannon, and climbed out into the hot, dry air. The heat hit him like a blanket covering his body, making him stop, forcing him to take a deep breath. He'd been enjoying the controlled comfort of the shuttle cabin, but for the moment he had to talk to Kor.

Ensign Adaro remained aloft in the *Columbus,* standing guard along with the three Klingon shuttles.

Sulu, Rathbone, and Kerdoch had discovered Kahaq's body thirty minutes after they started back. Kahaq had died while lying out in the open in the heat, without water, in full Klingon warrior dress. They had left the body there and returned ten minutes before. There was now less than one hour until sunset.

Kor stepped out of the shadow of the disrupter cannon and motioned that Kirk join him in the dome.

Inside the slightly cooler interior McCoy sat at the table, his uniform drenched in sweat, a large bottle of water in front of him. Kerdoch stood near the door, his rifle still slung over his shoulder. Rathbone and Sulu were sprawled on the cot, leaning back against the dome walls. They both looked exhausted.

"Great work," Kirk said to them, then turned and indicated Kerdoch.

"I agree," Kor said to the colonist. "Your deeds this day will be remembered."

Kerdoch only nodded, but even Kirk could tell the colonist was pleased at Kor's words.

McCoy scooted a large bottle of water toward Kor. "Drink. It's actually cold. I just made three trips to the well to refill our supplies in here."

"Good thinking, Bones," Kirk said. He'd been concentrating so much on the coming fight, he'd forgotten about important basics like water and food.

"No thinking involved," McCoy said. "If we don't drink enough in this god-forsaken heat and we die. Why anyone is fighting over this planet is beyond me. If you Klingons were smart, you'd let the Narr have the place."

"Doctor," Kor said, "after one more day of this heat, I might agree with you."

"Imagine what it's doing to the Narr in those armored suits," Kirk said. He took a long, cold drink from the bottle after Kor, then passed it back to McCoy.

"We must talk," Kirk said to the Klingon commander. While sitting in the *Galileo,* he'd had time to study the situation. They had managed to level the coming fight to some degree. With Sulu and Dr. Rathbone back in camp, all four Federation shuttles could be in the fight, along with the three Klingon shuttles. They were still outnumbered, twenty fighters to seven shuttles, but with the disrupter cannon the fight might be almost even.

Mr. Scott had also sent along two specially modified sonic disrupters he thought might have a chance of canceling out the antigravity controls in the Narr suits. That, along with the new weapons brought down in the shuttle and it seemed, at least for the moment, that the ground fight might be level.

But that still meant a fight. And Kirk didn't much like that idea.

"Talk," Kor said to Kirk, sitting down in a chair at the table and placing his hands flat on the surface in front of him.

Kirk pulled out another chair and sat facing the Klingon commander.

"Kor, we must trust the Narr. We must talk with them. Now. Before the fight."

Kor slapped the tabletop with the palm of his hand, making a sharp gunshotlike noise that echoed in the small dome. "Kirk, you have gone soft. Has the heat turned you into a coward, afraid of the coming fight?"

"I'll fight," Kirk said, his voice as cold and as hard as he could make it. He stared intently into the deep blackness of Kor's eyes. "If I must."

"So why talk?" Kor asked, never letting his gaze waver from Kirk's. "Humans always want to talk before fighting. It is your worst trait."

"Because, Kor," Kirk said, "the Narr have a valid claim to this planet and you know it."

"Possession is the only right Klingons recognize."

Kirk pointed in the direction of the Narr camp. "They now have possession of one area of this planet, and they control the space above it."

"And we will take it back," Kor said.

"As they are trying to do from you," Kirk said.

"Klingons do not surrender," Kor said. "We fight."

"I am not saying you should surrender. Just give me a chance to talk to them again."

"For what reason?" Kor said.

"To stop the coming fight," Kirk said. "The Federation agreed this was to be a Klingon planet, and we left. Kerdoch and his neighbors won this planet in a fair and honorable fight, which they fought without weapons. They fought using advanced agricultural methods."

"Klingons are superior in many ways, Kirk," Kor said. "We have won this planet. And we now defend it."

"As does the Federation beside you," Kirk said.

"True," Kor said.

"We honor our agreement," Kirk said. "And the Narr may honor an agreement, given the chance to make one. If we can't make one with them, then we will fight. I will stand beside you in defending this planet. I will die beside you honoring our agreement."

"The Narr have no honor," Kor said. "They destroyed a colony of farmers."

"A colony they thought was destroying *their* planet," Kirk said. "You would have done the same thing."

Kor waved his hand at Kirk, then stood and moved toward Kerdoch, the expression on his face noncommittal. Kirk had no idea if he had gotten through to the Klingon. Arguing with Klingons had always been an annoying experience at best.

After a moment Kor turned back to Kirk. "Talk if you want," he said.

"You must come with me," Kirk said. "Kerdoch

must also, to represent the colonists. The others can remain and prepare for the coming fight."

"This is stupidity," Kor said, half spitting the word onto the floor. Then he turned and headed for the door. At the entrance he stopped and turned to where Kirk still sat at the table. "Come. We will talk to the Narr. Then we will fight."

"Coming?" Kirk said to Kerdoch, who nodded.

Kirk smiled and shrugged at McCoy as he stood.

"Just make it back to shelter in enough time, Jim," McCoy said.

"Let's hope we don't need to," he said as he followed the Klingon commander out into the dry heat.

Kerdoch stood on the edge of a blackened field next to the human captain and Commander Kor, one of the most honored of all Klingon warriors. They faced the Narr camp, without weapons. Two days ago Kerdoch had stood in his own fields, working to help them grow, fighting back the weeds and the forces of nature. It had been a long two days. Much had happened.

Before him the Narr camp still poured black smoke into the air. The smoke pleased him. The Narr had burned his fields, attacked his home. He had burned their camp, destroyed their ships. It gave him a feeling of closure. For the moment the circle of revenge was complete for him.

They had stood facing the Narr camp, unarmed, for twenty minutes, letting the hot sun pound on them. Now the smallest of the two suns neared the horizon. The promised Narr attack would begin soon.

"They will kill us where we stand," Kerdoch said.

"Would you kill unarmed soldiers facing you?" the human captain said.

"No," Kor said. "It would be dishonorable."

"The Narr will act the same," the human captain said.

"You trust Narr honor?" Kerdoch asked. He did not believe the Narr were honorable. He stood in this field because he was willing to die beside Commander Kor and because he had come to trust the honor of the human captain. But he did not believe the Narr had honor.

Then he realized he had thought the same of humans just two days before. If the human enemies had honor, then the Narr might also. Enemies having honor was a difficult concept to understand.

"There," the human captain said, pointing.

Kerdoch could see five Narr in armor moving toward them through the scrub brush and rock. The human captain had been correct. The Narr did have honor.

"Keep your hands away from your sides," the human captain said. "We must show them we carry no weapons."

Kerdoch did as the human captain said because Commander Kor did also.

The Narr stopped twenty paces in front of them. Then the one in the center moved two steps closer and stopped again.

"I will talk for us," the human captain said. He took three steps forward and also stopped.

"We have discovered since we talked before," the human captain said, "that this planet does belong to you."

"Then leave this place," the Narr leader said.

"We will leave if that is what you demand, and if you give us safe passage," the human captain said.

Kerdoch could not believe what he was hearing. The human captain was surrendering for the Klingons. How could Commander Kor stand and listen?

"But," the human captain said before the Narr could respond, "first would you tell us your intended use of this planet?"

"To expand our food resources. At a time in the future we plan to grow our crops here."

"You do not seem to be farmers by nature," Kirk said.

"We are warriors," Narr said, straightening up slightly inside his armor. "We are not farmers."

"The Klingons are also warriors," the human captain said. "But they are also farmers. They work the land and grow the crops as if fighting a great war every season. They are great farmers."

Kerdoch marveled at the human captain's understanding of Klingon nature. But at the same time he was puzzled that the human captain failed to understand that Klingons never surrendered.

"The Klingons have already established a base on this planet," the human captain said. "An agreement could be struck between you and the Klingons, so that they could farm this planet. They would grow their own crops as well as yours."

The human captain was giving Kerdoch's hard work away. Kerdoch almost stepped forward at that moment, his anger was so strong, but Kor's raised hand stopped him. Kerdoch turned to question the commander.

"Let him continue, Kerdoch," Kor said, raising his hand higher, signaling Kerdoch to say nothing.

Kerdoch turned to listen to the treachery going on in front of him. At that moment he could not tell who he was most angry at. The human captain, or Kor for allowing the human captain to speak such words.

The Narr hesitated, then stepped closer to the human captain. "You suggest that the Klingons grow our crops on this planet? Is that correct?"

"Yes," the human captain said. "They would grow your crops as well as their own."

"They would grow them in exchange for the planet?"

The human captain nodded. "And I'm sure you would pay them a fair price for your crops. Details beyond that could be worked out later. But such an agreement would allow the Klingons to stay on this world, as they want. It would also allow you to expand your food base as you need, years ahead of your schedule. Both sides would win."

"I must confer," the Narr said, and turned away.

Kerdoch squeezed his fists tight. Why had Kor allowed the human captain to betray them?

The human captain turned and moved back to where Kerdoch and Kor stood. He was smiling and Kerdoch desperately wanted to smash the smile from his sickly human face.

"You are a crafty one, Kirk," Kor said. "You knew we would never surrender."

"Of course," Kirk said, laughing. "I never intended to surrender. But I had to get the Narr's attention."

"You gave away our planet," Kerdoch said, his voice almost shaking with his anger.

"You will keep the planet, Kerdoch," the human captain said. Then, facing Kor, he continued, "And the strategic advantage of its location, which is important to the Empire. Am I right, Commander?"

Kor bowed slightly, but said nothing.

Kerdoch felt his anger suddenly drain as if it were nothing more than the escaping air of a child's balloon, pricked by a needle. He looked at Commander Kor before turning back to the human.

The human captain continued. "You would also gain a strategic advantage over the Narr by controlling part of their food source in the future. And you will discover the locations of their home worlds in case a future conflict should arise."

Finally Kerdoch was starting to understand what Commander Kor had understood all along. It was why Kor was such a great warrior and he was only a farmer. His respect for the commander increased, as did his respect for the human captain, who had understood Klingons well enough to make such a deal.

"And what do you get, Kirk?" Kor asked.

"I get off this planet alive," Kirk said. "And a chance to cool down."

Kor laughed. Then he peered at Kirk. "You also get the continuation of the Organian Peace Treaty."

"That too," the human captain said, smiling.

"Human?" the Narr said.

The human captain turned to face the approaching Narr soldier.

"Do you speak for the Klingons?" the Narr asked.

"I speak for the Klingons," Commander Kor said, stepping forward beside the human captain. "I am Commander Kor of the Imperial Fleet."

The Narr soldier nodded and glanced at Kerdoch, who gave him a hard stare in return but said nothing.

The Narr soldier turned back to Commander Kor. "We will agree to talks based on the principles the human has put forth."

"You will withdraw your claim to this planet?" Kor asked.

"We will," the Narr said, "if you agree to produce a base amount of our crops on this planet each year, to be sold to us."

"It is agreed," Kor said. "We will talk."

"In twenty of this planet's days we will send a representative to this location."

"As will we," Kor said.

The Narr nodded to the commander.

Kor nodded back.

The Narr soldier turned, lumbering away in his heavy armor.

Kerdoch watched him go, not completely understanding that the fighting had been stopped that quickly.

"Come," Kor said.

Kor, the human captain, and Kerdoch all turned as one and moved back toward the colony across the blackened field. Kerdoch let his feet guide him, his mind still on what he had just heard.

After twenty paces the human captain laughed, "That armor must have been hot."

"Very hot," Kor said. "The heat must have reached his brain. He just gave away an entire planet." With that both the human captain and the commander laughed.

"Commander," Kerdoch said, still slightly confused, "what exactly occurred?"

"This human has given us a glorious victory," Kor

said. "One that will be talked and written about for generations."

"And you trust the honor of the Narr?" Kerdoch said. "They will hold their side of the agreement?"

"I have learned this day," Kor said, "that my enemies may have honor. It seems humans have honor. A warrior race such as the Narr must, therefore, surely have more. Yes, I trust their word."

"I think I've just been insulted," the human captain said.

"Ah, Kirk," Kor said, clapping the human on the back. "It is the nature of our relationship for me to insult you."

At that the human captain smiled. "And for me to insult you," he said.

"On that we are agreed," Kor said.

"I'm glad to know this relationship won't change," the human captain said.

But Kerdoch knew that it had. They were laughing together, something enemies rarely did.

Chapter Twenty-four

Vivian Rathbone sat for a moment at the controls of the shuttle *Balboa* as the *Farragut* docking bay pressurized.

After the final sequencing was finished, she let her hands drop into her lap from the control panel. They were shaking. And she was sweating, almost as much as she had in the intense heat of the plasma attack, even though the shuttle's climate controls were working perfectly.

"Well, I did it," she said to herself. It had been almost four years since she'd piloted any form of shuttle, and she had never piloted a starship shuttle like the *Balboa*. But when Captain Kirk told her she was to fly one of the shuttles back to the *Farragut*, she hadn't objected. One thing she had learned on her first landing party was that a crew member really had no limits. You did what you were ordered to do, even if it cost you your life, as it had Ensign Chop.

But it could have been much worse than just flying a shuttle and docking it on the *Farragut*. On the way from the colony to the shuttles Ensign Adaro, who had piloted the other *Farragut* shuttle, the *De leon*, had teased her that flying back to the *Farragut* was a lot easier than flying in battle against the Narr, as they were supposed to have done.

That was the first time she had heard that Captain Kirk had planned for her to fly the *Balboa* against the Narr fighters. Ensign Adaro had been right. This flight was a lot easier than flying in combat. But the idea of the captain trusting her that much had made the flight to the *Farragut* even more nerve-racking. She didn't want to do anything wrong that would let the captain know she might not have been able to handle any assignment he would have given her.

"Ma'am?" Ensign Adaro said over the comm line. He was already standing on the hangar deck. When she looked down he waved for her.

She punched the exterior comm line. "On my way."

She stood and looked around for anything she might have left behind. Then she laughed. She hadn't taken anything to the planet and had even less coming back.

The airlock door hissed open. As she passed through it, she patted the metal side of the shuttle. "Thanks," she said to it.

Inside her head she added, "and I'm glad we didn't have to fight together."

The young ensign looked filthy and very, very

sunburned standing among the *Farragut* docking bay crew. As she joined him the ten or so who made up the docking bay crew broke into cheers, standing and applauding her and Adaro.

She wasn't sure about Ensign Adaro, but she blushed. Then laughed.

Having them acknowledge that what she'd gone through and survived had been difficult, made her feel better. Made her feel as if she hadn't let Captain Kirk down quite as much as she feared she had.

"Enterprise," Ensign Adaro said, "two to beam aboard."

"Stand by, Ensign."

"Thank you for coming to our rescue," she said to those still applauding.

As the transporter beam took them, both she and Ensign Adaro applauded those around them.

"By my count," Projeff was saying on the screen in front of Scotty, "it's two ideas from the *Farragut* to your one."

Scotty leaned back. He and Projeff had worked well together. Someday they might even resolve that environmental control problem they'd been discussing on Starbase Eleven. But he wasn't going to let Projeff get the last word.

"I think we're even, lad."

"How do you figure that?"

Scotty smiled. "My first idea was on how to fix the shields. It worked."

"Not well enough," Projeff said. "I had to improve it."

"Your first real idea was on how to disrupt the Narr's antigravity suits."

"I wouldn't agree with that," Projeff said. "That was my second idea."

"But your first original one, lad."

"It's still two ideas to one," Projeff said.

"Not quite," Scotty said. "You see, we dinna get a chance to test your antigravity idea."

"What?" Projeff asked. "The simulations worked fine."

"So did my shield simulations," Scotty said. "But in battle they needed modifications. I'll wager in battle your weapons would have needed modifications too."

"There's no way to know that," Projeff said.

"And there's no way to know if your idea even worked," Scotty said. "So I see us as tied, one idea to one."

Projeff's eyes narrowed, but it looked as if he were using the expression to hide his amusement. "If we're tied, we need a tie-breaker."

"I agree, lad, but we're heading off to different parts of space."

"It would need to be a long term project then," Projeff said.

"That wouldn't be fair," Scotty said. "There'd be no way to know who succeeded first."

"True enough," Projeff said.

"So I challenge you, lad, to a duel of the minds the next time we share a shore leave."

Projeff grinned. "You're on, Scotty."

Scotty nodded. "It's been fun, lad."

"That it has, Mr. Scott." Projeff signed off.

Scotty sighed and leaned back in his chair. "An

even score," he whispered, "courtesy of the creative mind of the *Enterprise*'s chief engineer."

The turbolift doors hissed open, and Captain Kirk strolled onto the bridge. He had showered and shaved, then reported to sick bay as Dr. McCoy had ordered. Now, feeling better than he could remember and very happy to be alive, it was time to get back to work.

"Welcome back, sir," Lieutenant Uhura said.

"Thank you, Lieutenant," he said. "It's good to be back."

Spock nodded to him as Kirk stepped down to his captain's chair.

"Good work, Mr. Spock," Kirk said. "You handled the situation very well."

"Thank you, sir," Spock said.

Mr. Sulu had already returned to his post next to Ensign Chekov. Both seemed to be busy at their stations.

On the main screen the Narr ships had moved away from their positions over the colony. According to the report he'd been given before showering, they would remain in orbit for another twenty minutes finishing up repairs and the boarding of ground troops.

The three Klingon ships were grouped in a small triangle between the two Federation ships and the Narr ships. Hanging in space to the right of the *Enterprise* was the *Farragut*. Repairs to both starships had been mostly completed.

He sat down in his chair and activated his log. He gave the stardate and then winced. He might as well get the worst duty over first. Then move on.

"Let the record show," he said, his voice solemn

and low, "that Ensign Chop died doing his duty for the Federation, in a brave and noble manner."

Kirk paused for a moment.

"Mr. Spock?" he said.

"Yes, Captain?" Spock said.

"Have Ensign Chop's remains been returned to the ship?"

"No, sir," Spock said. "The ensign left instructions in his personal records that if he died on a landing party he was to be buried on the planet or in space. A detail was transported down twenty minutes ago. They buried his remains in one of the bunkers near the colony, next to other dead from the attacks. The colonists have promised to maintain the site with honor and respect."

Kirk nodded. The colonists would keep their word. He had learned that much about those people. He took a deep breath and put the ensign's death down inside him, where every death of every crew member stayed.

He could see all of their faces. He knew all of their names.

There were already far too many in there.

He let out a deep breath slowly.

"Okay," he said and reactivated the log back. "On a more pleasant subject, let the record show commendations for Lieutenant Sulu."

"Commendations also for Ensign Adaro, Vivian Rathbone, Dr. Leonard McCoy, Science Officer Spock, and Chief Engineer Scott."

He leaned back in his chair. On the screen in front of him the ships still floated above the planet. It was a place he hoped to never visit again. As far as he was concerned, the Klingons could have it.

"Lieutenant Uhura, hail the *Farragut*."

"Aye, sir," she said. She turned her chair slightly. "I have Captain Bogle on-screen, sir."

Captain Bogle's smiling face filled the screen. "Captain," he said. "From the looks of your face, your vacation was successful."

"Nothing like a little fun in the sun," Kirk said.

Bogle laughed. "Glad it was you instead of me. I hate too much sun. Give me a nice rainy day anytime."

Kirk laughed this time. "I just might agree with you on that right now." Then Kirk got serious for a moment.

"Captain," he said, "I want to officially thank you and your crew on behalf of the crew of the *Enterprise*."

"Accepted with pleasure, Captain," Bogle said, nodding slightly.

"And, Kelly," Kirk said, staring seriously at his friend's face, "let me convey a personal thank you as well."

"Kirk," Bogle said, "you're welcome. Just remember you still owe me a drink."

"I think it just might have to be more than one," Kirk said.

"I'll hold you to that, Kirk," Bogle said, laughing. *"Farragut* out."

The screen returned to the images of the ships orbiting the planet.

"Captain," Spock said, "the Narr ships are leaving orbit."

In a tight formation, the seven wing-like ships moved away from the planet. Between them they towed the hulk of the dead Narr ship.

Then, as one, they jumped to warp and were gone.

"Lieutenant," Kirk said, "signal Commander Kor that we are leaving."

"He's hailing us, sir."

Kirk laughed. "I thought Klingons hated to talk. Put him on-screen."

The Klingon's face filled most of the screen. "Kirk," Kor said, his voice back to the full, loud brassy sound Kirk remembered. "You have taught us much. We will remember this day for generations."

"I only honored our treaty," Kirk said. "As you would have done."

Kor bowed slightly, in what Kirk took to mean agreement.

"Kirk, someday our battle will come."

"Kor, I'm looking forward to it."

Kor laughed. "As am I, Kirk. It will be a glorious day. And a glorious fight."

With that the screen cut off. The planet on the screen looked almost empty without the Narr ships in orbit. But it was a nice empty.

"Mr. Sulu, lay in course for Starbase Eleven. This crew has some shore leave to finish."

"Yes, sir," Sulu said, smiling.

"Besides," Kirk said. "It's going to take me some time to level out this tan."

It took a moment before everyone on the bridge, except Spock, broke into laughter.

Epilogue

Kerdoch let his gaze travel around the large room filled with his family. The smells of the huge dinner still filled the air, even though his story had been a long one. He blinked and tried to focus on the present. When he told his story of that great battle with the Narr, he always seemed to take himself back. He relived the revenge cycle. The fear of losing his family. The hardships of battle.

Now, just from telling the story, his old bones were tired. Deep down tired. But he wasn't quite finished yet. He had to continue for just a moment longer.

All eyes were still on him. All attention was still focused on his story of that battle all those years before. Every year he held their attention with the story, and many knew it by heart. It seemed that this year he had mesmerized them again. It was not his telling. He knew that. No, it was the importance of the message of the story.

He took a deep breath and let the warmth of the room ease the tiredness in his old bones. Then he continued with the last of the story.

"Commander Kor and the Narr representative met, as they had said they would, twenty days later. Their agreement has stood for all these years."

He looked around at this family.

"But that agreement is not why we celebrate this day. Agreements come and go. But lessons remain always."

He stared down at his grandchildren, who sat at his feet. A five-year-old boy, his eyes bright with fire, stared up at him. "Young K'Ber, can you tell me the lesson?"

K'Ber sat back a moment, his eyes even brighter at the privilege of being picked by his grandfather to answer a question during the telling of the story. Kerdoch wanted to smile at his grandson, but instead kept very still.

The young boy finally said, "The enemy has honor."

"Good," Kerdoch said, smiling at the boy, who seemed to light up at the attention. "We learned that day to celebrate the honor of the enemy as well as the honor of the warrior."

Again Kerdoch looked up and caught his wife's gaze. She was smiling at him proudly, as was his oldest son. That day long ago he had been more than just a farmer, or a colonist. He had been a Klingon warrior. And the retelling brought back the pride he had felt then.

"As Klingons," Kerdoch said, "we have always

given honor to those among us who fight. Dying in battle has always been our most honorable death. But it must be remembered that to our enemies, we are the enemy."

Around the room a murmur broke out as his words sank in. They were words to be remembered by them all, as he had done all these years.

He stood and held up his arms over his family gathered in the large room. "Today I tell this story to remind us all to honor those who fight and those who die in battle. Let this Day of Honor be remembered always."

Around him his family stood, cheering, all talking at once.

Again he had done his duty. For another year the story would be remembered. And so would the important lesson that went with it.

1252.01

THE
STAR TREK®
ENCYCLOPEDIA

A Reference Guide To The Future

UPDATED AND EXPANDED EDITION

THE FUTURE JUST GOT BIGGER!

Beam aboard a completely revised edition of the definitive reference book for all *Star Trek* fans! For the first time, this updated and expanded encyclopedia brings together all four incarnations of the entire ongoing *Star Trek* phenomenon: the Original Series, *Star Trek: The Next Generation*®, *Star Trek: Deep Space Nine*®, and *Star Trek*®: *Voyager*™.

Meticulously researched and helpfully cross-referenced, this new edition features more than 2,000 photos—now in full color—and all new diagrams and illustrations created especially for this volume.

Michael Okuda and Denise Okuda
with Debbie Mirek

POCKET BOOKS

Coming mid-December
From Pocket Books

1412

Turn the page for an excerpt from Star Trek: Deep Space Nine: *Trial by Error* . . .

Two days ago, the *Toknor* had encountered the remains of a Karama ship—the Karama were a race known to do business with the Jem'Hadar. The ship had been almost completely destroyed, and there was ample evidence to attribute its destruction to extremely high energy weapons fire. Since establishing their recent presence in Cardassian space, officers of the Klingon Empire had gathered a considerable amount of intelligence on the Jem'Hadar. While it was true that the Jem'Hadar possessed formidable weapons, the *Toknor*'s computer could not attribute the Karama ship's destruction to any of them.

Two unknowns, Dolras thought, still observing the second one. He didn't like it. Could there be a connection?

Dolras had stayed near the Karama ship as long as he could, examining unremarkable long-range sensor reports. Then he had moved on, deeper into the Gamma Quadrant and farther away from Dominion space, all the while wondering what was waiting for them out there.

So far he considered the mission a success because it had resulted in a considerable store of new planetary and even some cultural data of the kind that could be analyzed to provide valuable trade and military intelligence. And Klingon mission parameters did not necessarily include the investigation of space phenomena, which ordinarily was all well and good to Dolras's mind. But this unidentified energy field had been following his freighter ever since the *Toknor* had left orbit around a small, rather unremarkable planetoid roughly one-quarter light-year back. Sometimes it was ahead of them, and sometimes it was behind. It almost seemed to be studying them.

At present the energy cloud lay dead ahead. But not for long, if Dolras had anything to say about it.

"Evasive maneuvers, Thrann," Dolras told his first officer. "Maximum impulse." He would see exactly what their little cloud did.

Thrann quickly complied.

Dolras watched as the ghostly patch of space, some five hundred meters across, appeared to remain stationary in the viewer as the *Toknor* changed course.

"The field continues to pace us," Thrann reported.

Dolras frowned. "How far are we from the wormhole?" They were in no immediate jeopardy, as far as he could tell, but this anomaly was becoming a real concern.

"At warp six, two-point-one days," Thrann said.

That was nearly the maximum sustainable speed for the *Toknor,* but Dolras knew he could squeeze warp six-five out of her for at least two-point-one days. And in any case, there was no reason to believe the anomaly was capable of warp speeds. The *Toknor* had been completing a sensor sweep, traveling at three quarters impulse since leaving the vicinity of the planetoid.

"Bring us one hundred eighty degrees about," Dolras ordered. He watched closely as the anomaly circled to the *Toknor*'s stern. Good, he thought.

"Set a direct course for the wormhole and prepare to go to warp. But wait for my order." Dolras looked up. "Kotren!"

"Sir?"

"Tell us something worthwhile!"

His science officer turned, forehead ridges damp with sweat, his expression intensely serious.

"I am still evaluating our data," Kotren said.

Our lack of data, Dolras thought. He knew Kotren was giving his captain and crew everything he had. Some years ago, Dolras would have censured the young officer even so, but not now. *Not yet,* he told himself. He had been in space for too many decades; these days, he preferred to save his energies for times that truly required them. Whatever phenomena his ship had encountered, it was clearly outside even the computer's knowledge.

Dolras steadied himself. "This thing is playing a game with us. I want to know more about it. Prepare a sensor probe for launch. We will investigate this energy field up close and find out why it insists on following us."

"At once!" Kotren said.

"The probe data may make it possible for you to determine the cloud's purpose," Dolras continued. If it has one, he thought. But he suspected it did, and he was intent on determining what that purpose was.

"The probe is ready," Kotren announced a moment later.

Dolras looked to the main viewer. "Launch!"

"Probe launched," Kotren said.

"On screen," Dolras said. The low-pitched *ping* of the departing probe resounded through the ship, and he watched the main viewer as the tiny machine propelled itself across the narrow gulf between the *Toknor* and its unwelcome shadow.

"We're receiving specific telemetry and sensor data," Kotren began.

Dolras watched the probe vanish into the energy field, almost as if it had been absorbed.

"The field is chiefly composed of positively charged plasma particles," Kotren continued. Then he fell silent.

"Continue!" Dolras demanded. He had to know what was happening.

"Sir, we have lost contact with the probe," Kotren said. "I am attempting to reestablish—"

"Then what is that?" Dolras snapped, leaping to his feet. He jabbed his finger at the screen as the probe—the same probe they had just launched—exited the thin, cloudy anomaly and arched back toward the *Toknor*. He took a step toward the screen.

"I see it, Captain," Kotren replied, glancing frantically from the screen to his consoles and back. "But we are receiving no telemetry. The probe no longer registers on our sensors."

Dolras narrowed his eyes. It did not register? How could that be? He could *see* it. "Turn it around and send it back," he said evenly, sitting again.

Kotren attempted to comply, then turned back to his captain. "We still have no control over the probe."

"Thrann!" Dolras shouted. "Regain control of the probe. If that is not possible, put a tractor beam on it!"

Dolras watched Thrann tap at his controls, then shake his head. He worked again, and Dolras watched the screen as the pale orange light of the ship's tractor beam reached out and engulfed the probe . . . and the probe passed through it.

"I cannot explain it," Thrann said, his voice tense. "The beam is having no effect. It is as if there is no probe there to lock on to."

"Then destroy the probe," Dolras said. He nodded to himself. That would certainly solve the problem. "Target disrupters."

"Powering disrupters. Target acquired," Thrann said.

"Fire!"

Dolras saw the beam strike out at the probe—and pass straight through it with no apparent affect.

As he noted the probe's course, Dolras needed no instruments to tell him what would happen next. "Shields up," he ordered. "Prepare for impact!"

He braced himself as the probe arrived at the *Toknor,* but instead of the expected impact and explosion, the probe passed through the shields with only a flicker of color, then continued into the ship itself. No contact was felt.

"Report!"

"No impact registered," Thrann said. "The probe seems to have vanished."

Dolras swore under his breath as he stared once more at the anomaly—this strange curiosity that was well on its way to becoming his most vexing adversary. Still, the cloud seemed to present no immediate danger of any kind, only an unsettling mystery to be solved. He frowned. He didn't like mysteries.

"Close to within two hundred thousand kilometers," he told Thrann. "Modify our forward disrupter array to emit a diffused electrostatic charge, reverse polarity."

"That could disrupt the cloud's entire energy field," Kotren said.

"Or it could send that thing, whatever it is, running for home. Either way there will be sparks enough to see what it looks like with a light shining on it."

Thrann acknowledged Dolras's comment and went about the task. A moment later he raised his head. "Ready," he said.

"Watch it closely, Lieutenant," Dolras told Kotren. "This is our only chance to learn something. Thrann, are we ready to go to warp?"

"Yes, Captain."

"Activate the disruptor array."

Again Dolras leaned back, watching the main viewer, as a bright red beam of electrostatic energy hit the cloud. It began to seethe with movement. Yellows, oranges, and pinks swirled this way and that. Dolras gaped. It was beautiful, almost mesmerizing.

Seconds later a blinding light burst from the cloud. Dolras shielded his eyes while the computer compensated for the increased brightness.

"What was that?" he demanded of Kotren. "Status!"

Warning klaxons abruptly sounded. Dolras tried to blink the white hot spots from his eyes, to no avail.

"We are being bombarded with an intense wide-spectrum radiation beam," Kotren replied. "Every system on the ship is approaching overload status. Recommend—"

"Go to warp, Thrann!" Dolras shouted. "Engage, engage!"

"Coming about," Thrann reported, hastily manipulating the helm controls. "Engaging now."

On the screen, the stars spun in a quarter circle, then sprang back to become long, narrow lines of light that seemed to stream away in all directions. Dolras took a deep, calming breath. Perhaps the disrupter array had been a mistake. But at least they were safe now.

"Captain," Thrann said after a moment, "the energy field is pursuing us, matching speed and course, continuing to accelerate."

Dolras felt a hardness in his stomach. Warp speeds, it seemed, were not an advantage.

"I have it on aft visual," Kotren said. "The field seems to be changing, taking on a distinct shape."

"Put it on the main screen," Dolras told him. "Maximum magnification."

To his surprise the image that sprang into view was nothing like the cloud. It had come together into a vague blocky shape, and though it was indistinct, he recognized the lines of a long hull and warp engines.

"A starship," Thrann said.

"So it would appear," Dolras said. But who were they? What did they want? "Identification?"

"None yet," Thrann said. "Our sensors cannot pick it up."

"Impossible," Dolras scoffed, clenching one fist as the frustration built within him. "I have never heard of a cloaking device like this, but now that it is down, we should be getting *some* readings."

"Their technology must be well beyond our own," Thrann said grimly. "I recommend firing on it, with or without a lock."

"First, open hailing frequencies," Dolras said. "Tell them to identify themselves and break off their pursuit, or we will open fire. Thrann, prepare a photon torpedo."

Both officers did as they were told.

"No response to our hails," Kotren said a minute later.

"Torpedo ready," Thrann said.

Dolras closed one eye and fixed the other on the dark object still following his freighter. He felt a twinge of earned pleasure. Enough was enough. "Fire torpedo," he said.

"Torpedo fired."

"Tactical onscreen," Dolras said, and the desired display filled the main viewer. He watched the computer's representation of the torpedo as it traversed the distance between ships. It appeared to strike the target precisely.

"Direct hit," Thrann reported. "No detonation. No effect."

"How is that possible?" Dolras said, coming halfway out of his seat, then lowering himself heavily back down. He clutched the arms of his command chair.

"The torpedo has vanished," Thrann replied.

"Fire again! Fire at will!"

Dolras watched a second torpedo track toward its target as precisely as the first, followed by yet another. Both quickly vanished, leaving their objective untouched.

"Torpedo detected on course toward us," Thrann announced, and Dolras heard the agitation in his voice. Despite their training and seasoning, his crew members had little actual combat experience. Still, they were Klingons: they would perform their duties, and he would do the same.

"Divert as much power as possible to aft shields," he said. "Target incoming torpedo."

"Enemy torpedo closing," Kotren announced. "Configuration unknown. I am reading it as a high energy plasma burst."

"Fire!" Dolras ordered. If they could detonate the enemy torpedo before it hit their ship, they would be spared the worst of its effects.

Thrann fired the *Toknor*'s fourth torpedo. Dolras tensed as it flew a brief intercept course and met the incoming torpedo exactly.

"No effect," Thrann said.

Dolras sat back. No such thing was possible, and yet . . .

"Brace for impact," he said.

As the words left the captain's mouth, the *Toknor* heaved suddenly forward, then shook with a violence even he was not prepared for. The aft screen went instantly white with brightness from the explosion. Around him, power relays overloaded. The bridge went dark, lit only by flashes and sparks from instrument panels as numerous systems shorted out.

Dolras held on to his chair, teeth bared, growling deep in his throat, finding no words to express his fury. Smoke filled his nose and throat. He watched his Ops officer scramble to put out a fire that had started near the science station. Blood and burn-marks streaked the side of his face.

Dolras forced his growl to become a speaking voice. "Status!"

"The impact of the plasma burst nearly collapsed the aft shields," Thrann reported. "I am attempting to compensate."

Dolras rose and made his way across the bridge to Thrann's station. The *Toknor* was already at warp six-point-three, the fastest speed anyone could expect from such a ship. He watched the readout change: warp six-point-four. His mission was to return with the information and samples he had spent so many months gathering—not a glorious mission, perhaps, but an important one nonetheless. He did not intend to fail.

"Continue on course for the wormhole," Dolras said. He tapped at the console's intercom control.

"Engineering, I want everything you can give me, do you hear? Warp seven would be a good start!"

"Yes, sir!" came his chief engineer's resounding reply.

Good, Dolras thought. Someone knew how to respond to an emergency.

"When we reach the Alpha Quadrant, we can arrange to rendezvous with a Klingon attack force," Dolras told Thrann privately. "Together we will know victory, and we will finally learn who is behind this."

Thrann nodded.

Dolras reached out and tapped the main controls, removing the tactical display from the main screen and restoring the external forward view. Then he stood back, staring at the image in silence.

"Captain?" Thrann asked, looking up, watching his captain, "what are you looking for?"

Dolras held steady for a moment, then he raised one hand and placed it firmly on his first officer's shoulder. "Stars," he replied. "I wanted to see the stars."

Look for STAR TREK Fiction from Pocket Books

Star Trek®: The Original Series

Star Trek: The Motion Picture • Gene Roddenberry
Star Trek II: The Wrath of Khan • Vonda N. McIntyre
Star Trek III: The Search for Spock • Vonda N. McIntyre
Star Trek IV: The Voyage Home • Vonda N. McIntyre
Star Trek V: The Final Frontier • J. M. Dillard
Star Trek VI: The Undiscovered Country • J. M. Dillard
Star Trek VII: Generations • J. M. Dillard
Enterprise: The First Adventure • Vonda N. McIntyre
Final Frontier • Diane Carey
Strangers from the Sky • Margaret Wander Bonanno
Spock's World • Diane Duane
The Lost Years • J. M. Dillard
Probe • Margaret Wander Bonanno
Prime Directive • Judith and Garfield Reeves-Stevens
Best Destiny • Diane Carey
Shadows on the Sun • Michael Jan Friedman
Sarek • A. C. Crispin
Federation • Judith and Garfield Reeves-Stevens
The Ashes of Eden • William Shatner & Judith and Garfield
    Reeves-Stevens
The Return • William Shatner & Judith and Garfield Reeves-
    Stevens
Star Trek: Starfleet Academy • Diane Carey

#1 *Star Trek: The Motion Picture* • Gene Roddenberry
#2 *The Entropy Effect* • Vonda N. McIntyre
#3 *The Klingon Gambit* • Robert E. Vardeman
#4 *The Covenant of the Crown* • Howard Weinstein
#5 *The Prometheus Design* • Sondra Marshak & Myrna
    Culbreath
#6 *The Abode of Life* • Lee Correy
#7 *Star Trek II: The Wrath of Khan* • Vonda N. McIntyre
#8 *Black Fire* • Sonni Cooper
#9 *Triangle* • Sondra Marshak & Myrna Culbreath
#10 *Web of the Romulans* • M. S. Murdock
#11 *Yesterday's Son* • A. C. Crispin
#12 *Mutiny on the Enterprise* • Robert E. Vardeman
#13 *The Wounded Sky* • Diane Duane
#14 *The Trellisane Confrontation* • David Dvorkin

Star Trek: The Next Generation®

Encounter at Farpoint • David Gerrold
Unification • Jeri Taylor
Relics • Michael Jan Friedman
Descent • Diane Carey
All Good Things • Michael Jan Friedman
Star Trek: Klingon • Dean W. Smith & Kristine K. Rusch
Star Trek VII: Generations • J. M. Dillard
Metamorphosis • Jean Lorrah
Vendetta • Peter David
Reunion • Michael Jan Friedman
Imzadi • Peter David
The Devil's Heart • Carmen Carter
Dark Mirror • Diane Duane
Q-Squared • Peter David
Crossover • Michael Jan Friedman
Kahless • Michael Jan Friedman
Star Trek: First Contact • J. M. Dillard

#1 *Ghost Ship* • Diane Carey
#2 *The Peacekeepers* • Gene DeWeese
#3 *The Children of Hamlin* • Carnen Carter
#4 *Survivors* • Jean Lorrah
#5 *Strike Zone* • Peter David
#6 *Power Hungry* • Howard Weinstein
#7 *Masks* • John Vornholt
#8 *The Captains' Honor* • David and Daniel Dvorkin
#9 *A Call to Darkness* • Michael Jan Friedman
#10 *A Rock and a Hard Place* • Peter David
#11 *Gulliver's Fugitives* • Keith Sharee
#12 *Doomsday World* • David, Carter, Friedman & Greenberg
#13 *The Eyes of the Beholders* • A. C. Crispin
#14 *Exiles* • Howard Weinstein
#15 *Fortune's Light* • Michael Jan Friedman
#16 *Contamination* • John Vornholt
#17 *Boogeymen* • Mel Gilden
#18 *Q-in-Law* • Peter David
#19 *Perchance to Dream* • Howard Weinstein
#20 *Spartacus* • T. L. Mancour
#21 *Chains of Command* • W. A. McCay & E. L. Flood
#22 *Imbalance* • V. E. Mitchell
#23 *War Drums* • John Vornholt

Star Trek: Deep Space Nine®

Star Trek®: Voyager™

Flashback • Diane Carey
The Black Shore • Greg Cox
Mosaic • Jeri Taylor

#1 *Caretaker* • L. A. Graf
#2 *The Escape* • Dean W. Smith & Kristine K. Rusch
#3 *Ragnarok* • Nathan Archer
#4 *Violations* • Susan Wright
#5 *Incident at Arbuk* • John Greggory Betancourt
#6 *The Murdered Sun* • Christie Golden
#7 *Ghost of a Chance* • Mark A. Garland & Charles G.
   McGraw
#8 *Cybersong* • S. N. Lewitt
#9 *Invasion #4: The Final Fury* • Dafydd ab Hugh
#10 *Bless the Beasts* • Karen Haber
#11 *The Garden* • Melissa Scott
#12 *Chrysalis* • David Wilson

Star Trek®: New Frontier

#1 *House of Cards* • Peter David
#2 *Into the Void* • Peter David
#3 *The Two-Front War* • Peter David
#4 *End Game* • Peter David

Star Trek®: Day of Honor

Book 1: *Ancient Blood* • Diane Carey
Book 2: *Armageddon Sky* • L. A. Graf
Book 3: *Her Klingon Soul* • Michael Jan Friedman
Book 4: *Treaty's Law* • Dean W. Smith & Kristine K. Rusch